Yesterday

Was a Long Time Ago

A Novel

Selena Haskins

Ordering Information:
Special discounts are available on quantity purchases by book clubs, book stores, corporations, associations, and others. For details, contact the publisher at the email address above.

Library of Congress Control Number: 2017903819
ISBN: 978-0-9859096-5-9
Copyright © 2017 by Selena Haskins

"When someone you love becomes a memory, that memory becomes a treasure."

-Author Unknown

PART I

FRESHMAN YEAR

1992

I'd been searching for love since my parents died in a car accident when I was eight years old. It seemed like love had gone to the grave with them and left me on Earth without a sense of purpose.

"Your grandparents will take good care of you," Uncle Walter said to me, with his hands resting on my shoulders.

My dark brown eyes glistened like shiny marbles as they became a pool of tears. I didn't want to leave my home in Richmond, Virginia, to go to my grandparent's home in Charlotte. Richmond was the only home I knew.

"It's alright, child. You're in good hands with us." Grandma's lips curved a smile at me, as I hesitated to climb into the backseat of the station wagon with my doll, Lilly, in my hand. I noticed I'd neglected to fix Lilly's yarn hair as I normally did, but I didn't care.

I remember tossing Lilly aside as I watched Grandpa shake hands with Uncle Walter, and then hug Aunt Lolita. My cousin Lisa stood aside with a frown on her face. She was upset that I was leaving, too. We'd gotten used to spending a lot of time together even though we fought a lot; we were still a family. When Grandpa leaned down and kissed Lisa goodbye, she turned up her nose and quickly wiped away his kiss.

Uncle Walter said to Grandpa, "Lisa's nine years old now.

1

Don't worry, she doesn't even like for us to kiss her anymore either."

"That's all right. They grow up too fast these days."

After our goodbyes that day, we headed to Charlotte.

"Buckle up everybody," Grandpa said, while the melodic tune of Jeffrey Osborne singing *On the Wings of Love* poured from the car's speakers. I imagined my parents as angels flying above the station wagon, and looking down on me from Heaven.

"Now Willie, you know we don't listen to secular music," Grandma said to Grandpa, and quickly turned the dial. She quickly looked over her shoulder at me. "Germaine, you'll have to excuse your Grandpa for playing that song. We only listen to church music."

I thought to myself, *Oh boy*. I had a feeling it was going to be a long ride to Charlotte that day. It would be another long ride to Washington, DC and Rockford University years later.

Here I was, away from home again, and I missed Charlotte, my grandma, and the gospel music she played every day that eventually grew on me. I even had a few favorites now, but while gospel music comforted me most days, I found myself writing poems and stories to keep from getting homesick. This morning was no different. I went to bed late last night after writing a love story, and now I was up early writing again, but this time I'd been writing in my journal. I felt compelled to write about my secret crush on Angelo Pearson. Ever since I wrote a piece on Angelo for the school's *American Youth Magazine* (AYM), I hadn't been able to stop looking at his featured picture on the front cover.

I was the first freshman to ever publish articles that attracted the attention of over 80 percent of the students on campus. Although some articles I got slack from, the article on Rockford's beloved football star, Angelo, was the student's' current favorite piece.

When I stood up from my study desk, I felt dizzy for a brief moment. My head swam from fatigue. I locked my journal in the desk drawer, grabbed the AYM magazine, and put it inside my backpack. Every writer treasured their most favored piece. A part of me felt like I was carrying Angelo with me since his face graced the cover. My English professor, Susan Schwartz, who was the editor-in-chief for the magazine said to me, "Brilliant work, Ms. Landry." She'd always spoken in a toffee-nosed style. I wasn't sure if it was how she articulated her words or if she was being a snoot.

"Headed to class, Germaine?" Shante grunted from the top bunk, as she stretched her long skinny arms toward the ceiling. Her hair was standing up like the feathers of an electrocuted chicken.

"Yeah, I'll see you guys later." I grabbed my biology book off a stack of R&B boy band CDs. I'd purchased them before I came to Rockford without my grandmother knowing.

"Oh, if Lisa wakes up looking for her Pink Lady pin, I set it on the dresser," I mentioned to Shante, and glanced at Lisa snoring on the bottom bunk. Her long wavy hair was sprawled over her pillow like spider legs, and the side of her mouth dropped a thin film of saliva. If only her Line Sisters could see "Miss Beauty Queen" without her makeup and snoring like a bear, she'd be ridiculed all over campus.

"I'll tell her." Shante nodded, and then flopped back on her pillow.

She and Lisa met in math class last year when they were freshmen. This year they seem to have a similar schedule for their sophomore classes, because they started late and allowed them to sleep in. It was a good thing or else they would be late every day. They had been out all last night on a scavenger hunt for the Big Sisters of the Pink Ladies sorority they were pledging for. Each week Shante and Lisa had to do something different. Some of the things were downright disgusting! The worst of them was when I walked into our room one evening, and the five line sisters were passing a raw egg mouth-to-mouth. The objective was to not let the yolk burst. I'd decided to write an opinion piece for the AYM about it. I titled it, *How Far Will You Go for the Sisterhood and Brotherhood?*

Unfortunately, it was most of the students' least favorite article. Thankfully, I was able to bounce back with my latest piece on Angelo Pearson.

SAY YES

As soon as my feet hit the pavement outside of Angela Davis Hall, I started running down College Street. I kept telling my feet to hurry, as the autumn winds blew my African braids back from my face. My feet crushed the dead leaves scattered on the pavement. It sounded like someone crunching potato chips as I sprinted down the street. I dodged and weaved through the pedestrian traffic of students on the sidewalk. A young man seemed to step into my path, and he bumped me so hard with his shoulder, my body jerked backward. I felt myself sway off balance from all the heavy books in my backpack. Like a bowling pin wobbling front to back, I tried to hold myself steady to keep from falling, but the heel of my shoes slipped on a small pile of leaves.

"WH-WH-WH-WHOOOOA!"

I landed on my butt! My backpack fell onto the ground, and burst wide open. Everything inside flew up in the air like a mini-tornado. The impact of the fall made my glasses come off my face, and I couldn't see where they landed. My butt hurt so bad, I could have sworn I'd broken my tailbone.

"Dag girl, watch where you're going!"

I blinked twice, trying to make out the face of a young man's voice yelling at me. His lips were scrawled, and his nose was flared like a bull. He balled his hands into fists, and I thought he was going to hit me.

"No, no, no, please don't hurt me!" I held up one hand in defense, while simultaneously searching for my glasses with the other. All I could feel was the cold concrete at first, and then I felt something round and smooth with handles. *My glasses! Thank you, God!* I scrambled to put them on.

I could see that the young man had a chocolate complexion,

and he was wearing a black hoodie. He wasn't alone, there were three others with him. He stood lopsided over me and I realized my glasses were bent. As he came into clearer vision, I noticed he was wearing a gold herringbone chain with a bulldog pendant. His hair was cut in a short fade with a zigzag part in the front. I knew him as Marcus. He was one of the upperclassman who played for the Rockford Raiders football team, and he was a member of the Bulldogs Fraternity.

"Sorry about that." I staggered to my feet, and dusted off the crumbly leaves that were sticking to my plaid wool skirt like the prickles from the legs of a beetle. Marcus's face snarled and then relaxed. I watched his thick lips curve a crooked grin. I smiled back, thinking perhaps there were no hard feelings. When he started laughing, so did I. I'm sure the way I'd fallen was pretty comical. What more could I do besides laugh it off?

"It was just an accident right?"

"If you say so." He laughed harder, and the three guys with him chimed in. I wasn't sure of their names, but I was pretty certain they traveled in the same circles. I looked at Marcus confused because I knew it couldn't be *that* funny. Suddenly, I felt a cold draft on my legs. I looked down and realized my pantyhose had fallen to my ankles.

"Oh no!" I quickly ducked behind a parked car and pulled them up. I knew the tights were too big, but Lisa let me have the extra pair she bought since I had run out, but I should've known better. Lisa was curvy and thicker in build than I was. She was also two inches taller than me. I was 5'5" and she was 5'7". The size of these pantyhose was Q, and I always wore petite. I felt so embarrassed, I wanted to run back to Davis Hall and never come out of my dorm room again.

"Clumsy nerd!" Marcus taunted, and then slapped high-fives with his boys. They started cracking jokes about how skinny my legs were. It was a painful reminder that I was born premature. It just happens that I have a small frame with a big head as a result. Thank God I could wear braids to hide my forehead, but there was nothing I could do about my bony legs.

"Hey, why're you guys just standing around watching this

poor girl pick up her own things from the ground?"

I looked up as I was gathering my papers. I was trying to stop them from flying into the busy Georgia Avenue streets. I recognized the handsome guy who came to my aid: Angelo "Ace" Pearson, the school's star running back.

"Here you go, miss." Angelo handed me the last of the papers, and I shoved them inside my backpack. I'd have to carry it like a purse now since the zipper broke.

"I'm sorry my brothers were rude to you," Angelo said, his hazel eyes meeting mine.

"It's okay. Don't worry about it."

"I'll handle them for you," he said, but I was busy admiring his curly hair and deep Tom Selleck-like dimples.

"I don't think it's polite for you guys to bash this young lady. That's not the way Bulldogs treat women."

"Why not, Ace? Payback is a mutha–"

"Chill out, Marcus, okay? Don't even go there."

"But Ace, how you gonna let this girl write lies about us in the school magazine?"

"I said chill, man! We have to respect our women. You guys know the rules. Besides, any type of news we get is good press for the Bulldogs. It puts our name out there."

I couldn't tell if Angelo was putting on airs or if he was serious about respecting women. You see, the Bulldogs had a reputation for dogging out women, which was part of the opinion piece I had written a month ago.

"Easy for you to say, Ace. The latest magazine article about you didn't mention nothing bad about *you*. Last I recall, you're a Bulldog too. King of our frat," Marcus contested. That's when I realized it wasn't an accident that Marcus bumped into me. He was still angry about the article.

"Forget about that. It's the past. Just go on to class and I'm going to walk this young lady to hers, got it?"

The guys frowned and grumbled something under their breath, and headed to their classes. I admired Angelo for having that kind of power. Even though what Marcus and the frat brothers did was wrong, I almost felt sorry for them after the way Angelo had reprimanded them like children.

"Let me help you carry your books," Angelo reached out his big hands. They were wide enough to catch a football, that's for sure.

"Thanks for helping me, Angelo."

"No problem at all, so tell me your name again. Is it Gina something?"

"It's Germaine Landry." I quickly answered, and sped up my walk. I was a little upset that he had already forgotten my name, even though I interviewed him just a month ago, and sat in front of his face for at least an hour.

"Really? I never heard of a girl with a boy's name."

"Mine is Germaine with a *G* not a J, and for the record it's a unisex name."

"Well excuuuse me. I guess inviting you out to the Bulldog's party this weekend would be too much to ask, huh?"

"I'm not interested, but thanks."

He opened the doors to the Arts & Science building, and I walked inside.

"Is that a no?"

"*No* is part of a universal language. I'm sure you understand that since you're no dumb jock, right?"

"Come again?"

"Never mind." I shook my head. I couldn't believe myself. Was I really this upset because he couldn't remember my name? Maybe I was just a nobody to him. This reminded me of the time I was in the eighth grade, and I had a crush on a boy named Myron. I had given him a small box of chocolates for Valentine's Day. He ate the chocolates, dumped the box, and didn't even say thank you. I was a nobody then, and maybe I still was.

"Maybe you don't know me, Germaine."

"Oh, I know you."

"You think you know me, but that article you guys did about me was all about football."

"Why does it matter if I know you or not? You didn't even remember my name." I reached for my books and freed his hands, as we stood outside of my classroom. He stepped in close to me, propped his arms against the door frame, and I felt caged in. He stood so close to me that my nose almost touched his midsection. I could smell the leather of his Rockford jacket mixed with the scent of his cologne that smelled like sandalwood and something sweet.

Suddenly, I felt nervous and turned on at the same time.

"I remembered your name. I knew your name from the minute you came here."

I puckered my brow. I felt confused.

"I know everything that goes on around this campus."

"Then why did you ask my name?"

"I was just making conversation, but I'd like to get to know you better, Ms. Germaine with a *G*." He softened his voice and leaned in close to my ear.

I felt awkward as I stood in front of him like a helpless child. I wasn't sure why he was looking at me so intense. It felt like his eyes were peeling my clothes off. I wondered what he saw. My breasts were the size of apples, I had a flat, cardboard-shaped butt, and I was so skinny if I turned sideways you could see my heart beating. I wasn't ugly, just average I think, so what did he see in me that was so pressing that I had to come to his party?

"I have to go." I twisted the knob on the classroom door, but Angelo quickly grabbed me and pulled me back from the door.

"If you knew me, Germaine. You would know that I don't like to be turned down. Take this VIP invite and bring your girlfriends." He handed me a colorful black and gold invitation from the inside of his jacket pocket.

Seeing that he wasn't going to give up easy I took it.

"If I come, I need to bring my roommates."

"Like I said. Please bring your girlfriends. The more the merrier."

"You may already know them."

"What're their names?"

"Lisa and Shante. They're pledging for the Pink Ladies."

"Oh yeah. They may just end up joining our sister

organization. I think one of my brothers used to mess with Lisa."

"Oh really?" I asked, pretending to be surprised. "Anyway, I gotta get to class."

"Before you go inside, you may want to step into the ladies room."

"Why?"

His eyes rolled down from my face to my legs. My pantyhose had fallen again.

I'm going to kill Lisa!

ANGELO PEARSON

"Ace! Ace! Can I get your autograph?" A young man asked as soon as I walked into Victor's Italian diner uptown with my frat brothers. I quickly scribbled my name on the back of his food receipt—a big capital A, lowercase c.e. and my jersey number 19.

"Thank you! Ya'll crushed Morgan State tonight, man, and you ran through those dudes like bowling pins!"

"Thanks, my man." I smiled proudly and watched the young buck hurry out the door to brag about meeting me to his friends.

I walked up to the counter and the young lady smiled widely. She twirled one of her braids around her finger.

"What can I get you tonight, Ace?" She batted her eyes. She didn't know me personally, but I was used to girls flirting with me.

"Why don't you run and get Vic for me, sweetheart?"

"Sure, anything for you, Ace." She walked toward the back, and within seconds Victor walked out of his office with his belly hanging over his belt. His arms were swelled like Popeye's with tattoos of skulls. I watched him wipe sweat from his forehead, and use a small comb to slick his black, greasy looking hair back into place. Victor was always sweating, maybe because he was a big guy.

"Ace, come here, son, let's talk." Victor motioned his hands, and I knew to meet him around back. I told my frat brothers to order anything they wanted and I'd be right back.

I met Victor at the back of the diner near the dumpsters. It always smelled like dead rats and piss, but I didn't care. I was there for only one thing.

"You's did a good job out there tonight, kid. I was in the

11

back watching the whole game and I's tell ya kid, three touchdowns ain't all bad, so here you go." He spoke in his native Italian accent, and handed me a ball of cash neatly wrapped in a thick rubber band.

"Remember kid, if you look out for me I's look out for you, got it? So, uh, the next game, be sure to score four touchdowns 'cause I's got a lot of money on the next one, got it?"

"I got it."

"Hey, remember this stays between us. I don't want no wise guys in our business, ya understand?"

"I got it, Vic."

"Those other guys who play ball with you are wise guys, especially the one with the eraser head."

"Marcus? He's my boy. He's cool."

"You better watch him, Ace. He always looks at me funny. I don't trust him. He's a schmuck. Any guy who eyeballs you is a schmuck, understand? I swear if he wasn't a friend of yours, I'd whack him!" Victor went on and on. He never gave me an opportunity to explain much. He always did all the talking and I had to listen. Nothing had changed since we met when I was a freshman, and he had offered me my first deal when I walked into his diner one day for lunch. I guess it was because Victor was the boss of his own diner and a bouncer at the IBEX club at night. He was used to telling folks what to do or making them do it with his fists.

"Find some new friends, kid, I'm warning, ya." He tossed his cigar to the ground and smashed what was left of it with the pointy toe of his dress shoe. I counted the money to make sure all three thousand dollars were there. I got paid a thousand dollars per touchdown. I'm sure Victor got paid twice as much. When I saw the amount was correct, I went back inside.

"Hey Ace, you're in deep thought over there, man," Marcus said, after he and the guys devoured plates of spaghetti, lasagna, and pizza. Our tables were filled with so many empty plates that you would've thought the guys had eaten at a buffet instead of a diner.

"I'm cool, just tired from the game tonight."

"So what did Victor want?"

"Oh that was just business. You know what time it is."

"Yeah, well, how much loot he give you this time?"

I looked over my shoulder to make sure Victor wasn't in sight, and I slipped Marcus a hundred dollar bill, but never said a word as to how much money Victor gave me.

"That's for the new kicks you wanted."

"You know I can buy my own sneakers."

"Selling weed? It'll take you a month!"

"You should tell Victor to let me in."

"Nah, he's trying to stay low key."

"Well, since you're being so generous, I won't complain." Marcus shoved the money into his pocket.

"Say man, what's going on here?" Eric asked, returning to the table after using the restroom. He took his hair pick and stuck it in the back of his thick red Afro.

"Nothing you need to know about, my man."

Eric was not just my frat brother, but my teammate. He played tight-end. I was running back, and Marcus was a tail-back.

"Yo homey, it looks like you got enough money there for the party this weekend, son." Tony rubbed his hands with excitement, as I quickly put the money away. I'd caused a scene already.

I met Tony my sophomore year. He was a transfer student from a small college in NY, and brought a lot of style to our fraternity. He was a nice dresser and smooth with the ladies. He designed our new frat jackets.

"I put up a lot of money for the party already, guys. I paid for the deejay, bought the booze, and the food. You guys can take care of the rest of that crap."

"We-we-we can handle the decorations and paper goods or whatever small stuff is left, Ace." PeeWee stuttered and cracked his knuckles. It was a nervous habit that irritated me, but he was a nervous kid. Our youngest frat brother that we recruited last year. His name was Ricky, but we called him

"PeeWee" because he was the youngest, and he looked like he still belonged in high school. Yet, PeeWee had more heart than the other recruits.

"Just so ya'll know, I invited Germaine Landry."

"Who?" They questioned, one-by-one.

"The girl who writes articles for the AYM." I reminded them, and then they broke out in silly amusement.

"Did I say something funny?"

"Yeah man, why are you inviting her?" Tony laughed.

"I got plans for that fresh meat."

"Aw shucks! I knew Ace had something up his sleeve. You gonna turn that country girl out, aren't you?" Eric seemed itching to know.

"Anybody willing to make a wager on it?"

"We're in. Fifty dollars apiece!" Tony exclaimed.

"It's not going down like that. I want a hundred dollars each. This one is going to be a challenge. I can tell."

"We-we-we don't have that kind of money, Ace." PeeWee's voice shook.

"Call your folks. Tell them you need it for books or something."

"Here, you can take back the hundred you gave me. I want to see Germaine rot for what she said about our frat." Marcus seemed anxious for revenge.

"Just so we know it happened. We gotta videotape it like we always do, know what I'm saying?"

"Cool." I shrugged, sipping the last of my soda. I caught the eyes of an elderly woman staring at me with her eyebrows pointed toward her nose. She looked like the bad witch in the *Wizard of Oz*, except she was short, and didn't wear a long black dress.

"You gotta problem, Grandma?"

"Yeah, why is she looking at you like that, Ace?" Eric wondered.

"I'm staring at you so I can remember what a bunch of fools look like." She raised her cane, as she approached us. I thought she was going to hit us with it.

"You'll reap what you sow if you do that to that young lady. The good book says so! 'What a man soweth he shall reap.'"

"Go on home, Grandma, and change your Depends." Tony shoved her back as she started toward me.

"Come on, Martha, mind your business now. Leave the young fellas alone before you get us both killed." Her husband tugged at her arm. The two walked out the door together, and I could still hear the old woman rambling obscenities about us, and cursing us to kingdom come.

When I got home later that night, there was a message on my voicemail from Germaine confirming that she was coming to the party. *Let the games begin!*

THE PARTY

Mary J. Blige poured through the speakers of my boombox. Her new hit, *Real Love,* was playing on *93.9 WKYS,* and I was sitting in the desk chair while Lisa did my makeup. Shante was on the other side of the room getting dressed. I still couldn't believe that Angelo asked me to the party, and Lisa and Shante couldn't believe it either.

"I don't trust that Ace," Shante admitted, as she walked over to the mirror on the back of her closet door. She checked to make sure she had zipped up her dress in the back.

"If I were you, I wouldn't be too quick to let my guard down. Not unless you want the same thing that he does."

"What're you talking about, Shante?"

"Come on, Germaine, I know you're not *that* naïve."

"I don't get down on the first night, Shante, so don't worry about me."

"Girl please, you don't get down like that, period. You got a padlock on your booty," Lisa teased.

"Wait a minute! You're still a virgin?"

"Gee, thanks a lot for telling her, Lisa! Just because I don't sleep around like you, that doesn't give you the right to tell my business."

Lisa burst out laughing.

"It's not funny, and Shante, being a virgin doesn't mean I have a disease."

"I'm sorry, I didn't mean to say it like that. I actually think it's pretty cool that you're nineteen and still a virgin, but whatever you do, don't tell Ace. The Bulldogs prey on the innocence of girls like you."

"She shouldn't just be worried about Ace, but Donna. I told her we can all go to this party, but she needs to be careful. Don't get caught up."

"Who's Donna?" I asked, trying not to blink as Lisa put the eyeliner on me.

"Donna is Ace's jealous ex-girlfriend. She's the President of the Pink Ladies, you've seen her before. She dyed her hair blonde and wears those blue contacts."

"You mean to tell me that RuPaul-looking girl used to be Ace's girlfriend?"

"She was his girlfriend until she cheated on him with his frat brothers. That's how she became President of the Pink Ladies. She let them run a train on her."

"How can she be jealous of me after what she did?"

"You know how it is... or maybe you don't, but for some people when they can't have what they want then they don't want anybody else to have that person either. Anyway, are you and Lisa ready yet?"

"We're all set," Lisa said, handing me the mirror, and I gave her thumbs up for a good makeup job.

The Bulldogs frat house was a ten minute ride uptown. The block was nicknamed Greek Row because of the fraternity and sorority houses that stretched along the block of Kennedy Street. The steps to the Bulldogs' house had three Greek letters painted in black, and a big bone made of stone hung over the threshold by spike chains. As we approached the steps, there were two frat brothers wearing their fraternity paraphernalia— a black hoodie with gold Greek letters.

"WOOF WOOF BULLDOGS!" the frat brothers at the door chanted their fraternity call. I could only shake my head at the silliness of it all.

When we walked inside, Snoop Dogg's song, *Gin and Juice,* was blasting so loud that I could feel the bass under my feet, and I thought I was going to catch a contact high from the marijuana people were smoking.

"Can you please fix that look on your face?" Lisa stopped me before we entered the living room crowded with people dancing.

"What look?"

"That nonchalant look. Even if you don't want to be here, just smile and fake it."

"Don't worry about Germaine. She'll be all right. She'll warm up."

They usually partied without me. It was the first time I'd ever been to a party, and so far I wasn't impressed at all. Back at home the young folks from church had gatherings, but they were modest. We would gather in the basement, drink punch, play board games, and sneak on secular music when our folks weren't watching. This party had S.I.N. written all over it, and if my grandmother knew Lisa and I were here, she would have a heart attack.

"Germaine, you're not going to ruin my fun tonight. I plan to lay one of these cuties," Lisa huffed in vexation.

"Is this better?" I forced a smile on my face.

"No, but just come on!" Lisa grabbed me by the hand, as we walked in close together trying to squeeze our way through the crowd. It was a bad idea to come to the party, and I could feel it in my stomach. The last thing I needed was for someone to see Lisa holding my hand, embarrassing me. I wasn't a child, but my grandparents wanted Lisa to look after me, which is why they convinced Rockford's Housing Department to squeeze me into the room with Lisa and Shante.

I quickly snatched my hand back and followed Lisa into the living room, trying not to trip and fall in the big red heels she'd loaned me. It was either I wear the heels or my patent leather loafers. I just wanted to be comfortable, but Lisa insisted I look sexy for Ace. I personally think my favorite pants suit and loafers would've fit just fine.

Lisa spotted someone she knew, and quickly said to me, "I think you can handle things on your own from here, can't you?"

"I'll be just fine, Lisa."

"Try to find out where Ace is or something. Don't just stand around like a wallflower. It makes you look lost and out of place," Lisa added, before walking away to dance with some guy who was eyeballing her from afar. She claimed she knew him, maybe she did or maybe she didn't. I could never keep up with Lisa. She'd never dated any guy seriously, and she seemed to get bored very easily with them. I'm sure if Uncle Walter knew how many boys on campus she'd bedded, he'd grab his shotgun and ask questions later.

Anyway, Shante and I walked into the dining room where one of the Bulldogs was serving drinks from a big punch bowl. He stood behind the table wearing a black T-shirt with a bulldog on the front, and dark sunshades, even though there was no sunlight.

"How much?" Shante asked him, as she reached into her purse.

"Five dollars."

I couldn't even see his eyes through his shades, they were really dark and I wondered how he could see us or anything else for that matter. Then I remembered the VIP invitation.

"No, wait, drinks are free for us, and so is the food." I reached in my purse and handed him our VIP card that Ace had given me. He barely looked at it or probably couldn't see what it said with those dark shades on. He served Shante a plastic cup of fruit punch that reeked of alcohol, and then proceeded to hand a drink to me as well.

"No thanks, I don't drink. I'd like a glass of water if you don't mind."

"Water? Who is this girl?"

"Don't mind her, she doesn't get out much, but we're working on that," Shante said to him, and then she intertwined her arm with mine. We turned around to face the living room and watched the people dancing.

It wasn't really dancing if you ask me, just a lot of bumping and grinding that would cause my grandparents to fall out of their rocking chairs if they saw it. I remember one day, I was caught watching *BET* with Donnie Simpson hosting a music video countdown, and Grandma caught me. She sat me down and prayed with me so long I fell asleep. I really did! She said, "I had to make sure you weren't cursed, child. You stay away from those music videos and things, that secular music is the

Devil!" Grandma was sweet, but she was always preaching to me.

"I don't plan to stay long, so let's make sure we get back by our midnight curfew." I glanced at my watch; it was ten fifteen.

"Leave a party before midnight? Nobody pays attention to curfew on the weekends. So don't worry, you won't change into a homely looking rag doll when the clock strikes midnight, Cinderella," Shante laughed.

"Look, you and Lisa can stay as long as you like, but I'm leaving before curfew. You guys will have to catch a ride back to school."

"Fine you ole party pooper. I'm about to get my dance on. You should try to have a little fun for once, Germaine." She kicked off her heels and headed to the dance floor.

"Hey there, you look lost." I felt someone tap my shoulder. I turned around and noticed it was Donna. I immediately felt nervous.

"No, I'm-I'm-I'm not lost. I'm just waiting for them to play something I can dance to that's all."

"Really? Me too. What sorority are you with?" she stared me up and down with a skeptical eye.

"Oh, I'm not part of any sorority."

"Seems like you could be an AKA. Some of them are pretty quiet."

"I'm not quiet with people I know."

"Aren't you Lisa's cousin? Your name is Germaine, right?"

I looked at her warily. "Yes, it's Germaine."

"I'm Donna." She extended her hand and I hesitated to shake it at first, but she extended it further with persistence. "I heard Ace invited you to this party by VIP."

"He did invite me, and I brought my cousin and Shante with me."

"He's my ex-boyfriend you know."

I nodded, suddenly feeling a world of butterflies in my stomach. I felt unsure as to where this conversation was going, especially by the smidgen look of skepticism on Donna's face.

"There's nothing going on between us, Donna."

"I'm sure there isn't. Besides, if Ace wants you, he just downgraded." She gritted on me and walked away with her nose snobbishly in the air.

Wow, I just got dissed! I'd had enough. My feet hurt from the shoes being too big. I felt high from the smoke in the room. I was hungry because the so-called "free" food was nothing but stale potato chips, weenies turned dry, and leftover pieces of cheddar cheese on a platter. I made a beeline out the door.

I stepped into my sky blue Toyota Corolla (a graduation present from Uncle Walter), sat down on the driver seat, and locked the door. I decided to wait a little while for Lisa and Shante, but then I would leave before midnight. I turned on the radio, and Tevin Campbell's *Alone With You* was playing on *WHUR 96.3*. He was singing the words I felt, except I wanted to be alone and *at home*. I had no one to be alone with anyway. This was becoming the story of my life. Lisa and Shante got all the guys, and what did I do usually? Bury myself in a good book or write one to relive my fantasies.

I looked up at the frat house and thought about going back inside to wait for Lisa and Shante. I could see the shadows of people dancing from the window. They were having a good time. It was much warmer inside than it was sitting in my car, so I headed back toward the frat house.

As soon as I twisted the knob on the door, a girl came running out, nearly knocking me down. She was topless and her breasts jiggled in every direction. I watched her closely to see where she was running off to. She stopped in the front yard, and swayed side-to-side before puking in one of the shrubs. I quickly turned my head.

"I got her! I got her!" One of the guys ran past me with his jacket in hand. He rushed to the girl upchucking in his front yard, and draped his jacket over her shoulders. I decided to go back to my car, because whatever was going on inside was getting too wild for me.

I was hungering to put my mind someplace else, and I wished I was back in my dorm finishing my manuscript that I was trying to get published. So far, college life was nothing like how I imagined it would be. I had envisioned myself becoming the girl I never was in high school by getting noticed more, being more sociable, and having more friends. Maybe I'd watched too many episodes of *A Different World,* none of that stuff was real. I was foolish to even think I would end up like Whitley and find a Dwayne Wayne. Maybe something was wrong with me. Was I the only one who saw some of the people on campus as strange, wild, and crazy? Or was *I* the one who was abnormal?

"Hello in there!" I heard someone shout, snapping me out of my thoughts and causing my body to jerk forward. I looked at the passenger window and saw a pair of hazel eyes staring at me.

"I didn't mean to scare you, but can you open the door?"

My heart was beating fast, pounding like someone beating a bass drum. Angelo had scared the crap out of me! I quickly sat up and adjusted my skirt as best I could, took my braids out of a ponytail, and pushed my new glasses over the bridge of my nose.

"It's kind of cold out here, Germaine. Do you think you could open the door before Christmas?" He shivered from his shoulders downward. I pushed the button to unlock the door.

"Sheesh, you tried to freeze a brother out here."

"Sorry, Angelo."

He climbed onto the passenger seat, and I could feel the cold fall air from his body as he sat down.

"Why did you leave the party?"

"You mean, you knew I was at the party?"

"I know everything. That's why they call me Ace."

"Are you high?"

"Only for you, baby," he reached over and slid his hand up my thigh. I jumped in shock, and smacked his hand as hard as I could.

"Stop it! I'm not that kind of girl!"

"OUCH! My hand is on fire!"

I rolled my eyes at him. How dare he think I was some

tramp that he could just roll up on me and do as he pleased?

"It was just a touch, that's all. Sheesh!"

"Just to think, I actually thought you respected women. Silly me, I should've known you were just putting on a front."

"No, no, I'm sorry. I'm a little . . . you know . . . buzzed or whatever." His eyes did a dance of their own without his control. I didn't like it at all. An intoxicated man was a turn off, no matter how cute he was.

"Please get out of my car."

"You can't be serious! Are you really saying that to me?"

I winced my eyes at him, giving him an evil stare.

"Listen, I'm *really* sorry and I promise I won't touch you again."

"Fine, you can stay for now."

"You know, you need to lighten up a little, Germaine."

"You mean allow you to disrespect me?"

"I don't believe this. At first you were too shy to say two words to me and now you're ready to knock me out like Mike Tyson? What's your problem?"

"I just don't like being disrespected, and another thing, why did you invite Donna to the party tonight? Isn't she supposed to be your ex-girlfriend?"

He blushed a handsome dimpled smile, as he took off his hat, and ran his fingers through his hair, loosening his curls.

"Well?"

"Do I detect a little jealousy? If so, I think that's sexy."

"Jealous? Why would I be jealous? I don't even know you, but it's tacky to invite your ex to a party with a girl you want to get to know."

"Donna is the president of our sister organization. That's how it goes. When we throw a party, we invite our sisters and vice versa."

"I bet."

"You know my hand still hurts. I hope I can catch a football at tomorrow's game, but if I can't it's your fault."

"I didn't mean to hit you that hard. Just enough for you to remember not to try that again."

"I find your feistiness to be very sexy."

"Please stop flirting with me. You're high and you don't mean it."

"Oh I do mean it, but I promise I'll be cool from now on."

"Good."

"Why're you sitting out here in your car, anyway?" he asked, curiously.

"I decided to pick my poison."

"Was the party that bad?"

I pursed my lips and gave him a look that said, *what do you think?*

"You don't know how to have fun. I bet your idea of fun is watching *Jeopardy.*"

"They said you're a junior here, but you act like you're still in high school."

"That's just the way you see it," he said, and then pulled down the mirror on the passenger side and checked his face. "You don't want to pass up on this," he stroked the smoothness of his cheeks.

"You're not short on confidence I see."

"If you hate me so much then why are you here?"

"I've been asking myself that all night. This was a complete waste of time. I should charge you for gas."

"I don't think I ever met anybody as uptight as you. I mean, do you wake up in the mornings, look at yourself in the mirror and say, 'damn, why did you wake me up?'"

"Angelo, stick to playing football. Comedy is not you," I said, leaning forward to turn the heat up in the car.

"So, where're you from, Miss Germaine with a *G*?"

"Charlotte."

"Charlotte? Well what made you travel this far when you have all those historical black colleges down South?"

"I wanted to get away from home. Besides, my cousin Lisa hyped up the school so much I wanted to see it for myself. It was either Rockford, Howard or Trinity. I chose Rockford for its diversity."

"Listen, let's clear the air about this article you wrote for the

AYM," he skipped the subject. "You said your cousin Lisa and her friend Shante are pledging, but you're obviously not. What is your beef with us and why did you go so hard in that article?"

"I think it's a complete waste of time and energy. Not to mention there's secret hazing that goes on."

"Not with our chapter, and there're plenty of benefits to being a part of a fraternity you know. We do a lot for the community, our families, and local schools. We even help our brothers and sisters to find jobs. Just last week we raised money to feed the homeless."

"The article I wrote was an opinion piece, that's all. Don't take it personal."

"I understand that, but aren't opinion pieces still supposed to state all the facts? See, even I know that. I bet you didn't expect that from a jock, right?"

"Look, for the record, I apologize for offending you and your brothers. It won't happen again."

"They'll be happy to hear that. You know, at least you're not the type of girl who's afraid to speak her mind. Just don't go so hard on folks next time."

"Point taken."

"Do you think we can have just one dance together tonight before you leave?"

I thought about it for a moment, and if I didn't dance with Angelo it would *really* be a waste of a night.

"Sure, one dance won't hurt. Let's go."

SOMETHING NEW

I was sitting outside of Davis Hall in my black Pathfinder waiting for Germaine to join me. I'd cleared my Saturday schedule since I was supposed to take Tamika to dinner, and then meet Stacey at the club later on. I lied and told them I had to ride back home for the weekend because my parents got sick. They were disappointed, but I would make it up to them later. I needed to get the ball rolling so I could win the bet on smashing Germaine.

While I was checking my beeper for missed calls, I heard someone knock on the passenger door. When I looked up, I saw that it was Germaine. I got out and opened the door, and helped her inside.

"I thought I was going to have to come inside and rescue you."

"Sorry I'm late. Lisa and Shante had to loan me something nice to wear."

"They've got good taste." I eyeballed her from head to toe. She was wearing a burgundy leather skirt, sweater, and matching burgundy leather boots. Germaine was a skinny little thing, but she was kind of cute to me. There was something about her bright eyes, and those thick sexy lips that curved wide at the corners when she smiled. I typically preferred my chicks with a lot of junk in the trunk, trendy clothes, and high heels. Germaine was the opposite. She was a cross between a plain Jane type chick and a church girl who wore long skirts. It was nice to see her dressed up in something trendy and sexy for a change.

"I love this song!" Germaine swayed her head side-to-side to Mint Condition's, *U Send Me Swingin.*

"Yeah, I was hoping you would. I figured playing their CD

would be a good start to what we have to look forward to.”

“I’m so excited! And, did you say P.M. Dawn is opening for Mint Condition?”

“Yep, they’re gonna kill it!”

“I can’t wait. I hope we have good seats too.”

When I came up on a red traffic light, I handed her the two tickets from the inside of my jacket pocket.

“Wow, front row seats?”

“A friend of mine hooked me up in exchange for an autograph of my football jersey.”

“Wow!”

“I take it you’ve never seen these groups in concert before.”

“I’ve never been to a live music concert, except at church.”

“Why is that?”

“My grandparents are very religious people.”

“So you live with your grandparents?”

She shook her head yes.

“Are your parents religious too?”

“My parents died in a car accident when I was a kid.”

I gently rubbed her hand. “I’m sorry.”

“No need to apologize. You didn’t know.”

“Must’ve been kind of tough for you growing up without your parents, and then having to live with strict grandparents, huh?”

“Sometimes. At least Grandma let me go to the movies and to the mall with my friends. It’s my grandfather who’s really quiet. He’s the only man I know who can watch the late night shows faithfully and not laugh. He’ll crack a smile, but that’s it.”

“Interesting, so do you have any brothers or sisters?”

“No, it’s just me. What about you?”

“I’m an only child too. I guess we finally have something in common.” I winked at her.

After the concert, Germaine and I couldn’t stop talking about how good of a performance the groups put on.

“. . . and when P.M. Dawn sang *Die Without You* oh, I could have melted!" Germaine blushed. "Thank you so much for taking me, Angelo. I'll remember this night forever."

"Sounds like we need to go out more often, Germaine, like every Saturday. There're a lot of things I can show you that you may like," I said, as I pulled up to the Southwest Waterfront in front of the Phillips Restaurant.

"I'd like that."

I opened the door for her, and helped her to step out of the truck.

"Did I tell you that you look beautiful tonight?"

"No."

"That was a compliment, Germaine."

"Oh, sorry. Thank you."

"Have you dated before?" I intertwined my arms around hers, while the valet drove off to park my truck.

"No, I haven't."

"Not even the prom?"

"The only way I could go was if I took a guy from church, and I never liked any of the boys at church, so I didn't go. My prom dress that my Uncle Walter bought for me is still hanging inside my closet back at home."

"That's messed up!"

"Yes it is. I wondered for so long what I missed out on, but oh well. Life goes on, right?"

I gently took hold of her hand, and kissed the back of it. "Life does move on."

After dinner, Germaine and I went walking along the pier. I draped my leather jacket across her shoulders to keep her warm.

"Are you at Rockford on a football scholarship?"

"Now see, you're stereotyping me. I thought we weren't going to go there tonight."

She chuckled. "I'm sorry, I didn't mean to prejudge you."

"You're right though. I am on a football scholarship, but I'm not a dumb jock just so we're clear on that. I still have to keep my grades up to maintain the scholarship."

"Good for you." She hit me with a playful elbow on my side.

I was beginning to find her cynicism slightly attractive. No other girl was bold enough to speak what was on her mind. They usually agreed with everything I said and wanted to do.

There was silence between us for a moment as we walked by other couples on the pier. The riffs from Mint Condition's *Swinging* were still in my head, and there was something enchanting about tonight that felt peculiar. I couldn't put my finger on it, but I wanted to stay out for as long as we could, although I knew Germaine had a midnight curfew.

I stopped walking and turned Germaine gently toward me so I could look into her beautiful bright eyes. I slowly removed her glasses, and gently stroked the side of her cheek. When she didn't smack me like she had done at the party, I figured she was giving me permission to go further, so I leaned down and gently kissed her lips.

She took hold of my hand and led me to continue walking. I guess she didn't want me to go too far with her, so I didn't force it.

"You look beautiful without your glasses on. Have you considered contacts?"

"I wear them sometimes, but they dry out so fast."

"You should give it another shot. Maybe try a different brand because I love your eyes. I'll even buy you a pair if you'll wear them."

"Sure, I'll try a different pair, but I can't pay you back."

"I don't want you to do that. Just accept it as a gift."

"Was Rockford your only choice for schools or did other universities offer you a football scholarship?" She skipped the subject.

"I had other offers, but I wanted me and Marcus to play together again like we did in high school."

"I understand."

"My dad was a little bitter since he wanted me to play for a division one school."

"What does that mean?"

"It means, since Rockford is not a division one school that I may end up going as a second-round draft pick in the NFL, but I'm okay with that."

"What about your mother? Was she happy that you came to Rockford? I mean, you guys are still on TV sometimes."

"My mom really likes Rockford, but she wants me to become a doctor, so I majored in medicine in case football doesn't work out."

"At least she wants you to have a backup plan, but what do you want?"

"What do you mean?"

"Sounds like your dad wants you to play football and your mom wants you to be a doctor, but you never mentioned if that's actually what *you* want to do."

My eyes perked up with surprise. "Good question. Wow! I guess I never thought about it since I never really cared too much for school in the first place. I just know I can play football."

"Are there other things you like to do? Other things you're good at, I mean."

I paused in my walk. "Hey, you're not trying to get information out of me for another article are you?"

"Of course not! I would never do that without your permission."

"All right, well, I can draw. As a matter of fact, I paint and I'm really good at it. As a kid, I spent my summers in Paris with my maternal grandparents, and my grandmother taught me how to draw and paint. My grandfather taught me how to speak French fluently."

"Wow, that's amazing! I *never* would've imagined that about you."

"Why not?"

"On campus, you're a very confident jock who only seems interested in girls and parties. Not art."

"That's why I said if you got to know me, you may like me."

"Hmmm. I see. Why don't you say something to me in French?"

"Okay." I thought about it for a moment, and then I said, *"Croyez-moi et je vais vous montrer des choses que vous ne l'avez jamais vu."*

"Oh that sounds so beautiful. "What did you say?"

"I said, trust me and I'll show you things you've never seen."

"Interesting. So, your mother and maternal grandparents are European?"

"You got it. I'm biracial. My mother met my father in France while he was in the military. He made a detour during his travels so he could visit France. As irony would have it, he met my mom, and brought her back here to the States, or the colonies as they called it back in those days."

"Interesting, and your father is . . ."

"Dad is African American. From what I know, my paternal ancestors were sold and worked on a plantation in Zanzibar, Africa before they were sold in Jamestown."

"Angelo, your story is amazing. I wish I knew that much about my family history. Everyone's private when it comes to talking about the past in my family."

"Same here, I know some of my family history, but there are some things I don't know about."

"Like what?"

"Well, I wonder why my paternal grandfather and my dad stopped speaking to each other when my father came home from the military. This was before I was born. Later on, when my dad decided to marry my mom and have me, they started speaking to each other again. Even my mother doesn't know why they stopped speaking."

"Family secrets are intriguing to me. Yours sound just as interesting as mine. For instance, no one ever told me why my mother was driving the night she and my dad were killed in that car accident," Germaine began to explain, as we sat down on one of the benches. "My dad knew my mother wasn't that good of a driver, and especially at night. Why did he let her drive, or did she insist? And I heard it was raining that night too."

"That is kind of mysterious." I rubbed my chin in thought.

"Maybe that's why I like journalism. I love the investigating part of it. I'm hoping one day I'll stumble upon an old article that will go into more details than the short articles I found."

"One day you will."

Our eyes gazed at each other. We had more in common than I imagined. I felt compelled to kiss her again, and so I did. I could tell she'd never been kissed. She kissed fast, hard, and rushed. I coached her to follow my lead, and within seconds, she got the hang of French kissing and flowed with a natural rhythm. I loved it! I wanted to kiss her all night.

After I dropped Germaine off at home, I felt good. It was one of the best dates I'd been on in a long time, and I really didn't want to go home. I was used to dinner and a nightcap or better yet, just banging a chick on the first night, and forgetting her name by the next day.

I felt an urge to call Germaine and talk some more when I got home. I wanted to know so much more about her, and to tell her more about me, so I picked up the phone and dialed her number.

"Sorry, Ace, Germaine is knocked out sleep," one of her roommates said. I was disappointed. On the other hand, it was probably best that we didn't talk. I needed to focus on the bet. This was going to be hard. Germaine was such a nice girl and she was genuine. She wasn't like all the girls who had dated me because of my looks and popularity. She actually seemed to take an interest in me as a person. This was going to be tougher than I ever imagined.

CLOUD NINE

The Kiss

Gently he reached out his hands,
pulled me in close to him.
I nestled in his warmth,
sniffed his cologne,
and became high.
His eyes looked drowsily
in love with me,
penetrating through my soul.
The anticipation heated my skin
and made my heart bounce.
As his lips approached me,
I closed my eyes and imagined
how good this was going to be.

When his lips brushed against mine
our tongues did a ballerina dance
of twirls and spins.
I didn't want it to end,
but when it did,
all I wanted to do was kiss him again.

Last night was my first date with Angelo, and it was wonderful.
The concert was phenomenal! Mint Condition killed it, just like
Angelo said they would, and P.M. Dawn sang my favorite song,
Die Without You. For the first time in my life, I'd been kissed.
Like, really kissed! Angelo is such a great kisser. I feel like I'm
on cloud nine. I could never imagine myself with a guy of
Angelo's caliber. I'm so used to writing about guys like him in

my stories, that I never imagined it would actually come true for me. In high school, I had no luck attracting the cute guys I had crushes on. I wasn't an ugly person, but most guys only knew me as the smart girl in the class who always dressed like she was going to church. A part of me questions what Angelo sees in me since I'm not like other girls. Yet, whatever he sees in me, I want to keep doing it so he will continue to like me, and kiss me the way he did tonight.

-Germaine Landry,
Journal Entry: November 8, 1992

AM I IN LOVE?

Germaine and I talked on the phone nearly every day after our first date. I would also walk her to all of her classes, invite her to my games, and we'd study together in the library. I didn't normally like studying, but since it gave me a chance to be with her when I wasn't busy, I took advantage.

I took Germaine on a tour of DC and to the surrounding area known as the DMV. We went to the movie theater at Union Station, and watched *The Bodyguard* which starred Whitney Houston. We went bowling in College Park, which is right outside the city. We also went roller skating at Crystal's Skating Rink. Sometimes we would grab a slice of pizza after roller skating, and then go to Iverson Mall to shop. I bought Germaine a whole new wardrobe. No more hand-me-downs or borrowing outfits from her cousin Lisa and friend Shante. I also took her to a hairstylist I knew, and had her braids taken out. She complained about her forehead being big, but once the stylist finished with her hair, the curls hid her forehead nicely.

During the week, we skipped the school cafeteria for lunch, and I would take Germaine to places like Ben's Chili Bowl for the best chili dogs, or Horace and Dickey's on H Street for a fish sandwich. For her birthday, I took Germaine to Clyde's—a fine dining restaurant in Georgetown. I also surprised her with a pair of earrings as a gift.

On Saturday mornings, after football practice, Germaine and I drove to the best breakfast spot in the DMV, the Red Barn. Of course to expand some of our eating out energies, I managed (with the help of Lisa and Shante), to talk Germaine into partying with us at the Mirage Nightclub, and the Kilimanjaro. Because of my football popularity, the bouncers at the door allowed the underaged Germaine to enter the clubs with the agreement she was not to be seen drinking any alcohol. We would dance the night away to Buju Banton, Patra, and Super Cat. Teaching Germaine how to reggae dance was the fun part, but the bumping and grinding was the exciting part for me.

Germaine was growing on me, and I was really beginning to like her alot. I tried not to open up to her as much and remember the bet with my brothers, but Germaine's personality was infectious. I couldn't help but be honest with her and share myself. I felt drawn to her wittiness and curt sense of humor. She wasn't like any other girl I'd dated before. Even though she was naïve to the social scenes, she had a certain level of maturity about her for a nineteen-year-old. She wasn't petty like the other girls I dated, nor clingy or jealous. In fact, it was me who called her the most and when I didn't hear back, I would feel nervous and think that maybe she met someone closer to her age.

Germaine had an innocence about her that was so genuine that I loved exposing her to the social things in life. To my surprise, she was opening my mind too, although more intellectually. I love how she appreciated the little things, like the birthday card I gave her with a personal note meant more to her than the expensive dinner at Clyde's.

I decided to do something even more special for Germaine before she went home for Thanksgiving. I sent her to Ms. Sylvia, a seamstress at a cleaners on Florida Avenue.

"Pick out a favorite color and fabric, and have her make you a nice dress. I'm going to take you somewhere special, so just let me know what colors you choose, so I can complement you with my own special attire," I had said to Germaine by phone. I used the last of my allowance money and borrowed money from Victor to rent a tuxedo and a limo. I promised Victor I would score four touchdowns in the next game in exchange for a special rented hall, and Victor hooked me up.

All heads turned when the stretch white limo pulled up outside of Davis Hall.

"Where is she going?"

"Yeah, who is that?"

"Is that Ace?"

Students who were sitting out front of Davis Hall, all started to talk. I even caught a few heads peeping out the dorm room windows as I waited anxiously for Germaine to come outside. The minute she stepped out on the front steps, she looked gorgeous. She wore a beautiful purple satin dress with silver shoes and a matching shawl. She was wearing contacts and her hair was styled in spiral curls that dropped to her shoulders. I approached her slowly, smiling as my eyes trailed her body from head to toe.

"You look amazing." I leaned down to kiss her cheek. I couldn't take my eyes off her. I was looking forward to a wonderful night.

A MEMORABLE NIGHT

My stomach bubbled with giddy excitement, and I knew Angelo could feel the sweat in my palm as we held hands in the back seat of the limo. We took a twenty minute ride out to Maryland, listening to all of our favorite songs before pulling into a parking lot in front of what looked like a ballroom.

"Call and let the guys know we're here," Angelo said to the limo driver, and then he took my hand as I stepped out one foot at a time. I didn't want to do anything clumsy to ruin my beautiful royal purple satin dress. I gripped the side with my free hand to make sure I wouldn't step on its length. The material felt so smooth against my skin, and I felt so pretty that I was almost sure I would do something to embarrass myself.

A cool breeze came over us, and Angelo quickly draped my shoulders with his tuxedo jacket to keep me warm. When I looked up, we were facing a well-lit canopy with the words *La Fontaine Bleue* in fancy script across the top.

When we walked inside, a tuxedoed man instructed us to follow him, and I could hear the sound of a piano playing softly in the background. Inside the ballroom was a huge shiny floor with a round table draped in white cloth, and seats decorated in white with huge purple bows tied around the back. There were beautiful place settings with shiny silverware and lit candles that bounced sparkles off the tube champagne glasses.

"This is so beautiful, Angelo. Why did you do this?" I gazed into his eyes.

"I'd rather let Natalie Cole and her father tell you." Angelo clapped his hands, and a screen dropped down slowly from the stage where it looked like a hired band would perform. Someone dimmed the lights, and then on the screen was the music video of Natalie Cole and her father, Nat King Cole, singing *Unforgettable*. My heart raced with an adrenaline rush that shot through my veins.

"That was—that was the theme of my high school prom night. How did you know that, Angelo?" I gasped, feeling so overjoyed that I could cry.

"I called West Charlotte High School."

"Oh my gosh!"

"I'm glad you like it."

"Like it? I love it!"

"Shall we dance?"

"You know I got two left feet."

"Follow my lead." Angelo gestured, his hands guided my every move and step. He moved his limbs like liquid with a perfect rhythmic flow. Yet he stood strong, with the correct posture, and guided me across the dance floor. I wouldn't have imagined this macho football stud actually knew how to ballroom dance.

"Have you had lessons in ballroom dancing?"

"My mother taught me. She and I dance all the time, more than her and my father."

"You're so different, Angelo. I don't see this side with you on campus at all. It's like night and day. When you're with your frat brothers you're this macho guy who calls all the shots, and on the football field you're a monster."

"Are you saying you want me to treat you like one of the guys?"

"Of course not. But maybe you should show a serener side to you, a side that is not so rowdy and reckless."

"Well maybe you should let people see how beautiful you are instead of hiding behind long skirts and oversized sweaters. Wear the outfits I bought you," he said. "And maybe you should speak up in your classes the way you do on paper, and not shy away from people who question who you really are. Because you're smart and beautiful."

"You're the only person who has ever told me that."

He spun me around, and dipped my body halfway to the

floor, and never missed a beat as I followed his lead.

"You know, I've read your manuscripts, and I think you have the power to make your readers believe what you say, but it's time for you to believe your own words and feel more confident about yourself."

"Maybe you're right. I guess it's hard for me to do. It seems so easy for you."

"You think so? The tough part about being popular for me is keeping it up. Living up to the expectations of people, so we both have something to work on. For now, no more questions or analyzing. Let's enjoy this moment."

"I already am. I feel like I'm dreaming and waiting for someone to pinch me."

"There's so much more I want to show you and do with you, Germaine, if you'd let me."

"I appreciate all of this, Angelo, but you know I've never been with a guy before." I felt ashamed and somewhat embarrassed to be nineteen and still a virgin.

"What?"

"I'm a virgin."

He burst out laughing.

"Stop it! I'm already embarrassed by it."

"Germaine, I wasn't talking about sex. I want to show you a world that you've never been exposed to."

I covered my mouth, mumbled against it. "Embarrassing."

"Don't be. When the time is right it'll happen when we least expect it."

"Thank you for not pressuring me."

"I would never do that."

Just then, the song ended, and we sat down and enjoyed the delicious gourmet meal. Afterwards, we danced, we sang, and we kissed under the lights from the chandeliers. It was an exclusively enchanting night. I felt like I was in a dream world.

When the limo stopped in front of my dorm, Angelo walked me to the front door. I threw my arms around his neck and kissed him, running my fingers through his corkscrew curls. The girls were watching. I could see them from my peripheral vision. I wanted them to see me.

Yes, girls, it's me, Germaine Landry the nerd, the writer, the country girl from Charlotte kissing the most popular guy on campus. Eat your hearts out!

CLEANING HOUSE

"Yo Ace, telephone!" Marcus shouted outside of my bedroom door. I quickly slid Ernest Gaines' *In My Father's House* under my pillow, turned off Shai's *Comforter,* and slid Wu Tang Clan's CD into the rotation instead. I then lay back on the bed against the pillow.

"Come in!"

Marcus walked into the room and tossed me the cordless phone.

"Who is it anyway?"

"Take a wild guess."

"Hey babe." I was sure it was Germaine and if it wasn't, I had nothing to hide anyway.

"Hello and, how are you?" she asked, her voice always sounded smoothly articulate, but calming. We chatted about nothing in particular. We were just happy to hear each other's voice. That's when I noticed Marcus was still standing in the doorway of my bedroom with his eyebrows pointing downward and his upper lip scrawled.

"Yo homey, don't forget our deal, all right?" Marcus shouted in a disgruntled tone, before slamming the door behind him. I assumed him and the brothers should have known by now that the bet for me to turn out Germaine was over with, as far as I was concerned. I sensed the brothers' jealousy when Germaine would come with us to the basketball games, bowling, and to the clubs. She was getting all of my attention and they weren't, so maybe they were still hoping that there was a bet, because then she would be gone from my life once it was over.

"Hold on, babe, someone's calling on the other line," I clicked over.

"Hello?"

"Ace, why I ain't heard back from you in weeks?" I'd recognize that loud ghetto voice anywhere.

"Oh, hey Tamika." I twisted my lips behind the phone.

"What do you mean, *oh hey Tamika*? Like I'm bothering you or something, dude? I been leaving you messages. Why you ain't call me back Ace? Huh? Why you ain't call me back?"

"I got a girlfriend now, Tamika. I told you that."

"Did ya'll just meet? 'Cuz just last month you were all up in my bed, not even caring that my sister was lying next to me sleep."

"Look Tamika, you need to find somebody else to bang, all right? I'm not that dude no more. I got somebody now."

"Whatever Ace. My sister already told me you hit that when I left for work. You lying cheating dog! But that's alright though, you'll be crawling back for this again soon, and you know what I'm going to say when you make that booty call? Go choke the chicken!"

She hung up, and I clicked over to the other line, but Germaine was gone. I'd taken too long. I called her back and apologized, made up a quick lie and said it was a long distance call for one of my roommates. She easily forgave me and we chatted about the new book she gave me by Ernest Gaines. I'd only read books for book reports, but I was halfway finished through Ernest's book and was ready to read another one. Reading had become my secret passion. I felt like I'd been living under a rock when it came to literature. All I paid attention to was football, my frat, and girls. That's when I knew I needed to clean house and set the record straight once and for all.

"Thanks again for the book, babe. If you others recommend, I'll check them out at the library, just let me know," I said to Germaine. Afterward, we said our goodbyes, and then I dashed downstairs to where the guys were. They were sitting in the living room playing dominoes and drinking beers. I walked over to the stereo in the corner of the room and turned down the volume. Das EFX was speed rapping with their usual swift tongues to their hit, *They Want EFX*.

"Yo homies!" I called their attention, and everyone looked in my direction. I stood in front of them barefoot, wearing sweatpants and a white tank top T-shirt. It was one of my lazy days. "All bets are off with Germaine in case you guys didn't know. I can't do that to her. She's my new bun," I explained to them. "For your troubles, you can have my Doug Williams football and my black book." I tossed my black phone book in the air, and immediately Tony and PeeWee leaped from the domino table to try to catch it. They could care less about the autographed football; they wanted my phone book of freaks.

"You getting soft on us, Ace." Eric shot a disappointing look at me, and then slammed his dominos down on the table. He took the autographed football and set it by his feet.

"Never that, brother, never that."

"I guess since you too weak to smash Germaine, maybe one of us should or all of us, know what I'm saying? Run that train on her like you let us do with Donna." Marcus wiggled his belt buckle as he took a swig of his beer.

"What the hell did you just say?" I stepped to him and balled my hands into fists.

"I'm just saying, if you can't then maybe—"

I yanked Marcus from the chair so fast, I scared everybody in the room. Everyone in motion stopped moving.

I pulled Marcus to my face. "You stay away from Germaine! When you see her you look the other way. If I ever catch you even looking like you flirting with my girl, I'll kill you with my bare hands. I swear on my mother, father, and my unborn children that you would be quick as dead, bruh. You got that?"

"Man, you know I was just playing. Let me go, man," Marcus laughed it off. I eased my grip off his collar, and turned him loose.

"Don't play with me like that ever again, because you know I never shared my girl with you. Donna banged ya'll voluntarily because I told her I would recommend her as president for the Pink Ladies. She failed my test of loyalty, and chose the Pink Ladies over me. Germaine would never fall for a weak test like that, so you need to respect our relationship."

"I got it Ace, but let's not forget that you stole my high school sweetheart."

"I thought you were over that."

"Easy for you to say. I really liked that girl, Ace, but you took her."

"For the record, she chose me."

"Yeah, but why even go there in the first place when you knew she was mine at first? You broke the code, homey."

"If you're not over that situation that's on you, but you better not ever let me catch you or anybody else in this house even smiling at Germaine or it's going down!"

"We get it, Ace, nobody's gonna holler at your girl, man." Eric stepped between me and Marcus. "We're brothers, no need to fight over some chick."

"I just had to make sure we all understood where I was coming from. But on the real tip fellas, it's high time we cut out all the petty pranks we been doing. We're about to be seniors next year. You don't see the other frats on this campus our age still doing some of the crap that we do. We're not freshmen, we're juniors."

"Listen to Ace, he even sounds like Germaine with that kind of talk." Eric laughed.

"Yeah, before you know it, he'll be carrying a briefcase to class," Marcus taunted. They all sat back down at the table.

"Let's get back to our game and make it quick. I got some fre-fre-fre-freaks to call!"

"Nah, hold up," Marcus said to PeeWee, and then he approached me, scratching the side of his temple in thought. "Ace, you owe me for not living up to the bet. Tony and PeeWee got the black book, and Eric got the football, but what about me, man? We cool now right? So what I get?" He held out his hand for money.

"You're still breathing. That's your gift."

"Man, whatever." Marcus waved me off, and the rest of the guys started laughing. "This dude ain't even hit it yet, and he ready to cut us off. Set up the dominos, Eric. Forget Ace!"

I couldn't believe they weren't taking me seriously. The only reason they wanted me to keep the bet with Germaine was so they could have my attention or possibly win my money. It was stupid. I don't even know why I initiated it in the first place. One thing was for sure, I was getting tired of the immaturity with my frat brothers, and the lack of privacy. The loud music, the pranks they pulled on people, and they were like leeches sometimes. Germaine said I should probably get my own place since I was complaining to her about it, and I was thinking I just may do that much sooner than later. Besides, she hated coming over to the house anyway. Can't say that I blame her now, especially since I can see her point.

MARCUS JOHNSON

I met up with Donna outside of the Studio Theater on 14th Street after her dance audition, and then we went to eat dinner at Tropicana, a Jamaican spot. After what happened between me and Ace last week, I felt like I needed to get back at him. He punked me in front of our other frat brothers. I was two seconds from punching him in the face. I was trying not to let Germaine come between our friendship, but Ace was letting her do that anyway. He was changing. Germaine had his nose wide-open and he was losing touch with the brotherhood and himself. I couldn't let that happen.

"What did Ace say about the bet? Is he still going to do it?" Donna asked me after small talk. As soon as she asked, I wished I'd never let her in on it, but she knew I was half-drunk last night when we were at the club talking, and it just slipped out.

"Ace reneged on the bet. He said he got feelings for Germaine now. I can't believe she got him on lock like that. We went to see Northeast Groovers crank out that song, "Water Dance" last week, and Ace rolled out as soon as Germaine paged him."

"What does Ace see in Germaine, Marcus? I can see if he liked Lisa. Every guy knows she a freak, but Germaine? She's a geek with nothing going on," Donna said, as she took the last bite of her chicken curry dish. I couldn't help but notice her cleavage since she was wearing a leotard. As she talked I wanted to reach across the table and squeeze her melons.

"You know, Marcus, Ace has hurt a lot of people. He's hurt me, you, and some of the brothers. I'm not saying I was perfect in what happened between us, but I was tested in the wrong way. Ace keeps doing his dirt, but somehow he's still president of the Bulldogs, and he's still the team captain of the football team despite the fact that he uses steroids and smokes weed. It's not fair, Marcus."

"He stays on top because none of us ever snitch on him."

"Exactly! We've been too loyalty to Ace."

"Maybe we can think of something to bring him back to reality, know what I mean?"

"I couldn't agree with you more, Marcus. I'm sure you're tired of being Ace's flunky anyway."

"What? I'm not his flunky."

"The sisters think so."

"I taught Ace everything I knew about football. If it wasn't for me, he wouldn't have a scholarship. The trip part is, Ace is really into art more than football. He plays just to please his dad. Hell, I'm the one who helped break the tie in the votes for him to become president of the Bulldogs in the first place."

"I believe you, Marcus, but you have to make our sisters believe you too. They can't see you now because Ace is in the way. If you want to lead the Bulldogs and become Captain of the football team, we need to make a plan to get Ace out the picture."

"You're serious about this?"

"Of course I'm serious!"

"I don't think we need to do anything drastic."

"What Ace did to me was awful, and you owe me this favor too since you were in on what he did to me."

"Alright, well, what do you have in mind?"

Donna spilled out all the details as if she'd been thinking about running the scheme for quite some time. When she finished telling me the plan, we shook hands, and parted ways. I wasn't sure if it was going to work or if I was going to do it, but Germaine needed to step-off and let Ace get back to hanging out with the Bulldogs again. They were always going out, and when they weren't going out on dates, she would come over to the house and stay in his room for hours. He was acting like he couldn't make moves without consulting with her first. Ace never been sprung like this over a girl before. Everywhere I looked, there was Ace with Germaine. They hung out on campus, at the clubs, after the football games, or at the library. They wasn't even letting each other breathe. If they weren't around each other they were on the phone talking for hours, and none of us could use it until he finished. Ace was sprung!

GERMAINE'S DESPAIR

It was spring, the quarter before our class finals, and I couldn't believe I got a *C* in my English composition class. I kept staring at the report of grades in disbelief. With watery eyes, I rushed across campus to the English department determined to report Professor Susan Schwartz to the head of the department. All those nights I'd stayed up late writing papers, and all those nights I worked on articles to help the AYM, and this was the thanks I got? A fat *C!*

I stormed inside the building, letting the main doors slam behind me, causing the student security guard to jolt to attention behind the desk. Our eyes met, and he could see I was upset. He parted his lips to say something about me slamming the door, but instead he swallowed hard, and decided against it.

"Um, if you could uh, just sign in, please." He spoke so softly I could barely hear him. A look of fear spread across his pale face. His cheeks flushed red for a moment, then turned back to his normal peachy freckled appearance as I scribbled my name and walked off.

The elevators chimed open, and Professor Schwartz stepped off. Our eyes locked in on each other. Her thin lips looked like a line and curved at the corners. She knew why I was there.

"Going somewhere, Ms. Landry?" she asked, her tone condescending. She stood with her shoulders back and neck stiff. Her red hair was pulled up into a bun and her green eyes that I once thought looked pretty only looked deceitful now. I knew she had just submitted our term papers to the English department like she said she would, but I didn't think it would be that fast.

"Professor Schwartz, I— Um . . . I'd like to talk with you

about my paper." *Don't stutter, be easy. Relax. You got this.*

Her eyes turned cold, and suddenly the confidence I'd walked in with felt like it was starting to dissipate. I thought of Angelo who often told me I needed to show the same brevity that I did with my writing, in person. *You can do this, Germaine.*

"Is that why you came here? Because if I didn't know any better, Ms. Landry, I would not think you were coming to see me, but you were going to see the department head."

"Well I—"

"If you have a problem with your grade, Ms. Landry, then maybe you should spend more time studying instead of moseying around campus with Mr. Pearson."

My eyes bucked in shock. I wasn't expecting that type of response. I didn't know what to say. I stood in front of her like a child with my mouth gaped open. The same way I did when my grandfather took away my typewriter when I sassed my grandmother for taking away my R&B music CDs. "You won't need this for a while," he'd said coldly, and walked out of my room. I didn't defend myself like I should have. I didn't think I could. My grandmother was overly strict with her rules and my grandfather supported her. Maybe I felt they would put me up for adoption if I didn't comply, and maybe I didn't say what I really wanted to Professor Schwartz because I was afraid she would fail me next time.

"Can I just resubmit a new term paper?"

"I'm sorry, Germaine, but if I let you re-submit your term paper, I'll have to let the other students with low grades do the same thing."

I blinked back my tears. I couldn't possibly show my midterm report to my grandparents. I earned two Cs and three Bs. This had never happened to me before. Never! I'd gotten straight A's all of my life. Earning a C was like a failure, and the Bs were like warning signs to me. I walked away slowly with my head hung low. There was nothing I could do.

"Germaine," Professor Schwartz called as I started to walk away. I turned around and her face wasn't cold and condescending, but sympathetic. "It's not the end of the world, but you need to take your writing more seriously," she gently expressed. "The pieces you write for the *American Youth Magazine* really show your talent, and I know you'll make a great writer one day, but your course work as of late shows a lack of focus and attention to detail. I hope you'll use the upcoming spring break to regroup."

My face warmed. Maybe she meant no harm. A slow smile formed on my face. "I will, Professor Schwartz. Writing means a lot to me. I promise to work harder and be more focused next time."

WHAT THEY WANT

As soon as my parents walked through the door, my mother was the first to complain. It was Parent's Day, and I hated when they came to visit.

". . . and you guys need to pick up your filthy socks off the floor, and put some food in this house. What's the matter with you boys? Why do I always have to tell you to clean up after yourselves?" my mother complained, as she emptied the full ashtrays and removed beer cans from the tables.

"Angelo, darling, why are you allowing your frat brothers to have this house looking like a pig's pen? At least hire a maid."

"Dammit Nadine, now that's enough already!" Dad shouted from the sofa. "It's a fraternity house, what do you expect? We go through this every time we come and visit."

"Ralph, it's time Angelo gets his own place. He's twenty-one and it's high time he starts living on his own instead of sharing a house with a bunch of filthy testosterones," my mother continued as she went into the kitchen. I heard water running, and then a loud humming noise. She had started the dishwasher. There was no stopping my mother when she was on a warpath. My frat brothers all threw up the peace sign to me with their two fingers, and rolled out!

"Son, you should've told them boys to clean up this house. You knew we were coming, and now we gotta listen to your mother's nagging," Dad said, puffing his cigar. "You know she always has something to say. That's how women are, they don't know when to shut up until you backhand smack 'em."

"Dad, that's enough!"

"I didn't mean much by it, Son, I didn't. Truth is, I haven't smacked your mother in a long time, but if she keeps ranting she's asking for it."

"Dad!" I jumped from the sofa and stood over him with my fist balled.

"All right. Settle down, boy."

I didn't think it was funny. As a matter of fact, he pissed me off.

"Sit down." He pointed. "Are you going to Freak-Nik for spring break this year down in Atlanta?" he asked, skipping the subject. I didn't feel like making conversation with him because I was mad at him and my mother at this point.

"Did you hear me, boy?"

"Dad, *boy* plays on Tarzan. I'm a man."

"Sure you are with your pretty self. You better not be turning into a pillow biter."

"A what?"

"You know, a butt-boy. I'm just making sure that's all."

"Dad, are you trying to say I'm gay?"

"I just want you to be careful, son. You hear me? My friends and I from the bagel shop see your kind all the time." He glared at me with those dark beady eyes of his. I wanted to smack him upside his bald, milk dud head.

"Your kind can attract either sex, you know."

"My kind?"

"You just make sure you're careful out here whatever path you choose. Make sure you use them Jim Hats, boy. You hear me?"

I rolled my eyes, ignored him and snatched the remote off the coffee table before us. I flipped the channels until I came across the Celtics playing the Magic. I liked watching Shaq. I knew he was destined to make Rookie of the Year.

"I'm finished, we can go now," my mother said, walking out of the kitchen.

I followed my parents outside to the car. They had driven the white Rolls-Royce, and left the Mercedes at home. On the way to campus, I thought it would be a good idea to explain my new career ambitions. I swallowed hard, thought about Germaine and all the conversations we had. Germaine suggested I try a more direct approach instead of mentioning my goals like a suggestion.

"Mother, Dad," I called from the back seat.

"Yes, Son?" Mother looked over her shoulder while Dad kept his eyes on the road.

"I'm going to Corcoran Art School if I don't make it to the NFL. I don't want to be a doctor. I want to be a visual artist. I can paint really well and—"

"Paint?" Dad shot an evil glare at me in the rearview mirror, cutting me off bitterly. "Here we go again. Didn't I tell you when you were in high school that you can't make money off art until you die? And then what's the point?"

"Dad, it's not about money with me. I should be able to do what I love."

"Angelo, darling, let's not talk about this anymore. You're too smart and too athletic to settle for a meager career like art." Mother put on a cordial smile, as she stroked the pearls around her neck. "You're going to be a doctor if you don't get drafted to the NFL. We've discussed this before, remember? Please give it a rest, darling."

"He better let it rest. You've never seen an artist doing commercials or getting shoe deals. Imagine the business your stardom will bring to my company. Besides, I've paid big bucks for folks to help advance your chances of making it to the league. You got one more year, boy. So don't blow it with oil paints and brushes. When I die, my company will be yours and your mother's, but not if you blow your football career. Those are my stipulations in my will."

"If you guys love me, you would let me be my own person and not live out your dreams, but seek my own."

"We do love you, honey."

"What's love gotta do with it, Nadine?" Dad rebutted. "I want the best for you, boy, and that's all there is to it. I don't want to hear about this art thing ever again. That's for punks."

That was it. There was nothing else I could say.

GET WITH THE PROGRAM

I heard the sound of screeching tires, and instinctively looked over my shoulder. I saw Angelo pulling up on the parking lot at the Raiders Stadium. I was waiting for him in the stands. He told me to meet him so we could talk.

When he opened the door, I could hear the tail-end of Samuelle's song, *Get with the Program* before he turned off the ignition and slammed the door. I wiped my tears, and started walking down the steps so I could meet him and tell him I was failing English. As soon as I got to the bottom of the last row, Angelo took off running around the track at full speed. He was running so fast it looked like he was kicking himself in the butt. When he finally stopped to catch his breath, I waved to get his attention. He didn't wave back, so I didn't think he could see me through the bright afternoon sun, and he took off running again.

"ANGELO!" I called out his name as he was coming around the track, but he kept going. I decided to place myself in his lane. He would have to stop or knock me down. The closer he ran toward me, the more he started to slow down, until he reached a complete stop and stood in front of me catching his breath.

"Hey, I was calling you, but I guess you didn't hear me." I crossed my arms and looked up into his eyes; they were filled with a look of determination to finish. He stretched his long, muscular arms to the sky, and then leaned down to touch his toes to keep his body warmed up. He stepped into the next lane, glistening with sweat, but he smelled good. He leaned forward and took a runner's stance.

"So you're just gonna take off running again and not say hello?"

"What's up?"

"Are you okay?"

"I just need to be by myself right now."

His tone was cold and sharp. I thought he would give me a big warm smile, a hug, a kiss, some other form of usual affection, but I didn't recognize this new behavior.

"Sometimes it helps if you talk about it."

"Your idea of talking is really stupid. I should've kept my mouth shut is what I should've done."

"What idea are you talking about?"

"You told me to tell my parents I wanted to be an artist, so I told them. They said I was crazy and you know what, maybe I am. I don't need this added pressure from you trying to change me."

I was confused. *Who is this person? And did you just swallow Angelo?*

"You made me look like a fool. I'm not some character in one of your books where people get to live out fantasies you know. You can't change me."

"Excuse me? Where's all this coming from?"

"Look, just because I showed you my artwork, I didn't mean for you to insist I become an artist. It's just a stupid hobby, and I don't need a freshman trying to tell me I need to get in touch with my *inner* feelings and follow my heart and . . . sheesh, what was I thinking?" He shook his head and laughed bitterly. "You know what, go back up there in the stands and leave me alone."

"Seriously? You want to be left alone? You asked me to meet you here."

"Well I changed my mind. You can leave me alone."

I couldn't believe what I was hearing. My eyes jumped nervously. I didn't understand what was going on.

"Why're you still standing there? I know you understand *English*."

"Don't insult me!"

"You know what, you don't have to go up there and sit down, you can just get lost!"

57

"I'm not a dog. You don't tell me to get lost, but since you're being very rude to me, I'm not just going to stand here and take it."

"Fine, bye!"

"Before I go, you need to know that art isn't just a hobby for you. Those art pieces I saw were breathtaking. They belong in a museum. And I wasn't just telling you to follow your heart. I was telling you to follow your talent and not to waste it, but I guess that's exactly what's going to happen anyway." I stormed off. I couldn't believe Angelo had turned on me like that. I was shocked!

"Hey, come back here, Germaine!"

I kept walking. I was not one of Angelo's frat brothers whom he bossed around. I was not one of the tramps who came to him after his football games, asking him to autograph their tits. I was Germaine Landry, a young lady deserving of his respect, so I kept walking.

"I said come here, Germaine!"

I kept walking. Next thing I knew I was being bear-hugged from behind.

"Stop! Get offa me, Angelo!"

"Where're you going?"

"I'm leaving you alone since that's what you want."

"I love you, and you can't leave."

"What you said really hurt me, Angelo."

"I'm sorry. I was really angry at myself, not you." He eased his arms from around me, and then lifted his hand to stroke the side of my cheek.

"I have a lot on my mind that's all."

"I should go so you can work out your feelings." I pushed his hand away.

"No, please stay. Don't be mad at me. I need you. I need you more than you know." He leaned down and planted a kiss on my lips, and my anger quickly softened. It was the first time Angelo told me that he loved me. It was the first time anyone had ever told me that they loved me.

With each kiss my heart began to forgive him, as he scooped

me up easily, like a feather that had fallen to the ground from a bird's nest. He laid me down on the grassy field and continued to plant feathery kisses all over me.

"I'm scared," I whispered softly in his ear.

"I will never hurt you. I promise to be gentle. Just hold me, close your eyes, and try to relax."

I gave Angelo permission to have my heart, soul, and body. As he pierced his love into my world, my nails dug into his lower back. He kissed me tenderly and caressed me to ease the discomfort, and I relaxed underneath his body. I couldn't believe what was happening. I was making love for the very first time. I gazed into his eyes and we both smiled and kissed.

I never imagined this would happen at Rockford's multipurpose stadium, where someone could've easily seen us. I didn't have a chance to suggest another location. The mood hit us too fast, and I may have changed my mind had we decided to go somewhere else.

Everything happened so fast, that within minutes it was over. Angelo pulled up his shorts and lay next to me, cuddling me in his arms. The remnants of pleasure and pain still throbbed between my legs as a light breeze came over me, reminding me that I was half naked, and needed to pull up my panties and skirt.

A plane flew above our heads, creating a looping pattern of white smoke across the blue sky that almost looked like hearts. I wondered if it was meant for us, as we lay in the corner of the far-end of the field, and earth seemed to engulf our bodies. I sure felt like I was flying high like the plane after what had just happened. I couldn't wait to pen the experience in my journal. My mind was already thinking about descriptive words I could use for details.

"Are you okay?"

I blushed. "I'm okay."

"I love you."

"I love you too, Angelo."

Crowning Your Love

When I let you into my world you took over my soul and birth me all over again. I was resurrected to a new life in the fiery pit of your heart, where lust breathed passions that rocked me into a stupor, drowning me in the whiskeys of your touch, the luscious luck of your lips. The scent of your undying manhood lingers with me in the morning, and reminds me how you rocked my world, and loved me into the depths of my soul so deep yet unreachable, beyond pelvic bones and spines, kissing me here, there, and tasting like bittersweet wine. For you have eaten every crumb of my love and there are no leftovers. For when I let you into my world you conquered your conquest, and here my dear is your crown.

-Germaine Landry
Rockford University, Freshman Year Spring 1993

LISA DUPREE-LANDRY

It was Parents' Day and my parents had waited around for Germaine to return to the dorm. Germaine's grandparents couldn't make it because Grandpa was feeling ill, and couldn't make the trip to DC. My dad had told them he would check on Germaine and meet with her professors, but Germaine was nowhere to be found. After waiting for over an hour, we left the dorm and joined Shante and her parents for dinner.

During dinner, we talked about the Pink Lady Sorority, and my mom was so proud of us.

"That's the best sorority you ladies could ever join. I hope you both get accepted," she said. "Lisa, the Pink Lady sorority is a family legacy. Your grandmother was a Pink Lady and so was your great-grandmother. She was one of the original founders of the organization at Howard University back in 1910. You ought to be very proud to carry on the family legacy, and it would do us proud if you end up becoming president of the Pink Ladies one day."

Seeing my mother smile gave me the greatest sense of pride and joy. I really felt that, besides my good grades, I was making my parents proud. I couldn't understand why Germaine couldn't see that joining the Pink Lady Sorority was an honor. But then again, her mom's side of the family had always been the social misfits, if you asked my mom.

From what I've heard, my Aunt-in-law Vera met Uncle Thomas in college; and got pregnant with Germaine on purpose when she found out Uncle Thomas came from money. Uncle Thomas married Vera and bought her a nice house in Richmond. I heard my mom telling my other aunts that she never liked Vera. She felt Vera was an opportunist who used

Uncle Thomas. The night of the car accident, I heard Aunt Vera was planning to divorce Uncle Thomas. She had told him she was still in love with some other man. They got into an argument, and the car veered off the road and killed them both. That's been the story on mother's side for years.

"Lisa, it's not like Germaine to not show up, so please tell her to call us when she gets in," Dad said, then hugged me.

"I sure will, Dad."

"I'm sorry your mother and I have to go. I have a business meeting first thing tomorrow morning."

"I understand, Dad." I waved them goodbye. Dad was a real estate broker, and when big companies called on him to make a purchase, he had to act quickly. My mom was such an understanding wife. She had retired a year ago as an elementary school principal. With my father's six-figure income, she'd decided not to work anymore, and my dad was just fine with her wishes.

Shante and I were eating popcorn and watching a rerun of *A Different World* when Germaine finally decided to show up. She was smiling ear-to-ear when she greeted us. I wasn't sure what was tickling her fancy.

"Look at you blushing. Did you finally give Ace some of that cookie?" Shante lifted her eyebrow.

Germaine blushed harder, and gathered her toiletries to go and take a shower.

"I knew it! I want the details blow-by-blow."

"I'm not going to kiss and tell."

"Oh boooo! You're so secretive, Germaine."

"Okay, fine it happened and it was . . . it was amazing. I feel like I'm floating on a cloud."

"With a glow on your face like that, it must've been good."

"Oh please! Knock it off!" I interrupted their silly banter. "While you were out getting deflowered, you missed my parents' visit. Did you forget that today was Parents' Day?" Germaine's happy cheeks sunk, and a look of despair came over her face.

"Oh, and when you call my dad, make sure you tell him *all* about your Bs and that fat C you got in English comp. I'm sure he'd love to hear all about your grades declining."

"Oh Lisa, you're such a killjoy, girl."

"No I'm not, but my cousin needs to get her mind on the books and keep her legs closed." I grabbed the phone and handed it to Germaine. "Call my dad, now!"

"You got some nerve Lisa. Last week you were with Kevin and Gerald, and this week it was Todd and Scottie. You should be happy for Germaine. Ask yourself why you're not."

"Back off, Shante! This is family business."

When Germaine hung up the phone, I watched tears fall from her eyes, and then I burst out laughing.

"Uncle Walter said I really need to do better next time, and that I need to call and tell my grandparents the truth," Germaine mumbled, dropping her chin, as she walked out slowly to go take a shower.

"That's what she gets! She knew better than to come to school acting a fool and giving it up to some jock. If she gets pregnant, I'm the one they're going to blame."

Shante looked at me and shook her head.

"What?"

"You're so wrong Lisa. So wrong."

THE PROMISE

Spring break came and went so fast, and the only reason I knew it was a break was because I spent it with my boo, Angelo. We went to Virginia Beach and hung out with other couples. Lisa and Shante came too, so my grandparents gave me the okay since we made it seem like we were a bunch of girls hanging out, although our boyfriends came with us.

Now it was May, I'd been studying for the school finals. Well, kind of. I was *supposed* to be studying for the school finals at the Edgar Allen Poe Library (we called it the "Poe" for short), but I couldn't concentrate. Angelo and I were in the back of the library getting a quickie in while our books and notepads were left scattered on the study tables. Lately, we couldn't get enough of each other. We were having sex all the time, including places I never would've imagined. First it happened at Rockford Stadium, then the back seat of his truck, the locker room, and last night it happened in the movie theater when no one else was around. Today was no different. We were fired up with passion and in a groove in the back of the library stacks. Suddenly, I heard footsteps approaching.

"You hear that?" I whispered in Angelo's ear. His eyes were half-closed and he was really into it, but my mood was instantly shot when I heard someone approaching.

"Stop, Angelo, someone's coming!" I quickly pushed him away from me and pulled up my panties and skirt. Angelo loved when I wore skirts now, it was easy access for him.

"Hurry up, Angelo!"

His hands shook nervously as he tried to pack away his stiffness, and fasten his jean shorts.

"Excuse me!" the librarian said in a southern accent. Her eyes zeroed in on us from head to toe. "Do ya'll need some help back here?" she questioned with her hand propped on her hip. She was a short elderly white lady with all gray hair, a fat nose with a mole, and glasses.

"Uuuhhhh . . . I'm looking for um . . . umm . . . this book right here." Angelo's voice trembled as he pulled a thick book off the shelf and tucked it under his arm.

The librarian looked at Angelo with skepticism, and then shifted her eyes toward me. I glanced down at my blouse and noticed I'd fastened it back unevenly.

"I'm afraid I'm gonna have to ask you kids to leave right now," she said, breathing heavily as her cheeks started to flush red. "This library is for studying and not fooling around, do you understand?"

"But we were just trying to find a book for class," Angelo tried to explain.

"Oh really?" the librarian snatched the book from Angelo, and read the title on the binder. "*What Happens to a Decomposed Body?* Humph, well, unless you two are studying to be forensic pathologists, then I suggest you leave this section right now!"

"That was so embarrassing." I said to Angelo after we left the library and went back to my dorm room. "I'll never be able to study in the Poe again."

"Don't sweat it. She'll forget all about us a week from now."

"I'm not so sure. Did you see the look on her face?"

"That was the fun part. Just knowing we could get caught turned me on." Angelo cupped my cheeks and kissed me, then lifted my skirt.

"Angelo, we really should study."

"You're right. We do need to study, but first I have a surprise for you." He turned his back to hide whatever he was doing, but I watched his hands search for something inside his pocket. Angelo turned around slowly with a velvet box in his hand.

"You didn't!" I gasped in surprise. My eyes lit up in amazement at the princess-cut diamond ring.

"Angelo, it's beautiful!"

"Do you really like it?"

I opened my mouth to say more, but no words would come out. I was speechless.

"It's a promise ring. This means you belong exclusively to me, Germaine, and I promise to be faithful to only you."

"Oh Angelo!" I pitched myself into his arms and kissed him.

Suddenly, we were interrupted by the phone ringing.

"I better get that," I said, breaking the kiss.

"Hello?"

"You have a collect call from Olivia Roberts. Will you accept the charges?"

"Yes."

"Germaine baby, it's Grandma. Are ya okay, I been looking for you and Lisa?"

"I was at the library, and Lisa's in class. Is everything all right?"

"Baby, there's something I gots to tell ya. Are ya sitting down?"

"Not quite. Are you okay, Grandma?"

"I'm at Charlotte Community Hospital."

I gulped. "Hospital? Why? What's going on?"

"Your grandpa had a heart attack!"

"What? I'm-I'm-I'm on my way!"

"But what about your final exams, baby?"

"They're not until next week. I can drive home now and be back at school by then."

"I don't think it's a good idea for ya to be on the road after what I done told you. Can Lisa ride witcha? As a matter of fact, I'll call and see if ya Uncle Walter can buy ya'll plane tickets. That'll be faster."

I hated when Grandma asked Uncle Walter for that kind of money, especially since he was already providing for me. Although he never had a problem with it, Aunt Lolita did. She would always complain when Grandma asked for any extra help, and then Lisa would rub my nose in it like we were some charity case. This was a trip I wanted to take by myself and not with Lisa. Besides, Grandpa Roberts was my maternal grandfather—no blood relation to Lisa.

"Okay, Grandma, if you think that's best," I lamented. Right now wasn't a good time to contest the matter, despite how I felt. We said our goodbyes, and I started packing.

TIME FOR A CHANGE

"Germaine, whatcha done did to ya'self? Are you wearing lipstick and eye shadow? And where're your glasses? What happened to your braids?" Grandma shouted the minute she saw me walking through the terminal at Charlotte Douglas Airport.

"It was time for a change, that's all."

"A change? For who? Christian gals don't wear short skirts like that or makeup. Ya keep wearing makeup like that and ya fittin' to attract the wrong kind of attention," Grandma said. She was still wearing the same brown curly wig she'd always worn since I was a kid, and the same brown dress with yellow paisley designs. I had never seen her in pants, not even pajamas.

"Come on, get in the car." She quickly motioned us like we were kids. Lisa kept laughing because Grandma was getting on me about the way I looked, but Lisa had way more makeup on than I did. Grandma didn't say anything to her. In fact, she and Grandpa rarely disciplined Lisa when we were growing up. Maybe they felt they couldn't discipline someone else's child, who knows? But I always felt it was unfair.

As soon as we got back to the house and settled in, the doctor from the hospital called. I could tell it wasn't good news. There were too many pauses in the conversation and Grandma's face was pale like she'd seen a ghost.

Her jaw dropped, "Oh God!"

Lisa and I rushed to her side as she broke the news that Grandpa had passed away.

A few days later, I was sitting in front of Grandpa's all-white casket, graced with beautiful yellow and white flowers. Family members I rarely saw all claimed to have known me since I was a baby, and they offered their condolences.

Strangers who knew my grandpa spoke highly of him, but I didn't even recall them visiting our house. I hated being there and seeing my grandpa lying cold in a casket. The scene reminded me of when my parents died. I just wanted to be by myself like I was when I was a kid. I wished I could snap my fingers and be someplace else, but I couldn't, so I channeled my thoughts and started to daydream about a new story idea. Perhaps this time, my new story would get accepted by a publisher since my last two didn't.

I'm going to write a story about a girl who was an orphan. A troubled girl, a deeply troubled girl, I thought as the minister preached.

"And Brother Roberts was a good man who would give you his last dollar," the minister preached. "He was a hard worker who never missed a day of work even when he was sick."

The orphan girl would one day find love, but then that love would break her heart.

"We'll miss Brother Roberts, but we'll pray that Sister Roberts and her family find comfort in each other in the coming days."

"Amen." Grandma clapped her white gloved hands together.

And one day the book will be a bestseller.

"Amen," I mumbled under my breath, except I was more in agreement with the story idea I had in mind to write.

After the funeral, we went back to our house, and I immediately went upstairs to my room, and closed the door. There were a few guests who came over after the funeral, but I was done putting on fake smiles and pretending that everything was going to be okay. No one knew that for sure.

I lay across my queen-sized bed that was made up with the same pink floral quilt I'd left behind. The walls were covered with a paisley pink wallpaper, making me feel like I'd stepped into a time machine and it was 1965 instead of 1993. Strangely, I never noticed how dated everything was until I went away and saw how other people my age lived.

69

I picked up my phone, which thankfully was no longer a rotary phone, and dialed Angelo's number using the calling card that Angelo had bought me as a gift.

"Yo wassup, it's Ace. Leave a message and I'll hit you back."

I didn't want to waste my minutes by leaving a message, so I hung up. I propped the pillow under my chin and stared blankly at the wall. That's when I heard a knock on my bedroom door.

"It's open," I murmured, voice muffled against the pillow. In walked Uncle Walter. He stood near the door and leaned his chocolate body against the door frame. His mahogany brown eyes looked directly at me, and crinkled at the corners as his lips curved a smile. He always looked like he was in a pleasant mood, even at a time like this.

"I came up here to make sure you were okay. Your grandmother's worried about you, Germaine, and so am I. You barely said two words the entire funeral. You looked lost. Are you alright?"

I slowly sat up on the bed and crossed my legs in front of me.

"I'll be fine, Uncle Walter."

"You know, maybe it wouldn't be such a bad idea if you transferred back home for next year. Johnson C. Smith is a good school and so is North Carolina A&T."

"Uncle Walter, I'm very happy at Rockford."

"I know, but it's not a good idea for your grandma to be alone right now."

The phone rang and interrupted what I was going to say next.

"Hello?" I answered, it was Angelo. "Hey, I'm-I'm sorry but I can't talk right now. Bye." I quickly hung up, not wanting to get into trouble. I'd left my promise ring at school so my family wouldn't notice it.

"That wasn't a boyfriend calling, was it?"

"Um . . ."

"It's okay, Germaine. I'm glad you made friends. On second

thought, maybe you should just make sure you come home more often to visit your grandma. I'll pay for your airfare. Whatever it takes to help with the new adjustment since Grandpa is gone."

"Thanks for understanding, Uncle Walter, and please don't tell Grandma I have a boyfriend."

"This stays between us as long as you bring your grades up this semester."

"I will."

"You know, I was young once too. I know what it's like to be in love," he said, looking off in thought. "Did I ever tell you that your father and I had a fight over your mother?"

"No."

"I saw Vera first, but Thomas claimed he did. For a whole week, we both showered her with flowers and gifts to see which one of us could win her over."

"Who won?"

"Thomas."

I laughed.

"You think that's funny, huh?"

"Kind of."

"Well, I sure do miss Vera and Thomas."

"I do too."

"I'm sorry. I guess it was selfish of me to mention them at a time like this."

"That's okay, Uncle Walter. I'd never heard that story before. Lisa tells everyone that my mom went after my dad for his money. I never knew you guys sought her out."

"Lisa said that? What does she know? She wasn't even born. It was *her* mother who came after me, not your mom. Vera wasn't an aggressive person. She was kind of quiet like you. She was focused on school and wanted to be a nurse. Thomas and I first met her during freshman year at VSU in the library. I always said she was the one who got away, and Thomas was lucky. I moved on to Lisa's mom, and then your mother told me she was marrying Thomas. I was really surprised, especially since— well never mind."

"No, please tell me."

"Some other time. You have a lot on your plate right now."

"Okay."

"Say, listen, if you guys need anything I'm just a phone call away, okay?"

"Uncle Walter, next year, can I have my own dorm room?"

"I couldn't agree with you more. Your grandparents meant well, but I never felt it was a good idea for you and Lisa to share a room. It's time for you to spread your own wings, but don't fly too far away that you get caught up with some guy. Promise?"

"I promise."

When Uncle Walter left the room, I felt so much better knowing at least one person in the family understood me.

SUMMER

I missed Germaine. We'd been talking on the phone every day. I let her call me collect to save money on her phone bill, so her grandma wouldn't know about me. "You need to come clean about us to your grandma, especially before I visit," I had said to her. Sneaking around just to talk to Germaine made me feel like a kid when I was a twenty-one-year-old man, and I didn't like it.

I planned to visit Germaine next week, and booked us a hotel at Wrightsville Beach, which was only a few hours from her Charlotte home. I've been saving money for the trip by working at the corporate office of Iron Motors, as assistant accountant.

"Boy, it's high time you get up outta this room!" Dad yelled like he was still a sergeant in the Army; his abrupt entry into my room without knocking quickly interrupted my thoughts.

He stood in the doorway, dressed in beige khakis, black patent leather shoes, and a matching Oxford shirt and tie buttoned to the neck. He took a poised soldier's stance with his arms at his side, and gave me a stern look as if I were a target. His face was smooth, unblemished, and he was clean-shaven like always. His bald head was as shiny as his shoes. Dad needed to get a grip on himself, though. This wasn't the military and I was not a soldier.

"It's eight o'clock, boy. The lawn outside needed your attention before sunrise, and you're still in bed like a lazy lima bean," he fussed. "Saturdays don't mean a day off for you, so get to it now, boy."

He slammed the door behind him and I heard his feet stomp down the hallway against the shiny wooden floors. Now I remembered why I'd stayed in DC every summer since freshman year. I had gotten tired of Dad ruling me with an iron fist, but if I had stayed in DC with my frat brothers, I would have to share my living space again, and pay rent. I really needed to find my own place and soon!

When I finished cutting the grass, I took a shower, got dressed, and picked up Marcus. We rode to the Inner Harbor for the Baltimore Summer Festival and had ball! The food was good, the beer, music, and there were lots of sexy women to dance with. When the festival ended, we rode back to Marcus's place.

I pulled up on West Fayette Street in West Baltimore where my paternal grandparents used to live in the 60s before they died. Since then, the neighborhood had become badly infested with drugs.

I watched young drug runners ride their bikes up and down the busy streets of clustered row houses. They were hollering out nicknames for the drugs they were selling. The lookout boys watched the corners for the police, and if they spotted somebody, they would shout, "Five-O!"

Marcus's house was near the corner of West Fayette where the drug addicts hung around talking to each other in slurred speech. Unfortunately, it was the same corner where Marcus's father had had an overdose. He died when Marcus was ten years old.

"This is why I gotta get my family up outta here, man," Marcus said to me as I parked my truck out front of his rowhouse. I hoped it would still be there when I came out. We caught a few of the youngsters eyeballing us with a strange look.

"Yo, what set ya'll from, homey?" A young man who looked a few years younger than me started walking across the street toward us. His friends followed closely behind him. He lifted his shirt so we could see that he was strapped with a gun.

"Back off, Tank, they cool!" Another young man, wearing a red cap ran up to Tank and pulled him back. "That's Marcus and Ace, they play football at Rockford. Don't even mess with them. Ya'll looking at future Baltimore Raven stars right there."

Tank, or whatever his name was, slowly backed away, but he was ready to put holes through us just because he'd never seen us before.

"Yo Marcus, let me know if you need to re-up, man!" the guy in the red cap shouted, right before we stepped inside the house.

"I'm good. Thanks man!"

The irony of Marcus's situation was that he hustled weed on the side. He always had, ever since we went to Blake Academy High School. Marcus was there on a football scholarship, but my parents had paid for my tuition because they could afford it. When we got to college, however, I urged Marcus to stop selling weed. He griped, "First of all, how you gonna tell me not to sell the weed you smoke? Second, you get an allowance from your peeps, but I don't. Rockford is making money off us playing football, and what we got? Just a free education and that's it. A dude like me still gotta eat and take care of home, you feel me?" He was right. It was contradictory for me to judge him. Although I witnessed his dilemma, I would never fully understand his plight.

We walked inside his house, and I flopped down on the plush sofa, and turned on the TV with the remote, while Marcus called up his girl. He asked her if she had a friend who could partner up with me so I wouldn't be the third wheel at the club tonight.

"Heeey, Ace!" Marcus's mother walked into the living room from the kitchen. She was wearing a tight jean skirt with a fitted top with the words *Hot Thang* written in a glittery script. She was a small-framed woman, but she was popping in all the right places and could put the young girls to shame.

"It's all good, Ms. Terri."

"It sure is, with your fine self. Hey Marcus, run to the store and get me some cigarettes."

"But we just got in the house. You've been here all day, and now you sending us to the store?"

"No, I'm sending *you* out to the store. Ace is a guest."

Marcus shook his head. "Is that all you need? 'Cause I ain't going back out for none of your errands."

"Marcus, don't back talk me. Now go on to the store and you best bring me back my change." Ms. Terri handed him a five dollar bill.

Ms. Terri was only sixteen years older than us, and she could easily be mistaken for a school-age student. Marcus was her oldest child and she also had a younger son, Gregory, who was thirteen. Gregory looked up to me and Marcus and focused on playing football. He was impressed by his big brother earning a football scholarship to Rockford, and he wanted the same for himself. Marcus was a good football player. Truthfully, he was a little bit better than me, but Coach had his favorites. I'm sure my father's money had plenty to do with me being one of them.

As soon as Marcus left, Ms. Terri looked at me with a devious grin on her face. Her eyes took in my biceps and my hairy muscular legs. I knew what she wanted. I was more than just a guest in her house, and always had been.

"Come on over here, Ace. You know I don't bite." She gestured with her pointy finger from the opposite end of the sofa. She slid down close to me, and spread her legs open. I noticed she wasn't wearing any panties, and her middle looked like a Chia pet.

"Can't believe you're still a child molester."

"Child molester? Boy, I was your first love. I taught you everything you know. I'm the reason them chicken-heads out there are addicted to you. I'm the one who taught you how to work that big woody you got, so don't forget it!"

"I was thirteen, and you should've known better, Ms. Terri!"

"Boy, don't get smart with me!" She rolled her eyes, and quickly sat up on the sofa.

"Why you keep coming back to get some of this if I molested you? You even hooked school to come get you some of this nooky," she reminded me, trying to make me feel bad, and for a moment it worked. I always questioned why I kept coming back for her in those days. I guess I thought it was fun that I was banging an older woman. Quite a few of my old running buddies smashed Ms. Terri actually. I stopped messing with her when I fell in love with Keisha. Marcus thought Keisha was my first, but all along it was his mother. I still feel bad for what Ms. Terri did to me, and for my part in it, which is why I like to smoke weed sometimes. It helps me to block out things I don't want to remember, and ease the tension I feel a lot of the time. It's the one thing that Germaine suspects every once in a while, but I usually blame my frat brothers, and say they were smoking around me when I'm unable to mask the smell.

When Marcus came back with the cigarettes, he threw the pack at his mother and nearly hit her in the face.

"Where my change at?"

"It's my change now, I'm out. Come on, Ace, let's go."

I could tell Marcus was still bitter about his mother's battles with drugs in the past, and leaving him behind to be raised in and out of foster homes until he was fifteen. Sometimes she would stop using drugs for long stretches, and then something bad would happen in her life to put her back out there in the streets. So far, she'd been clean for several years and this was the longest stretch. She had even found a job. She still had one vice left though: screwing younger men my age now. I guess she figured she'd wait until they were legal, so she wouldn't end up in jail. Who knows?

"Marcus, I thought you said you were going to take me to the movies?" said a kid's voice from the darkness of the stairwell. I looked over my shoulder and spotted Gregory sitting on the steps. My eyes bucked in fear. None of us saw him sitting there and I wondered how long he had been there and if he saw and heard his mother coming on to me.

"Tomorrow, buddy, I promise. We'll go see that new joint, *Jurassic Park*." Marcus slapped him a five.

"All right." Gregory nodded, and headed up the stairs. "Oh . . . good to see you, Ace." He looked over his shoulder and gave me a leery side-eye look.

"You know what, I need to drain the weasel right quick, Marcus. I'll meet you outside."

"All right. Hurry up man, my girl got a friend who wants to meet you."

When I got upstairs, I crept down the hall to Gregory's room and slowly eased the door open. He was connecting his Sega Genesis to the TV. On the other side of the room against the wall was a stockpile of brand new boxes of sneakers. His bed was half-made, and a bag filled with video games sat next to him. I knew Marcus always took care of Gregory, but there was no way that dime bags of weed could afford what Gregory had.

"Pssst . . . yo Gregory," I hissed.

He looked up from the game. "Yo, wassup Ace? Come on into my crib."

"Here's something for the movies tomorrow." I slipped him a ten dollar bill.

"Wow, ten whole bucks? I wonder how many things I can buy?" Gregory twisted his lips, and shoved it in his pocket like it had the value of a quarter.

"You can use it to buy popcorn."

"My boys got me covered."

"I see." I glanced around the room. "But what do your boys want from you?"

"Nothing, they like me 'cause I can play football so they buy me stuff that my brother can't. Why? You got a problem with that, Ace?"

"Does Marcus know?"

"Yeah he knows what's up, but what am I supposed to do while he's at school? My ma's job don't bring home the kind of money I can get from the dope boys, know what I'm saying?"

"Gregory, you need to leave those guys alone. They're bad news."

"Man, you ain't got the right to tell me what to do when you used to bang my mother."

"Shhhh!"

"Yeah, I thought so. Get to steppin'!"

I couldn't believe I was getting punked by a little bastard kid, but I didn't want Marcus to find out. I kept my cool, even though I wanted to snap Gregory's neck for getting smart with me. Oh well, I guess at the end of the day, it was Gregory's life to live. If he wanted to get caught up out there, I had to detach myself emotionally.

CHOICES WE MAKE

Seeing Germaine at the Charlotte Douglas International Airport in her new transformation made me feel proud. I had known there was beauty behind her glasses, drooping pantyhose, and plaid blazer jackets. This new caramel coated beauty had her thick eyebrows shaped, lips glossed, toes and nails done, and she was officially my dime piece. Her outer beauty complemented her inner beauty now.

We were both smiling like we hadn't seen each other in years. We kissed for a long time before getting into Germaine's little Toyota Corolla. We drove to Wrightsville beach, and checked into the hotel.

As soon as we got to the room, we got down with the action. All that pent up energy I had inside of me, I gave it to Germaine. Every girl I thought about screwing, including Marcus's girlfriend's friend, I never took it there. I kept those energies reserved for my girl. If I had to wait one more week or even one more day, I doubt if I would've remained faithful. It had been two months since I was last with Germaine, and that was the longest time I've ever waited to have sex.

"Whew! You really put it on me." Germaine wiped the sweat from her forehead.

"You put it on me too, babe. I taught you well," I panted, out of breath. I could feel every muscle in my body finally relax. I propped the pillow behind my head, and watched Germaine ease out of bed. She went and took a shower, and when she came out of the bathroom, she started getting dressed.

"Wait, where're you going?" I asked, sitting up on my forearms.

"I need to get back. My grandma must be worried sick about me. I've been gone for more than a few hours now. It's almost eight o'clock," she explained hastily, slipping her Daisy Duke shorts back on, with a matching top.

"Hold up, you promised to tell her about me, remember?"

"You know she would never approve of you Angelo."

"Let me get this straight, we planned this trip weeks ago, but you never told your grandma about it?"

"I told her I was meeting friends from school at the beach."

"Let me guess. You got your grandma thinking your friends are girls, right? Just like you did during our trip to Virginia Beach at spring break."

"Kind of," she mumbled, searching the room for the rest of her things.

"What do you mean *kind* of? Germaine, you need to fix this! Call your grandma right now and tell her the truth."

She tilted her head. "You can't be serious."

"I'm serious!"

Germaine grabbed the phone, but hesitated to dial at first until she saw me watching her every move. I listened to every word she said to her grandma, who was yelling on the other end of the phone.

When Germaine finally hung up, she took a deep breath.

"Wow, she's really pissed at me."

"I'd be mad at you too. You shouldn't have lied to her, Germaine. You've made it hard for me. She probably thinks I put you up to it."

"Aw, I'm sorry, pookie." She gave me a flirty kiss, and we laid down on the bed where she began to read poetry from her composition book.

LOVE MAKES NO SENSE

Invisible

The dream was clear with every turn of a shadow.
Desires poured through my heart like a bow and arrow.
I want to love him, but is he really mine?
He teases and taunts me and I ignore all the signs.
Should I expose myself like a forbidden fruit?
Should I subject my heart to what could be untruths?
Should I commit to something when I'm unsure?
Not knowing exactly what the future has in store?
It's so much easier to go unseen,
than to be visible waking up from a dream.

"Wow, that's deep," Angelo said, after I read the poem from my composition book.

"Being with you makes me feel like I'm dreaming. I've written stories about handsome, smart and athletic guys like you, but I never knew I would actually end up with one," I said, and gently kissed his lips, and rubbed my fingertips over the keloid fraternity brand mark on his chest.

"I'm afraid like everyone else I love, that one day I may lose you, Angelo."

"You shouldn't feel that way, babe."

"But I do."

"Why?"

"There's been so much death in my family."

"I know babe, but you can't be afraid of getting close to people because you're scared they may die."

"You know what's strange is that I was angry at myself when I cried at my grandfather's funeral."

82

"Why?"

"My Grandpa was a strange man. One minute was happy and jolly, and another minute he would seem really depressed, and not say a word for days. He and Grandma were complete opposites. She would tell me stories about her days growing up, and we'd share laughs about shows we watched on TV, while my Grandpa would stare blankly at us, as if we weren't really there. I sometimes felt that he went along with Grandma religiously, but he was never into church like her. I'd overhear him playing secular music in the garage while he fixed neighbors' cars. One day, while he was fixing my bike, he opened his tool cabinet, and a bunch of *Playboy* magazines fell out. He quickly picked them up, and I pretended that I didn't see them. I never told my grandma, but after that day, grandpa was very nice to me, at least for a little while.

I always hoped that one day he would show a different emotion towards me, instead of treating me like I was invisible. Every time I made the honor roll I'd look for him to say something meaningful or reward me, but it never happened. It was my grandma who fixed my favorite dish or took me to the mall to buy something I wanted. Despite me not ever really knowing my grandpa, I cried at his funeral. Love is so confusing."

"No it's not. I think you cried because he was your grandpa, and in his own way he did show that he cared about you. You don't need any other reason than that," Angelo said, making everything sound more simple than I was making it out to be, as usual.

"Maybe I would feel differently about it if he showed me the same affection he showed Lisa."

"What do you mean? You just said in so many words that he was stoic."

"With me, but not Lisa. His eyes would light up every time he saw her. He would always tell her how pretty she was, and show her off to the neighbors. He took her to get ice cream and to the parks to play. He told me to stay home with Grandma. He said, "Keep ya grandma company, we'll be back." I'd wait on the front porch for him and Lisa to come back. I never understood why he didn't take me with them when they went to the park."

"Maybe your grandpa showed Lisa that affection because he only saw her during the summers."

I sucked my teeth. "Are you on my side?"

"Of course, babe, but you over analyze too much. You don't *think* love, you *feel* love, and you don't *justify* love you accept it. Your poem makes you seem unsure about loving another person. You know you loved your grandfather, and you know you love me. You have to trust your heart babe."

"I do, but everyone I love leaves."

"Babe, I'm not going anywhere. Now let's lie back down and enjoy this moment together."

"Okay. Maybe you're right. I'm so glad you're here, Angelo."

"Me too."

MAKE SURE YOU'RE SURE

Angelo and I were enjoying spending quality time together at the beach for the weekend. I still felt like I was dreaming and waiting for someone to wake me up. I wrote down every moment of our time together in my journal, and took so many pictures with my instant camera that I ran out of film. On our last day together, we stopped at a carnival.

"Come on, this will be fun!" Angelo quickly parked and hopped out of the car.

We played games, rode the Ferris wheel, and ate cotton candy. Angelo ended up winning two stuffed animals for me, and a bag of goldfish from playing Shoot the Duck.

"I told you that would be fun," Angelo said, as we headed back to the car with our hands full of stuffed animals. Angelo placed everything in the trunk, except the goldfish.

"Hold up—I think I forgot something, I'll be right back. Just wait in the car."

After sitting in the car for fifteen minutes, I suddenly felt an urge to use the bathroom and wished Angelo would hurry up. I didn't know what was taking him so long, and I didn't know what he ran back to the carnival for. At first I thought he may have left his wallet or something, and then I thought maybe he went back for more funnel cake. As my thoughts wandered, I suddenly heard tapping on the window. I was sitting with the AC running since it was hot outside.

I looked up and it was Angelo, so I rolled the window down.

"Is everything okay?"

"Yeah, everything's cool," he said, huffing out of breath with one hand behind his back. "I just wanted to give this to the little girl who never got her ice cream from her grandpa." He brought his arm forward and handed me a chocolate ice cream cone.

"Aw Angelo, this is so sweet, thank you."

"Now that's the beautiful smile I always want to see."

After driving for about twenty minutes, I saw a sign that said, *Welcome to Charlotte,* and I suddenly felt sad. Angelo would be heading back to Baltimore later today. His flight was at five o'clock, and I wouldn't see him for another month and a half when school started. What was I going to do with the rest of my summer? Watch Grandma play bridge with her friends? Go to the state fair? I'd done those things before. Now that I'd seen so many other things in DC that I could be doing, I realized just how boring my life had been, and how much I'd been living in a bubble.

"You can make a right here on Roberts Place, my house is the light blue house with the walk-around porch. It's toward the back of the cul-de-sac."

"Isn't that your family name?"

"It is. My family was one of the first to build a house on this land, so it's named after us."

"That's pretty cool. My father has a three-million dollar company, and we don't even have a street named after us."

"So what, it's no big deal."

"Sheesh, what's wrong with you?"

"Nothing. Just park right here in the driveway."

"This is definitely the country," Angelo's eyes gazed at the green hill pastures in a distance, and then looked down at the sidewalk made of red brick. My house was in the suburbs of Charlotte, and not too far from a small town called, Davidson.

"Hi Germaine, how ya doin'?" my neighbor, Ms. Milly, shouted from across the street.

I waved hello. I really didn't feel like being bothered, but Ms. Milly was nosy. She walked across the street wearing a lavender house dress, pink sponge rollers, and slippers with her crusty toes hanging out like a tortoise.

"Who dis Germaine?"

"This is my boyfriend, Angelo. Angelo, meet Ms. Milly, she used to watch me as a kid while my grandparents went to work."

"Nice to meet you." Angelo shook her hand.

"Lawd have mercy he fine! You done went up north and caught a good fish, child." She laughed so loud and hard that her false teeth popped out of her mouth. She caught them in her hands. Angelo and I tried hard not to laugh, but we couldn't resist.

"If I was only twenty years younger, I'd be all over you like gravy on rice." Ms. Milly gurgled a bunch of slobbery words we could barely understand. Then she shoved her dentures back in her mouth.

"I bet you'd eat me without teeth, wouldn't you?"

"Don't pay any attention to him Ms. Milly. Come on Angelo, we need to head inside."

We walked inside my house and I immediately caught a whiff of mothballs and cat pee. Grandma always put down too many mothballs trying to keep away mosquitoes during the summer. This time she'd really overdone it.

"Pew, smells like my cat, Puppy, took a leak in here."

"You have a cat named Puppy? The poor thing must be confused."

"Oh, hush Angelo. Have a seat in the living room."

"Grandma, I'm home!"

"Be right there in a minute. Is your company with you?" she yelled from upstairs.

"Yep!"

"I beg your pardon!"

"Sorry, I meant yes *ma'am*, Angelo is here with me."

"I'll be down in a minute. Offer him something to drink."

"You're not thirsty or hungry are you?" I asked Angelo, as he rested the stuffed animals at his feet, and I placed the goldfish inside the fish tank with my oscars.

"I'm good, but you can crack a window or something, it's hot up in this piece." He unfastened the top button of his polo shirt. I opened the front window and propped it open with a wooden stick. We never had an AC unit and always used fans, but that wasn't helping much today.

"I see your grandma is a collector." Angelo browsed around

87

the living room, passing walls of historic newspapers, antique plates, and framed stamp collections.

"That's a very polite way to put it."

I loved my grandma, but it was true that she and Grandpa had been packrats for many years. They still had the original newspapers from when Dr. Martin Luther King Jr., held the march on Washington. It hung on the wall inside a picture frame.

"Why, hello there!" Grandma came walking slowly down the stairs on her cane. She had a fall and hurt her hip a few months ago, and had never fully recovered.

"Nice to finally meet you, Ms. Roberts, I'm Angelo Pearson." Angelo stood up from the sofa and gave Grandma a hug. She then sat by the window, and Puppy immediately jumped in her lap.

"I wish I could say the pleasure is all mine, but I don't appreciate it when a young fellow ain't got respect enough to meet his girlfriend's folks."

"Grandma, I told you that was my fault."

"Germaine, he got a mouth, he can speak for himself."

"You're absolutely right, Ms. Roberts. I should've reached out to you sooner. I apologize."

"Mmm-hmm. Don't try to flatter me, young man. I'm a woman of God."

"Yes, ma'am."

"Tell me about yourself. Where're you from, and whatcha folks do for a livin'?"

"I'm from Baltimore. My mother is a director for a medical foundation. My father owns Iron Motors."

"I've heard of Iron Motors. They show the commercials all the time. Ya Daddy own that company, huh?"

"Yes, ma'am. We're competing with Jiffy Lube and Valvoline."

"Whelp, sounds like ya got good working folk, but where do ya'll worship?"

Oh boy, I knew that was coming. Angelo please say something she approves of, I thought nervously to myself.

"Uhm, nowhere in particular. We're pretty free-spirited."

"In other words, ya don't go to church do ya?"

"Once in a while. Maybe on Easter, Christmas, you know, those occasions."

"Germaine comes from a religious family, did she tell ya that?"

"Yes and I respect that."

"I don't believe thatcha do. Ya spent the weekend together and I doubt thatcha had separate beds."

Angelo cleared his throat and swallowed hard. "Well . . . not exactly."

"Looka here, Angelo, what're ya plans with my granddaughter?"

"Plans?"

"Yes, plans! Are you fittin' to marry her?"

"Marry her?"

"Stop repeating what I'm asking ya, son."

"Listen Ms. Roberts, I know you're concerned about Germaine. I would never hurt her. I love her very much." Angelo gently squeezed my hand. "As far as my plans are concerned, I was hoping Germaine and I would finish school first."

"What's your plans after graduation?"

"NFL hopefully. If not, med school. Run my own private sports medicine practice. If Germaine and I are still together, then I guess we'll get married."

"*If* you're still together. Germaine, are ya listening to this? He's not sure about your relationship."

"Grandma, we're both still young, it's okay. I'm happy where we are now."

"Humph, a girl ought to expect more from a young fella she's fooling around with."

"I guess this is a bad time to ask if I could visit Angelo in Baltimore next week for the 4th of July weekend? It's just that I'd like to meet his folks too."

"Germaine, I'm disappointed witcha lying to me and sneaking around, and now you're asking me if you can run off with this young man I barely know?"

"I'm sorry, Grandma. I just didn't think you would let me date anyone, so I kept it secret."

"I never said ya couldn't date, I just preferred you dated someone who believed in the Lord. You done changed, Germaine. Ya language done changed, the way ya dress, and it seems like Angelo is making you a worldly young lady. Not the God-fearing young lady I done raised you to be. I'm worried about his influence on ya."

"I'm not a bad influence, Ms. Roberts."

"Young man, if I were you I would nip my lips right about now."

Angelo leaned back against the sofa and didn't say another word.

"I wantcha to be careful, Germaine, ya understand what I mean? Angelo is a city boy and things move fast for the folks up north. I just wantcha to finish school and getcha degree. It's whatcha mama and papa woulda wanted, and ya grandfather too."

"I'd like more freedom!" I snapped, frustrated words spilled from my mouth before I could think twice about stopping them. Grandma's shoulders flinched in shock.

"I'm sorry for yelling, but you have to understand that going away to college has taught me how to take care of myself on my own. I'm not a child anymore, Grandma. I'm a young lady and you have to understand that. Even Uncle Walter said I should spread my wings," I said, as I removed my promise ring from my pocketbook and placed it back on my finger. I wasn't going to let Angelo be a secret anymore.

"Oh my!" Grandma held her hand over her chest, and even Puppy's ears perked up in surprise.

"Don't worry, Grandma. It's just a promise ring."

"Oh dear heart, I pray for your soul out there in this crazy world. I knew this day would come, but I ain't expect it so soon. I'm just scared for ya, baby. Are ya sure 'bout this here situation?"

"We'll be just fine, Grandma. If I make a mistake it will be mine, not yours."

"I hear ya, baby. I can't say that this is easy for me to accept, butcha Uncle Walter warned if I kept squeezing ya too tight you'd break free. I wasn't expecting it to happen today. Lord have mercy!" Grandma became choked up and started crying.

"Everything will be all right, Grandma. I promise."

"My sweet baby is all grown up. Yes indeedy. Lawd hand mercy."

"I promise I'll call you every day while I'm in Baltimore."

"I guess it's your decision to make."

"Thank you, Ms. Roberts. I promise Germaine will be in good hands."

BALTIMORE

Angelo's house was in a quiet tree-lined neighborhood in North Roland Park. The house was a single-family home made of red bricks. It sat on a beautiful grassy lawn with water sprinklers creating a midair figure eight. I couldn't hear a pin drop when we stepped out of Angelo's Pathfinder. Angelo took hold of my hand, and I could feel the sweat of his palm. I wasn't sure why *he* was nervous. I was the one who should be feeling nervous.

"You ready?"

"Are you? You're the one sweating bullets."

He laughed, and tried to play it off like he was cool, but I knew him.

"Relax. You'll be just fine." I wiped the sweat beads from his face and kissed his lips. I always gave him affection to calm his nerves, even before his games, I would be right there in the tunnel to give him a hug and kiss before he ran out to the field.

"Everything is always better with that kind of sugar."

I was amazed the minute we walked in. The corridor was broad and spacious, the floors were shiny and made of dark cherrywood. When I looked up, I noticed a huge crystal and gold chandelier hanging above our heads in the corridor. A double staircase with an overlook faced us. Along the walls were beautiful oil paintings, including a portrait of Angelo and his parents. I felt like I was inside a mansion, although it was a big colonial style home.

"Did you paint those?"

"Yes, when I was in high school. I won an art competition with those."

"High school? Wow, they look professional, Angelo."

"Thanks."

I could hear Angelo's mother's high heels clicking against the floors the closer she got. I could see the resemblance between her and Angelo. She had long flowing hair past her shoulders and hazel eyes. She wore a lavender two-piece pants suit with matching shoes. I could tell that even without her makeup she would look just as beautiful.

"Hello, you must be Jasmine," she said, with a beauty pageant smile that didn't appear authentic, but polite.

"Hi, it's nice to meet you." I shook her hand.

"Mother, her name is Germaine, not Jasmine."

"Pardon me, I'm sorry. That was Angelo's ex-girlfriend's name."

"That's quite all right," I said with a faint grin, feeling a little awkward.

"Germaine, this is my father, Mr. Pearson."

I shook Mr. Pearson's hand. He was a short man with a bronze complexion. His wife was slightly taller than he, but it could've been her heels that gave her height over him. He was wearing black slacks with a lavender dress shirt, buttoned to the neck. I wasn't sure if it was intentional that he and Mrs. Pearson complemented each other in their dress.

"Nice looking young lady you got, son. You've done good." Mr. Pearson roughly pounded Angelo on the back.

"Angelo, you can put the girl's belongings in the guest room upstairs," Mrs. Pearson said. I thought, *girl's belongings? I do have a name, and you need to get it right!*

Angelo carried my small suitcase upstairs while I followed his parents to the closed-in patio. It was surrounded by huge glass windows with a nice view of the swimming pool outback.

"Germany, I've heard so much about you. Angelo tells me you're from the South," Mrs. Pearson was saying, pouring us glasses of wine. She never asked if I drank, but I assumed it was the custom of the French, since she was European and from Paris. She then offered me hors d'oeuvres from a silver platter. I placed a few pieces of the fancy looking cheese and grapes on my small plate.

"Yes, ma'am, I'm from Charlotte."

"Oh, please don't call me *ma'am*. I'm not that old."

"Sorry."

"What're you studying in school, Germina?"

"My name is *Germaine* and I'm studying journalism."

"That's right, it is Germaine. Tell me, why do you want to be one of those nosy reporters always in other people's business?"

"I'm sorry you feel that way, but our job is to cover news stories and inform the public. I wouldn't consider that nosy, but informative." I tried not to sound defensive, but she was forcing me to stand up for myself, which is something I was starting to get used to doing.

"You know, I like Germaine. She's got her own mind," Mr. Pearson said, nodding his head in agreement. I can't say that I was happy he co-signed my statement since he had been staring at my legs the whole time. He reminded me of a dirty old man.

"Humph, she's got her own mind all right, but no one respects journalists. They talk too much and at the wrong time."

"I disagree, Mrs. Pearson. Journalists are very powerful people with a great responsibility in how we share information. Our political leaders and those within our community, trust that whatever news we bring to them will be helpful. Our research has even helped protect this country."

"Germaine, it's a two-edged sword. At times you guys have helped protect and at other times, you've been the cause of wars in this country as well. I hope you know which side of the coin you're on—heads or tails."

"I'm back. What did I miss?"

"As for my son, he always chooses *tails*."

"Everything okay?"

"Everything is fine, Angelo." Mrs. Pearson answered before I could. "Have you told Germaine that you're going off to medical school in Boston after you graduate?"

"That's if he's not drafted," Mr. Pearson added.

My mouth gaped open. This was news to me. I cut Angelo a look as if to say, *what is she talking about?*

"I'm actually not sure which graduate school since we're just waiting to see if in fact I will get drafted," Angelo responded timidly.

"Maybe this *thing* between you and my son is really temporary, Germaine," Mrs. Pearson said. She poured her husband another glass of wine, and sat back down next to him. I noticed she started staring at my hands.

"Even that promise ring on your finger is temporary. You see, Angelo gets tired of his new toys easily, don't you Angelo, darling?"

"Toy? Mrs. Pearson, Angelo and I are in love. I believe in us. We'll be together no matter where he goes."

"I admire your little crush on my son, but so many girls like you have walked through my doors and—well, let's just say they never came back."

Angelo cleared his throat loudly. "I think it's time for lunch, are you hungry, Germaine?"

All I could do was nod my head yes, because I was in such disbelief. I felt like I was in the *Twilight Zone* and couldn't believe this was really happening.

"What're your plans while you're here?" Mrs. Pearson asked, as the maid set up lunch. We were given a tray with a bowl of tomato soup and grilled cheese sandwiches.

"Angelo, do you want to tell your mom what our plans are?" I asked, since he hadn't said much. He'd just sat there, allowing his mother to interrogate me up to this point, while his father kept a flirty grin on his face.

Angelo wiped his sweaty forehead.

"We're going to the harbor, eat crabs on Uncle Joe's boat, see the aquarium, catch a movie, and whatever else Germaine would like to do."

"Hopefully after all of that, she'll want to do *the do*." Mr. Pearson laughed.

"Excuse me?"

"Don't tell me you're not having sex, Germaine. As fine as you are, if I was younger, I'd smack it up, flip it, and rub it down!"

95

"Ralph, don't be rude." Mrs. Pearson smacked his leg. "Besides, I've seen more attractive girls come through my door. This one is as skinny as a beanstalk."

"I'm done here!" I stood up abruptly, and almost knocked the tray of food over.

"Angelo, I'd like to go somewhere right now!"

"It's okay, baby. Sit down," Angelo tried to calm me, but I rushed out of there like the house had caught fire.

"Germaine, baby. Wait!"

WHEN SPARKS DON'T FLY

The next couple of days, I took Germaine to the Baltimore National Aquarium, the zoo, and to Camden Yard to watch a collegiate baseball game. She had very little to say to me, and our conversations were cut and dry. Whenever Germaine got angry, she would ignore me, and I hated that!

Uncle Joe invited us to ride with him on his boat for the 4th of July. Germaine seemed happy to go. For her it was another opportunity to leave my parents' house. We had a good time eating crabs on the boat, and we watched the fireworks later that night. Yet, as soon as it was time to head back to my house, Germaine didn't seem as happy. She gave me the cold shoulder again.

I turned down the volume to H-Town singing *Knockin Da Boots,* and pulled my truck over to the side of the road. I was not going to ride all the way back to my house in silence.

"Germaine, how long are you gonna keep this up?"

"What do you mean?"

"You know what I mean, don't play games."

"Do you really have to ask, Ace?"

"You only call me Ace when you're mad, so what's up? I'm tired of you ignoring me."

"Your mother has belittled me every day since I've been here, and your father has been flirting with me, and you never say anything."

"You seemed to hold your own without me. There was nothing for me to say."

"You were supposed to defend me and our relationship the way I defended us with my grandma."

"What was I supposed to say?"

"Do you really have to ask?"

"Babe, I know you're upset that things aren't turning out to be as fun as we planned, and I'm sorry you had to go through this."

"You got that right. Besides the boat trip with your Uncle Joe and cousins, I've been miserable!"

I took hold of her hand and kissed the middle of her palm.

"Please try to cheer up, Germaine. I'd like for us to spend our last couple of days together having fun. I've got football camp next week, and we won't see each other for another month. This is *our* summer, baby. I don't think we should let my parents ruin it for us."

"Angelo, you can't just turn a blind eye to what your parents are doing. I can't take another night in your house. I deserve to be respected."

"I understand. I'm just as shocked that they acted like this. How about we check into a hotel?"

"I'd like that."

The hotel was a quick fix. At some point, I would have to talk to my parents about Germaine, but for right now, I just wanted to see my baby happy.

BACK TO SCHOOL

It was Greek Week, a time when all the fraternities and sororities gathered for friendly competition to recruit new members. Last year, I had watched the new recruits for the Bulldogs walk the burning sands as they crossed over. Not literal burning sands, but they had to carry lanterns while they marched for a mile to campus, and endured name calling, and having objects tossed at them. The big brothers did anything to make them quit the line and fall out of unison. Angelo said it was a test of their manhood, but I felt it was too much. I liked Greek Week better than watching the frats crossover, and I loved the shows they put on. So I agreed to stop by today's events to see just how good the Bulldogs were at stepping.

Greek row was packed with campus students, and most of them knew me as Angelo's girl now, so they let me pass through toward the front of the stage so I could get a closeup view of the fraternity competition. Angelo was on the stage that the university had built for today's events. He was standing front and center wearing a black fitted T-shirt, black jeans, a gold crown, cape, and a black eye-mask like Zorro. I could tell it was my baby by his muscular stature, regal nose, pouty lips, and curly hair sticking out the sides of the crown. The stage had been set up near the Greek gardens where all the fraternity and sorority benches were.

By Angelo's command with his rod, his frat brothers began to step to George Clinton's '80s classic, *Atomic Dog*. The brothers performed a complex routine of footsteps and hand clapping to the beat of the song. When the guys finished their routine, the crowd cheered so loud that my ears were ringing. I had to admit the dancing was amazing.

Angelo stepped forward to the microphone, and the crowd

went ballistic! You would have thought he was Prince or Michael Jackson. They began to chant his name for what seemed like minutes. He then motioned his hands for the crowd to calm down so he could speak, and by his command the audience hushed.

"Greetings my beautiful black people. What you just witnessed was the Bulldogs. One of the best black fraternities on this campus."

"*WOOF WOOF,*" the line brothers shouted in the background.

"Now, I'd like for you to give it up for our lovely sisters, the beautiful Pink Ladies," Angelo shouted over the microphone. They were dressed in pink biker shorts and black leotards with scripted pink letters. Among the newly recruited five girls were Lisa and Shante. They stepped to the center and performed to En Vogue's *Hold On.* When the dance ended, they held up mirrors to each other and blew kisses. I laughed because I couldn't believe the freshmen were impressed by the silliness of all of this.

"One of these ladies will be taking my place as the Fraternity Sweetheart and President this year, who will it be?" Donna shouted into the mike. "Will it be the lovely Lisa Dupree-Landry?" The crowd cheered, including some of the frat brothers. "Or will it be Monica Dawson?" The crowd cheered just the same. "A winner will be announced soon so stay tuned."

After the show ended, I headed to the library to write another article for the AYM. Since it was Greek Week, I decided to write a piece about the latest events. This time, I wrote an unbiased piece expressing the history of black Greek life on campus. I also talked about the week's events, highlighting the achievements in the community, as well as the importance of unity amongst brothers and sisters. A week later, when the magazine was released, I received lots of accolades from fraternities and sororities alike. The piece was so popular that Professor Susan Schwartz shared it with an editor at *The Washington Post.* The editor offered me an internship for next summer. I couldn't have been happier!

WARNING SIGNS

Even though the whole fraternity and sorority thing wasn't something I agreed with, I wanted to support Lisa and Shante at their initiation party tonight at the Embassy Suites. Besides, I couldn't have my baby Angelo there alone surrounded by a bunch of pretty girls. I knew his appetite, but I wanted to make sure he came home to eat.

"This is cute. What do you think?" Shante asked Lisa and me, holding up a short black dress.

"Hmm...it's okay."

"Yeah, there's something that's just totally cabaret about it, maybe if you add a shimmery scarf with it, it will bring it out more." Lisa added, eyeballing her outfit head to toe. Lisa was a fashion connoisseur.

"What about my outfit guys?" I spun around to show it off. I'd purchase it at Landover Mall.

"Germaine, that's a cute skirt, I love the leather, but as the Big Brother's girlfriend, I think you should wear a different blouse. I know ruffle shirts are in, but you want to look sexy. Here, try this." Lisa handed me a fabulous off the shoulder silver sequin top to go with my skirt.

"This is beautiful, Lisa, are you sure you want to let me wear this?"

"Cuz, I'm so happy right now that I want everybody to look good."

"Well, I know I've never said this to you guys, but seeing as though you worked hard to become Pink Ladies, congratulations to you both." I gave Lisa and Shante a hug.

"Oh my gosh!" Lisa suddenly started shaking, and broke out in a sweat.

"What's wrong, Lisa?"

"My heart is pounding."

"Call 9-1-1!" Shante rushed to the phone.

"No, don't do that, it's okay." Lisa inhaled deeply. "I'm just overwhelmed."

"I'll get you some water." I hurried out the door. As soon as I returned, the school nurse was attending to Lisa. I assumed Shante had called her.

"She's okay, it was just a panic attack," the nurse said. "Honey, you ought to stay home and rest."

"No way, I'm a Pink Lady, and tonight is initiation night. We get to celebrate."

"Fine, but you need to see a doctor about your anxieties. This is the second time I've visited you this week."

"Second?" Shante and I both said in unison.

"You girls look out for Lisa, okay? She cannot drink any alcohol with the medicine I just gave her. It'll make her drowsy and distort her judgment."

"We'll make sure."

"Whatever!" Lisa threw up her hand. "I got this. Let's go!"

PINK LADY

I was determined to forget all about my panic attack. I needed to be here tonight for the Pink Lady initiation party. I'd worked too hard and too long to become a Pink Lady, and Donna knew this. I'd put in more work than any other line sister. I'd gone above and beyond the call of duty. "You're the best recruit we've had in years," Donna had told me. I was a Legacy recruit, because my grandmother was one of the founding members. I'd been given my pin early out of respect for my grandmother's legacy, and because I worked hard. I couldn't let my anxiety control me. Just think how embarrassing it would be if I didn't show up. After all, I was going against Monica to become the next president of the Pink Ladies.

SWV's Remix, *Right Here,* was pouring through the speakers as we danced in the hotel ballroom. The Pink Ladies' car wash, held last month, helped us to raise enough money to have the party. We donated half of the proceeds to a few DC public schools, and used the rest to have the party.

The crowd was jamming on the dance floor, and shouting, "S.W.V.!" I forgot all about what had happened earlier as I guzzled down one drink after another, feeling a quick buzz come on. I surely didn't feel anxious about anything anymore. Shante and Germaine were so busy dancing and engaging with others that they didn't see me taking shots.

"Lisa." I felt a tap on my shoulder. When I turned around, the room spun with me. I was drunk.

"Donna is looking for you," my Soror, Nicole said to me. "She's outside." I took two steps forward and almost lost my balance.

"Come on, girl, you're drunk and I don't want you to fall." Nicole said, wrapping her arm around mine, and leading the way to the exit.

"Hey, wait! Where're you guys going?" Shante shouted, she happen to look in our direction. She rushed over toward us.

"I should've kept a closer eye on you, Lisa," Shante said, grabbing hold of my other arm. "Where're you guys going, anyway?"

"Outside. Donna wants to see me."

The cold autumn breeze instantly made me shiver since I had left my coat inside. Donna and two other sorority sisters were standing at the bottom of the stairs of the hotel. They were waiting for me.

"Heeey Donna, you wanted to see meeee?" I asked, words slurring from my boozing.

"Yes, I wanted to see *you*. Not your sidekick from Ohio." Donna cut Shante a look that said, *beat it!* Shante took the hint and slowly turned my arm loose. She stepped back, but not too far away. I was sure she could still hear us.

"The vote to make you Fraternity Sweetheart and future President is a tie between you and Monica."

"So now what?"

"I'd like to make a proposition for you."

"Suuure, I'm all ears." I hiccupped.

"My proposition will be in room 508 in ten minutes."

"Wait, I don't understand."

"You will become the new Sweetheart the same way I did."

"Oh my!" Shante yelped in the background.

"Ok. Cool." I replied, not fully comprehending.

"He'll be there in a minute. Here's the key."

When I walked back to the party, Germaine was dancing with Ace or at least trying to. He was swaying side-to-side and trying to kiss on Germaine, but she kept pushing him away.

"Angelo, stop it, not in public!" Germaine was saying to him.

"Come on baby, I'm horny. Let's get a room upstairs and handle our business." Ace gave her a forced kiss that looked like he was trying to shove his tongue down her throat.

"I said no! You're drunk!" She pushed him, and then stormed off.

Ace dizzily turned around, and almost bumped into Shante and I.

"Lisa baby, you lookin good. Your cousin is trippin'! You need to go talk to her for real."

"You're the one trippin'. You know she hates when you're drunk or high." I countered.

"Say bro, let's go upstairs. I got some smokes," Marcus offered Ace a blunt, as if he needed that.

"Cool let's go. Are ya'll coming too?" Ace asked me and Shante. I figured it was time enough to go upstairs by now.

"I'm going up to 508. Donna said I should meet some guy there, or was it 506?"

"508? Really?" Marcus looked puzzled. "That's my room."

Shante looked at me fearfully. "Lisa, I told you this was a bad idea!"

"Girl, stop trippin'! Donna probably wants me to hang out with my Big Brothers. If I'm going to be the Fraternity Sweetheart they probably just want to make sure I'm ready, right guys?"

"Of course, we have to make sure you're qualified that's all."

"Lisa, please don't do it!" Shante cried. She was fresh on my heels as we walked to the elevators. She propped her hands against the elevator doors to keep them from closing. "Something fishy is going on and you're too drunk to see it!"

"Girl, move out of our way!" Marcus shoved Shante, and pressed the button for the fifth floor. I could still hear Shante yelling for me not to go upstairs, but the higher we rode up on the elevator, the more her voice faded away into the background.

When we got to the room, Marcus turned on the TV, offered me and Angelo some weed, so we were just passing the bud around, no big deal. He asked me why I wanted to be president and what made me think I was qualified. I thought if this was what Donna had in mind then this was going to be an easy walk in the park. The higher we got off the weed, the more the conversation changed.

"Lisa, have I ever told you how beautiful you are?" Marcus said with a flirty grin, and then he took off his shirt. . .

TELL ME I'M DREAMING

I searched for Lisa and Shante, but I couldn't find them.

"Are you looking for your cousin?"

"Have you seen her?"

"She went upstairs. The brothers have to interview her and make sure she's ready to be president, but they should be finished by now. Go on up. They're in room 508."

"Is Shante with them too?"

"I think so," Donna said, with a deceitful grin. I figured it was because she didn't like me, but I didn't care. I still didn't give two cents about her either.

"I'll go grab them and let them know I'm ready to go."

"You do that," Donna said, snickering something under her breath to one of her sisters, and then they both giggled. They were all so immature.

When I stepped off the elevator, I followed the sign with an arrow pointing to the left for rooms 500-520. As I approached the door, I could hear what sounded like a woman moaning. I wondered if I had the wrong door. I looked up at the big bold numbers- 508 to make sure, and then I knocked.

"Who is it?"

I recognized the young man's voice. "Marcus, it's Germaine, is Lisa in there with you?" I heard the sound of the door locks unclicking, and then the door opened with a loud screech.

"Yeah, she's over there," Marcus said with a devilish grin, as he stood in the doorway wearing only boxers. I thought that was odd. I assumed he was one of the brothers who was supposed to be interviewing Lisa. It also puzzled me as to why the room was kind of dark. The only light I could see came from an outside lamp pole. It helped me to see the shadows of two people under the covers on the bed. I wondered if it was Lisa, and who was she screwing around with this time?

"Let me turn the lights on so you can get a better look."

When Marcus flipped on the lights, my heart instantly dropped to my feet. I froze in the spot I was standing in. Angelo was plunging into Lisa while her legs were clamped around his waist. He was so into it that he didn't stop to see who had turned on the lights.

"Oh my gosh! It's Germaine!" Lisa looked over Angelo's broad shoulders.

Angelo moaned. "What did you say?"

"Get offa me, it's my cousin you idiot!"

Angelo looked over his shoulder. "Oh snap!"

Both of their faces suddenly turned pale as if blood had left their bodies.

"Germaine, I can explain this!" Angelo leaped out of bed, and I hurried out the door.

WHEN IT ALL FALLS DOWN

I tried to catch up to Germaine, but I didn't want to run too far since I was naked, and it would've caused a scene. I hurried back to the room to grab my clothes, and found Marcus laughing by the whole scene.

"Say man, what's funny?" I asked, angrily, as I put my clothes back on.

"What goes around comes around."

"Wait . . . you knew about this?"

Marcus ignored me and started putting on his clothes. He'd had Lisa first and she asked me to join them. At first I refused, but she did things to me that I simply couldn't resist. Things Germaine wasn't experienced with yet. At some point, Marcus got out of bed and it was just me and Lisa. He snapped pictures of us, and at the time I didn't question it, because as Bulldogs we did things like that to women we conquered. Suddenly, I realized it was bigger than a Bulldog's shenanigan.

"You set me up!" I rushed over to Marcus and threw him up against the hotel room wall.

"Stop it! Why are you two fighting?" Lisa cried. "Donna said you knew about this."

"Donna?" I questioned her angrily, as I slung Marcus to the floor. I could feel the anger swell up from the pit of my stomach. I felt like a TNT bomb ready to explode. My brain was filled with mixed emotions as I tried to figure out how Donna and Marcus got away with this, and why they would set me up.

"You kept giving me drinks and you offered me weed on purpose, didn't you?" I punched Marcus, while I still had him pinned down. He tried to fight me off of him, but I overpowered him.

"Look, I'm outta here, you guys can fight all you want, but I need to go explain this to my cousin."

"How could you do this to me Marcus? We're supposed to be brothers!" I punched him over and over again until he blacked out. I checked to see if he had a pulse and he did, so I grabbed my things and split.

As soon as I saw Donna downstairs, I stormed toward her like a raging bull. She happened to look up while she was talking with her friends. She tried to back away from me, and nearly knocked over the punch bowl.

"You set me up!" I grabbed her by the throat, and squeezed until I saw her veins protrude.

"SECURITY! SECURITY!" The Pink Ladies started running in different directions in a panic of fear.

The police came, and it took all five of them to pull me off of Donna. She was left gasping for air, and eventually recovered with a medic's help. The cops muscled me to the floor, read me my rights, and then handcuffed me. Onlookers who were staying at the hotel stopped to see what was going on. Even the deejay had stopped playing the music. He had a numb look of disbelief on his face.

"Come on here, you punk!" One of the officers shoved me out of the hotel, and then all five of them had to force me into the back of the squad car.

"You know you messed up now, boy." One of the officers with a full beard said to me, as he restrained me in the backseat, and then sat next to me. I glared at his badge and noticed it said, 'Johnson' with a few numbers underneath.

"Man, screw you!" I hawked spit at his face.

Johnson punched me across the jaw, and I felt pain throb like a toothache.

"This young cat thinks he's all that. I bet you won't try that again." Johnson laughed sarcastically.

"My father and I are gonna sue you for police brutality!"

"I wasn't brutal to you. You spat at me, and I had to let you know that I don't play that crap. You young punks at Rockford think you're all of that because you can run a football, but you can't break the law and expect to walk."

"I didn't break any laws."

"Choking out that girl was assault, and she's pressing charges. Just who do you think you are anyway?"

"He's the kid whose father owns Iron Motors, right?" the officer sitting in the front passenger seat asked.

"Yeah," I mumbled.

"Well so what! From where I'm sitting you ain't no kind of man for what you just did, and I'll tell your punk for a father that I said so."

"You'll pay for this! You watch and see."

"Are you threatening me? Man, pull this car over. I'm sick of this spoiled brat sitting back here talking trash!"

The cops drove to Anacostia Park by the river, and dragged me out of the car. They pushed me into a woodsy area, and I knew something bad was about to happen, but I was handcuffed so there was nothing I could do to stop it.

In an instant, Johnson charged toward me, and tackled me to the ground, and then he clobbered me with fists.

"That's enough!" One of the cops bellowed out, and Johnson stopped pounding his fist into my flesh. They dragged me back to the car and drove me to the police station.

"I bet next time you won't talk that junk," Johnson threatened me with his nostrils flared like a raging bull. "If your punk for a father got beef with the way I handled you, I got no problems with kicking his butt too!" Johnson walked away and left me in a pissy cell next to a big man who looked like his name was Bubba.

Cheater

I hate you with a venomous fire,
you're a wolf behind a sheep's clothing,
a guilty-as-charged liar!
I could kill you like a cat on its ninth life,
revoke your gift for eternal life.
Strip away your destiny. Rob you of every penny,
because you're a cheater!
A snake in the grass with two heads
who used me!

Your love for me was a fake feeling
disguised with fraud and plotting schemes
that stole my heart and left me empty
and feeling numb because I finally
thought I loved someone.

You slept with my flesh and blood,
a dear cousin I truly loved.
She came from my father's roots,
tugged from weak limbs
and pledged allegiance
to the Pink Ladies,
never choosing what was right over them.

I was supposed to matter
more than a prank and laughter.
It was no accident, but done on purpose without purpose.
And she called herself a lady,
risking everything for the throne,
letting him love her from neck to tailbone.
You can never justify this betrayal and mistrust
that got stuck between the lusts of your left and right thighs,
high or not!

Selena Haskins

You were wrong as two left shoes,
and left me bruised without a clue.
How can you look in the mirror
and be proud of what you see?
If you died today or tomorrow, I'd say,
'Rest Without Peace!'

-Germaine Landry (1993–Sophomore Year)

SO MANY TEARS

I cried. I cried all that night when I found Lisa and Angelo together, and I've been crying ever since. I barely made it to any of my classes that following week. I would stare blankly at the chalkboard or fall asleep during the lectures. I was still hurting, and I shouldn't have been there at all. Although Lisa apologized since then, it didn't matter. Each time I thought about what happened, it made me cry even more. I wanted to spit fire in Lisa's face and watch her burn. How could she stoop so low? What was in it for her?

Oh, I got it, this was why she was all of a sudden President of the Pink Ladies. She had to sleep with the President of the Bulldogs to become the Fraternity Sweetheart or whatever they call it. I asked Lisa, "Was it worth it? Was it worth ruining my life and my relationship?" She would ignore my cries for answers and seemed to feel embarrassed by them. She'd pack her books and leave the room to keep from responding to me.

Every day since then, my mind kept playing the scene of the two of them having sex, and the look of pleasure on Angelo's face made me sick on the stomach.

Every time he rang my phone, I told Shante to tell him I didn't want to talk. After a while, we all just let the answering machine pick up. How could Angelo say he loved me, but sleep with my cousin? How could Angelo share himself with another girl the way he did with me?

I tried to stop thinking about it, but every time I closed my eyes I could see them together. I felt my stomach bubbling again, so I quickly stood up from my bed. I thought I was going to rush down the hallway to the restroom, and hurl to the porcelain gods like I'd done all last night. The stress these past few days was making me sick. I was supposed to meet my study group this afternoon, but I couldn't stand for them to see me like this.

"I can't do this anymore!" I cried.

Instead of feeling sorry for being such a fool, I became enraged. God knew I tried to forgive Lisa, which is why I was still there in the same dorm room, but I couldn't bury my anger another day. I was feeling like a bubble ready to burst. Since Lisa and Shante were at class, I had to find a way to release my rage.

I opened Lisa's closet door, and glanced over everything that was neatly arranged from casual outfits to dressy, all color coordinated and by different designers. I yanked each piece off the hangers and started shredding them with a pair of scissors.

I then went for her expensive jewelry collection, and popped diamond necklaces and pearls, and watched them fly across the room—pinging anything in sight. I stepped on the custom pieces and smashed them to the floor until they looked like colorful specks of dust. I took her favorite white mink coat and drew the word, *SLUT* on the back with a black Sharpie. When I saw nothing else in the room that I could destroy, the realization of what I had done was scattered before me. The room looked like a hurricane had hit it. I suddenly panicked. "I need to get out of here."

Just as I opened the door, Lisa and Shante walked in.

Shante walked by me. "What the hell?" Her eyes pulled back at the sight of the disaster in the room. I stood there for a moment, panting and sweating. I surprised myself by my menacing behavior.

"Wait a minute!" Lisa stepped in further. "Are those my Anne Klein shoes? And my Donna Karan cashmere sweater?" Lisa kneeled down to retrieve her damaged goods. Each item she found ruined made her more enraged. Lisa abruptly stood, then turned toward me with her nostrils flared, and lips pulled tight. She charged at me, and we went for it.

We fought all over the room—kicking, punching, and scratching until we ended up on the floor brawling wildly like two alley cats fighting over the last can of sardines. I didn't even notice that Shante had run out the room to get the

Resident Assistant and Security.

"Stop it! Stop it right now!" Dorm Security struggled to pull Lisa and me apart.

"You whore!"

"I'm not a whore!"

"That's enough!" the RA stepped in between us. "Lisa, you get your things and move out of here tonight. We're putting you in another room with someone else."

"What things? She destroyed all of my stuff."

"Well, grab whatever is left, and let's go."

"She can't stay here, either!" I pointed at Shante, who gave me a staggered look. "That's right, heifer, you get out too, because you knew! You knew Lisa and Ace were screwing each other that night, and you were supposed to be my friend, but you didn't tell me. When our paths crossed when I was leaving the hotel, you didn't say one word because you knew!"

"I tried to talk Lisa out of it, but she did it anyway. By the time I saw you, you were running out the hotel. I figured you already knew. What else could I have said?"

"Shante, we're moving you down the hall with Kendra, whose room is next to mine," the RA interrupted. She made both Shante and Lisa move out of the room, but I was able to stay.

"This matter will be reported to the Dean. I'll let her decide whether you girls get suspended or not."

When everyone had left the room, I was left behind to clean up the mess I created. I didn't know that one moment of rage would wreak havoc on my relationship with Lisa and Shante. Yet, I wasn't the one who started all of this. This was Lisa's fault.

Now the three of us had been split apart. I finally had the room all to myself, but I didn't want things to end this way. On the other hand, it was probably better for us to separate. All of us had been walking around the room on eggshells after what had happened. We were barely speaking to each other anyway. Now the tension was gone, and the culprit, Lisa, would have to bunk with somebody else.

IN THE DOG HOUSE

"The Press showed up at our house last night, and I told them you got carried away at that party last weekend," Dad said to me, after he had bailed me out of jail. Mysteriously, they couldn't find some paperwork that was needed to let me out. I'm sure Mr. Johnson, the cop who kicked my butt had something to do with me spending a week in jail. He probably wanted the media to find out.

"You're screwing up, boy. The NFL is watching the moves you make, and you go out and do something stupid."

"Did the story make it to the papers?"

"Of course it did. I read it just this morning at a bagel shop with a friend. I couldn't believe they would print that after I told them everything was fine. I guess they investigated further," he explained. "On top of that, I met up with Donna to give her ten thousand to drop charges against you and stop talking to the Press."

"Whew, she wanted that much?"

"That's not the end of it. Now I'll have to cough up three thousand to give to that student, Mario. He'll need to take the urine test for you again."

"Mario is good for it. He always has been, even when I dope up before the games."

"That's not the point, you peanut brain! I can't keep covering for you, Angelo. You're breaking the bank with your stupidity, and making my company look bad."

"I get it, Dad, alright? It won't happen again. I promise everything will work out. It always does."

"You better hope so, because the stock for Iron Motors has already dropped 5 percent!"

"Sorry."

"Sorry ain't good enough, boy. You need to make smart decisions from now on because I'm not gonna keep coming to your rescue. Now get outta my car!" He came to an abrupt stop right in front of the frat house that made my body jerk forward. Before I could shut the door good, he sped off without a goodbye.

Inside, I could see the frat brothers talking, but then they stopped when they noticed me walking through the front door. I glared at Marcus who was sitting on the sofa still brewing a blacked eye. I looked at the other brothers who all had gloomy faces like someone had died.

"You guys couldn't come and bail a brother out? You been sitting around for a week while I was in a pissy jail cell? What's up with that?"

"Yo, you should ask yourself what's up, my *brother*!" Marcus stepped to me, and I got ready to black his other eye. "You call yourself a brother? You ain't nobody's brother!"

"You don't have a right to be mad at me. You set me up!"

"I wasn't gonna go through with it, but when Gregory told me you used to bang our mother, I couldn't forgive you for that. I heard about them other dudes having sex with her, but I never thought my own best friend would do me like that."

"That's messed up, Ace!" Tony shook his head, and the other brothers started to sympathize with Marcus too.

"I was just a kid. She could've gone to jail for having sex with a minor."

Marcus swung at me, but I ducked just in time, and tackled him to the floor.

"Nah, we not having that today!" Tony and Eric fought to break us apart. It was a struggle, but eventually they were able to pull apart.

"Look Ace, you been slipping, man," Eric stated. "You shouldn't have never treated Marcus like that. We're all supposed to be brothers, but you done let Germaine come between us, and we knew you before she did. Now look at what it's cost you. You got locked up, Donna pressed charges, and all this is because of Germaine."

"Man you sound like a fool! All of this is because of Marcus and Donna setting me up!"

"You're blind Ace. Germaine got you booty whipped."

"Man, you tripping! I've done everything for this frat. You guys been riding my coattail since freshman year!"

"Just get your stuff and get out!" Marcus interjected.

"So, is this why you guys are up so early? You punks been plotting to kick me out the frat house?"

"S-s-s-sorry, Ace." PeeWee hung his head low.

"I've done everything for you guys. I paid all the bills in this house, I loaned you my truck, bought you clothes, and shared everything with you guys like brothers. Take a look around you, I even bought the furniture you're sitting on, and you're kicking *me* out? Guess what? All the TVs, the furniture, and everything else that *I* bought, is coming with me. Believe that!"

"Ace, I'm sorry it's come to this. You've been like m-m-my brother." PeeWee teared up. With him being the youngest and still immature, I believed he really didn't want to do this, but he was pressured by the rest of the brothers.

"PeeWee, it's all good. Don't sweat it, kid. At the end of the day, I'm still the King of the Bulldogs."

"Not anymore, son!" Tony stated in his New York accent. "We called the headquarters this morning since you made the papers."

Tony reached over and grabbed the newspaper off the coffee table and tossed it at me. My picture made the front cover of the sports section of *The Washington Post*.

"We can't have this kind of bad press. The guys at headquarters gave us two options. Either suspend you for the rest of the semester or entirely. They left it up to us to vote."

"And you're out!" Eric got right to the point. I was stunned, because second to Marcus, Eric was a really good friend. My parents actually enjoyed his company more than Marcus, whenever he came to visit us in B-More.

"You can't be serious!"

"You can call the headquarters yourself to check."

I knew they were telling the truth. Besides, even if they

weren't, I knew I wasn't wanted there anymore.

"So you guys voted me out after all I've done for you?"

"You mean after what you *did* to us, right?" Marcus bickered.

"Don't take it personal, Ace. We're still cool, but you can't be frat no more, homey." Tony reached out his hand for me to shake it.

"Nah sucker, you can step off with that."

I went upstairs and took my dear sweet time packing. When I finished, I took a long hot shower after being in that stinky jail cell for a week. I then went to the refrigerator and packed all of the food. I called for a U-Haul truck, and I was moved out by the end of the day. I left the brothers with nearly an empty house. Just as empty as my heart felt to leave.

I had my furniture put in storage until I could figure out where I was going to live. I needed money. I checked into a hotel in the meantime, but I knew the cash I had on me would only last a few days, including the money I had in the bank. I called my dad, hoping he could find me an apartment. He didn't want to hear from me, not with worse news.

"You got yourself in this mess, you get yourself out!"

I was in a bind. I had no choice but to call the one person I always knew who had money—Victor.

"Look kid, I know somebody who knows somebody, and they can get you an apartment on Connecticut Avenue where all the uppity folks live."

"Cool, I'd like that."

"But ya gonna need two grand for the deposit," Victor said to me. I had met up with him at the IBEX nightclub later that night where he worked part-time as a bouncer. During the day, he managed his diner. The IBEX was a spot me and my frat brothers would pay to see the strippers. Obviously, those days were over with now.

"Vic, I don't have that kind of money. Just spot me 10Gs; you know I'm good for it."

"That's a lot of dough, kid. You'll need to score every

touchdown and win the championship next weekend for that kind of bread."

"I got it. Don't sweat it!"

"Here's 5Gs for now, and don't worry about it kid, okay? Everything's gonna work out. I'll have the apartment keys for you's in the morning so meet me at the diner, got it?"

"Got it."

"Now kid, I gotta warn you. If I lose this kind of money I'm a dead man, but you's a dead man first, I can promise you. Are you hearing me, son?"

"I got this, Vic. Have I ever let you down?"

"Nope, but don't do it now 'cause we got big dough on the table, kid, are you hearing me? Ya don't wanna become a scooch. I don't like a scooch."

"I promise, Vic. I got it covered. I swear, man."

"Sure ya do kid." He puffed his cigar and winced his eyes against the thick film of smoke. "Say, did some wise guy introduce you to their fist or what?"

"Nah man, the cops busted me up like this for talking smack. It's funny you notice it, but my dad didn't say a thing about it."

"Your dad is a schmuck and a scooch. He's using you as his meal ticket. I'd never use you, kid, it's fair game with me, ya understand?"

"I know, and thanks for helping me out Vic."

"Don't worry about it. Now get outta here kid. I's gots work to do."

THAT'S THE WAY LOVE GOES

Germaine hadn't returned my calls in over a week since I'd been out of jail. I had even called her from my jail cell, reversing the charges to my parent's phone. I sent her flowers with a card apologizing, and I sent her emails. I tried to catch up with her on campus, but she must've left early for her classes or later. I desperately needed to talk to her. I needed to hear her voice and see her face. Tonight was the Rockford Championship game against Howard University, and I needed Germaine. She was my lucky charm.

I felt so desperate earlier that I went by her dorm room. One of the girls who knew me, let me sneak in since I was no longer allowed there because of what happened. When I didn't get an answer at her door, I decided to leave her a personal note. I wrote:

Dear Germaine, I know I'm the last person on earth you want to talk to right now. I apologize for hurting you. I miss you and I still love you. Please meet me this afternoon at 2 o'clock at the Botanical Gardens. We really need to talk. I hope to see you there.
– Angelo

So I'd been sitting here at the Botanical Gardens waiting to see if Germaine would show up. I chose the Botanical Gardens because it was far away from Rockford and private. I hoped Germaine remembered where it was, because I had to meet the team by 3 o'clock since the game started at 6:00. It was already past 2 o'clock now, and I needed to get back to school ASAP. I was sure Coach and the guys were wondering where I was. My father was also probably going nuts since we talked before every game, and I hadn't called him.

Where are you, Germaine? I searched the garden, eyes darting more wildly with each passing second. The temperature was dropping, so I slid my hands in my jacket pockets. As I moved quickly down the even pathway of pretty mums, pansies, and other colorful perennials of fall, I saw Germaine at a distance by the conservatory.

She was wearing black jeans, a purple Rockford hoodie, and sneakers. Her hair was pulled back in a ponytail, and she looked like she was planning on going to the game tonight. I felt so relieved that she'd showed up that my chest began to relax, and I stopped in my tracks and waited as she approached me. However, the closer Germaine came toward me, the more I saw her face forming into an evil stare. Her nose and mouth twisted in unison and her eyes narrowed on me.

My smile quickly dissipated, and I reluctantly uttered, "Hey, how are you?"

I didn't see it coming, but she smacked me hard across the face. I felt my jaw sting like fire and flashes of light flickered across my eyes. I didn't know how much more of a beating my face could take. I blinked a few times to bring my eyes back into focus, and that's when I saw Germaine storming off.

"Germaine! Wait!"

"Stay away from me, Ace! I don't want to see you again! Not ever!" Her voice ripped through the air.

"Germaine, I'm sorry!" I tugged at her arm.

"Yes you are *sorry,* Ace!" Her eyes looked pained and angry. "Marcus called me right before I came here to meet you, and he told me everything. EVERYTHING, Ace!"

Each word Germaine shot at me felt like poison shooting through my veins. It was slow and painful, as she went into all the details about the Bulldogs' bet on her. She also found out how I tested Donna's loyalty. Marcus even showed her our cabinet filled with videotapes of all the girls we'd had sex with since freshman year, and then he told her about me and his mother. Just when I thought Germaine was through with sharing all that she had discovered, she tossed the sex pictures of me and Lisa at my chest. My mouth gaped open as I tried to think of a way to explain everything, but I felt dumbfounded. The pictures were a further reminder of what Germaine had already seen up close and in living color. Marcus and Donna had really stuck the knife in Germaine's and my relationship. It hurt. It hurt so bad and I felt so low that I wished the solid ground could steady me.

"You are cold, heartless, and cruel! I feel like a fool. How stupid of me to think that you were a changed man and that I was someone special to you."

"But you are special to me, Germaine."

"No I'm not! I don't know who this guy is that's standing in front of me."

"Germaine, that's not true. You know me! Everything I did for you was because I loved you. I still do."

"Love? How dare you say you loved me!"

"But Germaine, I—"

"Stop saying you love me! Love doesn't betray people, love doesn't cheat, love doesn't run schemes. You've been gambling, using drugs behind my back, and you nearly choked Donna to death at the party, I heard. You slept with my cousin, and you screwed your best friend's mother, so I don't know you, because the guy I fell in love with would never do those things!"

"Germaine, if you could just let me explain—"

"Explain? You can't explain your way out of this, Ace, and you can't call your father and ask him to buy me back either. He can't save you this time."

"Please tell me how we can fix this, because I need you, Germaine."

"We can't fix *us* because you don't understand how broken *you* really are."

"Germaine, you don't really mean that, do you?"

"Broken people hurt people, and that's exactly what you did to me. You really hurt me Ace," she said, her voice shook, as her features began to buckle, and I could see her eyes filling with tears. When she blinked, they streamed down her cheeks.

I felt choked up. It pained me to see the hurt I'd caused her.

I reached out to try and hug her. "Baby I'm sorry."

"Don't touch me! We are through. Done! If you come near me again I'll call the police!" Germaine stormed off.

I blinked back my tears, and swallowed the lump forming in my throat. I tried to keep my composure, but as my emotions swelled inside of me, my chest started to shake uncontrollably, and my hands trembled.

"GERMAAAAINE, PLEEEASE DON'T GO!" I bellowed out from the pit of my stomach, but she kept walking. I felt so hurt that my legs felt weak, and I dropped to my knees. The only thing I could do was cry. "Oh God, what have I done? What have I done?"

ACE IS TRUMPED

It was the Mid-Eastern Atlantic Conference Football Championship (MEAC), and I was supposed to be ready for this game. As much as I hated to do it again, I gave myself a shot of steroids in the butt so I could last, but mentally and emotionally I was a mess! After I did what I felt I needed to do in the men's room, I joined the guys in the locker room huddle. I pulled up a chair and joined the circle. As I sat down, I stared at the Rockford Raiders symbol in the middle of the carpet floor. It was a raider riding a horse, looking like he was ready for war. I didn't feel like a raging Raider, I felt more like a wuss on a pony. I raised my chin and looked up at the whiteboard, as Coach drew a bunch of Xs and Os that looked like broken hearts to me. His pep talk to get us hyped before the game came in one ear and went out the other.

"So that's our game plan, now let's get out there and get us another championship!" Coach Jacobs shouted, as the school band started playing our anthem song, and we could hear the crowds cheering from outside. It was time to head out to the field.

As we ran through the stadium tunnel toward the bright lights of the field, I didn't get the same adrenaline rush I would normally feel. The crowd in the stands were screaming and waving our Rockford Raiders school banners. Some of the fans wore face makeup of purple and black, and some shouted my name as I ran to the field toward the sidelines. All the camera crews were there since this was the MEAC Championship. I forced a smile whenever the cameras turned my way, but deep down I wasn't feeling it.

After we won the coin toss, we rushed out to the middle of the field. The quarterback (QB) called the play and broke the huddle. As we formed the line, I felt light-headed from the start. *We can't fix us because you don't know how broken you are,* Germaine's words echoed through my mind. I didn't even remember the play the QB called.

I glanced up at the stands, and normally I could spot Germaine sitting a few rows above the team's bench, cheering for me with two purple pom-poms. The seat was now taken by a white girl with blond hair. She was bouncing up and down cheering for us, but I rolled my eyes feeling upset that it wasn't Germaine.

"You good, bro?" Sammy, my teammate, discerned the distracted look in my eyes. All I could think about was last year on this same field, Germaine had given herself to me. She loved me enough to let me be her first love. She trusted me with her heart, and I promised to never break it, but now it was broken. Everything we had built together was broken, and I couldn't fix it.

"I'm good." I nodded my head at Sammy, wishing in the back of my mind that I could undo all the damage. Despite my dad always saying that money could fix anything, I knew in this case that he was wrong.

"Seeet. Hut hut!" the QB yelled, and I was caught off guard as the formation line broke, and each player ran in the direction they were supposed to. The loud crackling of pads and helmets sounded like pieces of metal being crushed by a scrap machine. I ran down the field, turned around, and the football was spiraling down toward me. I didn't even know if I was supposed to catch it or if this was a play called for Marcus.

The crowds shouted from the stands, and the cheerleaders chanted along the sideline. I had to make a quick decision. The whole school, along with most of the city of Washington was attending this game. I could see the TV cameras from my peripheral vision following the action on the field. The ref was running alongside me with his eyes glazed on the ball that came down quickly. I stretched my hands as far as I could to try to catch it. I jumped for it, but it was too soon. My timing was way off, and I fell flat on the field. The football bounced out of bounds and out of reach, just like Germaine.

"BOOOOO!" The crowd didn't waste any time showing me their displeasure. The team quickly huddled, and the QB called another play. That's when I noticed a sinister look in Marcus's eyes. I knew he'd picked this day on purpose to tell Germaine the truth, and to give her those pictures to add fuel to the fire. He didn't want my head to be in the game.

The QB broke the huddle, and we formed the line again according to the play. I ran for the ball, and this time I caught it.

"YAAAAY!" The crowd cheered as I ran up field, dodging and weaving through defenders. "GO ACE! GO ACE!" The cheerleaders chanted. I kept running, but then I felt someone from the opposing team pull me back by my shoulder pads. My feet were still moving, but next thing I knew, another defender came running toward me head-on. I tried to dodge him, but I was already being pulled from behind. I took a hit so hard that my helmet popped off my head. I lay on the field staring up at the night's sky and the bright lights from the field, as teammates ran to my side.

"You all right, Ace?"

I shook my head, and slowly stood up. My knees buckled as I tried to steady my balance.

"I'm good . . . I think."

I limped over to the sidelines, and flopped down on the bench feeling winded and dizzy.

"That was a good run, son, you got us a first down. Take a rest for a minute," Coach Jacobs said, rapidly chewing his gum. "We'll run the next two plays for Marcus."

Marcus gave me a funny smirk as he donned his helmet. He wanted to be the star of this game. I knew this was all part of his plan. He and I had run so many schemes on other people throughout our lives that I knew how he operated. I was ready to throw in the white towel and call it quits. This wasn't a good night. I didn't feel like going back out on the field and getting banged up again. If Marcus wanted to be the star of the show, so be it. He could have the spotlight tonight. Right now, I felt privileged to sit beside the waterboy rather than go back on the field knowing my head wasn't mentally in the game.

"Yo, Coach, I'm shaken up. Maybe I should be checked out for a concussion."

Coach Jacobs walked over closer to me. He examined my face and checked my head.

"I don't see any knots or scars. What're you trying to say to me, boy?"

"My head hurts, Coach. Maybe I need to be checked out by the team doc."

"Are you kidding me? You've taken plenty of hits like that before. Now you hydrate, and if Marcus doesn't get us another first down or a touchdown, you get back on that field and win us a championship, boy!"

"But Coach—"

"That's an order!"

While I hesitated to get back on the field, the Howard University Bisons scored a touchdown off a fumble from Marcus. He had lost control of the ball. I laughed as Marcus returned to the sidelines cursing himself for messing up both plays.

"Dude, you can never be me!" I scoffed at him. I then put on my helmet and walked back onto the field while my teammates ran out to quickly set up the offense. Marcus was trying too hard to get the accolades I normally got, instead of playing his own style of game. He could've scored for us, but had tried to show off.

The QB called the next play for me that Coach told him to run. "Up the middle Ace, psych 'em out and run up the middle," the QB whispered to me, before I took the line. I thought, *yeah, sure, piece of cake. Whatever you say.* The truth was, I was pissed off by the Coach calling me *boy* because things weren't going his way. He called me *son* when things were good, just like my dad. Coach Jacobs wanted to win this championship to keep his job. Winning was bigger than me. Even though we had won the previous year, the rumor mill from the athletics department was that Coach Jacobs' old ways of doing things were no longer working. We had barely won last year because Coach refused to listen to the younger offensive coordinators.

The ball was spiked, and the QB passed it off to me. I faked out my defenders and started running up the middle. It felt like my legs were freezing up on me. The quicker I tried to run, the slower I felt, despite the steroids. It was as if weights had been placed on my ankles. I was going nowhere fast.

"RUN ACE! RUN!" I could hear the crowd. I could see the end zone straight in front of me. For some reason, I wondered, *why should I run? Who am I running for?* Suddenly, I was tackled from behind, and this time when I fell, I fumbled the ball. Howard retrieved it, and ran all the way up the field to earn a first down.

"BOOOO!" the crowd roared, and started throwing empty bottles on the field. I dodged and weaved the bottles, and safely made my way to the sidelines as the defensive linemen ran out onto the field. Security went up in the stands to control the crowd, but it didn't stop one diehard fan who was shouting obscenities to me with his fist balled.

"Hey kid, I know you heard me!" the man who was cursing me out shouted. Instinctively, I looked over my shoulder. "Yeah, you! You suck!"

The man was right. I did suck. I dropped my head and made my way to the bench. When I sat down, the other players slid down to the far end away from me, shaking their heads in disgust at my performance.

We lost the championship game 30-17. I had scored only one touchdown, but had turned over the ball several times or been sacked at least a dozen. Eric had scored the other touchdown, and our kicker made the score seventeen, but it wasn't enough. Howard University became the MEAC Champions. I was sure Victor was somewhere plotting to kill me, so I would have to figure out how to get him his money back and fast.

As I staggered toward the tunnel to the locker room, feeling beat up physically and mentally; a short reporter appeared through the crowd. He stepped in front of me and shoved a microphone toward my mouth.

"Angelo, I'm Mark Duncan from NBC4, that was quite a game you had there, do you have a moment?"

"Not really."

"But it will only take a few minutes," he insisted. I gave him a look that said, *make it quick.*

"As a senior, is this how you planned to end your football career here at Rockford?"

"I don't think anyone plans to lose."

"Some are already saying that you lost tonight's game because you were partying recently and got into trouble with the law. What do you have to say about those allegations?"

My dad appeared from out of the crowd, and rushed up to the microphone before I could answer.

"It was a rough game with all those crazy practices. I blame Coach Jacobs. He had these guys practicing day and night, but my boy here is NFL ready, believe me!"

"There were a few scouts here tonight, Angelo, do you think they would be impressed by your performance?"

"Well, I—"

"The scouts should look at Angelo's whole football career over the past three and a half years that he's been here at Rockford," Dad interrupted again. He yanked the microphone from Mr. Duncan, and started repeating his marketing lines in front of the camera.

"...and for all you fans out there, since my boy here made one touchdown, you get ten dollars off an oil change at any Iron Motors this weekend!"

Mr. Duncan snatched the mike back.

"As I was saying, Angelo, was this performance because of partying too much or did you throw this game to meet the gamblers' request?"

"Gamblers? What gamblers? My boy doesn't gamble!" Dad didn't know anything about it because I kept it from him. The only person who ever knew were Marcus and Donna. I didn't have to guess that Marcus leaked it to the media.

"That's all the questions for now sir," Coach Jacobs intervened. I was glad he saved me. I didn't know how to answer that question.

After the game, my Dad and I drove to the Union Pub on Capitol Hill. It was our ritual to get drinks after important games.

"What happened to you out on that field tonight, boy?"

"I don't know," I shrugged, then guzzled down two more shots of Tequila. "Bartender, give me one more for the road!"

"No, he's had enough!" Dad interjected. "Son, you need to get your mind right, do you understand? There were scouts at tonight's game. Now we gotta figure out a way to fix the rumors about you gambling. I want you to talk to the Press and tell them you don't gamble, you made a mistake by going to that party, and tonight you were too sick to play. Got it?"

"I'm not gonna do that, Dad."

"Excuse me?"

"I said, no!"

"You need to fix this!"

"Why do I need to fix this? It's not about me, it's about you."

"I don't have time to argue. Now get the Coach on the line right now and tell him you want a press conference first thing tomorrow, and that's an order!" He shoved his cell phone toward me. He didn't seem to care who was looking, which only made me feel more disrespected and embarrassed.

"I'm done here." I got up and walked out of the pub.

"Wait! Angelo, come back here, boy!" Dad shouted, and I could hear the sound of his footsteps quickening behind me.

"What do you mean you're done?"

I turned around sharply. "I quit! I'm done with football!"

"Is that right? Well you don't get to quit. You owe me for all the money I invested into your future."

"I always was a commodity to you, Dad. It's a shame that you don't care about me as a son."

"Boy you sound like a sissy."

"No, I sound like a man who wished he had a father who

cared enough about him tonight to make sure he wasn't unconscious after taking that hit. I sound like a man who wished his father would've talked to him about life, and showed him how to treat women so he wouldn't have lost the only woman in this world he ever loved. I don't owe you crap! YOU owe me!"

"You're out of line, boy. You better watch yourself."

"Or what?" I stood over him, giving him a stare down.

"That's it! Don't you ever come back to my house again! Give me the keys!"

I tossed the keys to the ground, and watched him bend over to pick them up. I was tempted to give him a hard kick in the butt.

"You'll never be nothing without football!"

"We'll see about that!" I climbed into my truck and drove off full speed, leaving him standing by the curb coughing from the smoke.

SECRETS

In the middle of eating Thanksgiving dinner, Lisa had another panic attack, and had to be calmed down by her mother. We had been suspended from school, and we couldn't return until after the Thanksgiving holiday. The news was a big disappointment to our family, and Lisa became overwhelmed by it all when Uncle Walter lectured us at the dinner table.

". . . and you young ladies shouldn't be fighting over some guy, anyway," he continued, while Aunt Lolita damped Lisa's forehead with a wet cloth.

"Are you done, Uncle Walter?"

"No, I'm not. You watch your tone, young lady." His eyes jumped with surprise. "Now I don't like the person you've turned into as of late. Your grades are dropping again, and you keep giving your grandma attitude, I won't stand for it!"

"Well then, can I be excused?"

"Did you not just hear what I said? No, you cannot be excused, I'm your father and you're both going to sit right here at this table until I finish saying what I gotta say! Two sisters shouldn't fight like this over a man!"

A cloud of silence came over the room. I wasn't sure if I heard him correctly. I glared at Lisa who looked at me from across the table with the same perplexed look in her eyes.

"Did you—did you just say you're *my* father?"

Uncle Walter huffed, wiped the moisture from his brow, and started pacing the dining room with his hand hovered over his mouth. Lisa and I stared at him in confusion, thinking maybe he had too much alcohol in his eggnog.

"It was a mistake!" Aunt Lolita yelled in his defense.

"I didn't mean for it to come out like that, but it's no mistake," he said, then turned to Aunt Lolita and rested his hands on her shoulder. "It's time they know the truth."

"What truth?" Grandma stood up from the table, taking the words right out of my mouth.

My gaze ping-ponged between him and Aunt Lolita, then I stood up and ran upstairs to my room, and slammed the door. I flopped on my bed and cried my eyes out. I couldn't believe what I had just heard. Before I had a chance to process what had happened. I heard Grandma calling for me outside of my door.

"Go away!" I cried. I couldn't believe what Uncle Walter had just inadvertently blurted out. Lisa was my half-sister? How could that be?

"Germaine, open this door right now so we can talk," I heard Uncle Walter demand.

"I think you've said enough!" I squeezed my eyes tight, as tears streamed down my cheeks. Next thing I knew, the door burst wide open. The bottom lock popped off and landed on the wood floor. Uncle Walter stood in the doorway with Grandma by his side.

"I just talked to Lisa and she's just as devastated as you are right now," he said, leaning down to pick up the lock off the floor and he placed it on my dresser, and promised to fix it later.

"Please don't say anything else. I've been betrayed enough."

"Germaine, please let ya father explain," Grandma walked in and the two of them sat on opposite sides of me on my bed.

"Everything I told you before was true, except I didn't tell you about the one night your mother and I had slept together. Vera was helping me with a term paper for class. We were in my dorm room, and it was getting late. Between the good music that was playing in the background, and the glasses of wine that I shared with her, it created a certain mood between us. One thing led to another, and we were intimate. She ended up pregnant, and out of fear of what Thomas would say and her parents, she wanted me to marry her. I couldn't do that to Thomas, not to mention I was seeing Lolita. Instead, Vera rushed Thomas to the altar, and led him and her parents to believe that you were his child.

That night the accident happened, was the same night I had told Vera I was coming over to tell Thomas the truth. I was tired of him being a father to you when I knew you were mine. Vera finally agreed to tell Thomas, and that night they were both killed in a car accident. I told your grandfather I wanted to get custody of you, but he wouldn't let me until I confessed that you were mine and not Thomas's. I did a DNA test to prove it, and it came back positive. Your grandfather and I had it out that day. He wanted me dead and said that one day I would pay the price for what happened to Vera. I guess that day has come, and I'm sorry, Germaine."

"So why didn't you let me live with you?"

"Well, two reasons. One, I felt responsible for your mother and my brother's death. Although Vera was grown, her death left your grandparents without a daughter, so I figured they could start all over again with you. Two, Lolita wasn't happy with the idea of raising another woman's child."

"Sheesh, and I always thought thatcha gave Germaine to us 'cause ya couldn't handle her and Lisa," Grandma mentioned. This was news for her too. I assume my Grandpa kept it a secret from her. Maybe that's why he never said much.

"That summer of 1983 is when Grandpa Roberts and I agreed to let Germaine be raised by you guys."

"So Grandpa did love me?"

"Of course he did child!" Grandma hugged me.

"He wanted to take you away from me the way I took his daughter, but your Grandma did all the raising if you ask me."

"Now Walter, don't you speak that way."

"Well, that's another discussion for another day, I guess," he said.

"This is just making my head spin."

"I'm sorry, Germaine. I just didn't want you and Lisa getting caught up in a love affair with the same guy. You both should learn from my mistake."

***

When they left my room my mind began to put together all of the pieces to my childhood. I'd always wondered why Uncle Walter insisted Lisa and I spend time together each summer and why I would visit them every other holiday. Then there were the gifts—expensive gifts he'd buy for my birthday and Christmas. He would also give my grandparents money each month after my parents died. I just thought he was helping out. No wonder my Aunt Lolita never really liked me. It all made sense now.

A WOMAN SCORNED

When we returned to school after the Thanksgiving break, Dean Patterson met with all of us in her office. When I say all of us, I mean, me, Lisa, Angelo, Donna and Marcus. I found out that Angelo was telling the truth. Donna and Marcus had set up the whole thing, but that still didn't mean that Angelo and Lisa had to fall into their trap.

I told Dean Patterson that I couldn't understand why she had suspended me and Lisa, and not Angelo, Donna, and Marcus. She explained that what happened was off campus, but the fight between me and Lisa happened in the dorm. Dean Patterson had also made me pay for the damages to Lisa's property out of my scholarship money, despite the fact that I told her that Uncle Walter, I mean, my father, had already given Lisa the money to replace her belongings. Still, Dean Patterson explained that she had to do what was best for the university.

After the useless meeting with Dean Patterson, I went back to my dorm room. I started packing away everything that reminded me of Angelo: pictures, ticket stubs from movies and concerts, his autographed football jersey, and the promise ring that reminded me of how he *broke* his promise. I even tossed out my birth control pills. I tried hard to remove Angelo from my space. I hated him—at least at first I did, until sadness slithered its dark cloud into my heart, and pushed away all the happiness from my being.

When I finished packing "Angelo" away in a box, I felt tired from the long day. I lay across my bed and stared at the empty bunk beds where Shante and Lisa used to sleep. I was determined to make my room a sanctuary from now on. I didn't need anything or anyone. Trying to make friends and be social with others had caused too much trouble in my life. It was better to be by myself.

When I woke up the next morning, I got up out of bed and turned on my computer. While I waited for it to boot, I brewed myself a cup of coffee. We weren't supposed to have a coffee maker in our room, but I had snuck one in at the beginning of the semester. Shante had brought her heater back from Ohio, and Lisa brought back her single electric burner from Virginia.

We used to turn on the heater at night to keep warm, since our room never seemed to get warm enough during winter. We would use Lisa's burner to cook hot dogs and Ramen Noodles when the cafeteria had closed for the day, and we were still hungry. We would even cook food for others in our dorm and charge them money. Sometimes we made enough money for all three of us to go shopping or get our hair done. During dorm room inspections, we would discreetly hide the items in the laundry room. I laughed to myself at the thought of how rebellious the three of us could be, but those days were over now.

Once my computer booted up, I tried to pick up where I had left off with my manuscript, but my mind drew a blank. I couldn't stop thinking about Lisa being my half-sister. I tried typing a few poems, hoping to spark some creativity, but when I went back to the manuscript I couldn't think. Usually whenever I wrote a story, it played like a movie inside of my head. This time, however, my mind was like a snowy TV after the programming had gone off air. Feeling frustrated, I decided to go take my shower, so I could head out for breakfast at the cafeteria.

"HEEEY, GERMAINE!" It was Kendra Thompson from down the hall. Her hair was wrapped in an African garb. She was standing at the sink cleaning her face when I came out the shower to brush my teeth.

I mumbled. "Hey, Kendra." I really didn't feel like being bothered. I didn't know her that well, but whenever I ran into her, she would talk so much that I thought my ears were going to bleed. I guess she felt because I was quiet that I was actually listening to her—I wasn't.

"Sorry 'bout you and Ace. Heard ya'll broke up, no?" Kendra asked, and I could hear her Jamaican accent.

I kept brushing my teeth, hoping she would take the hint and leave me alone.

"Is it true, gal? It's been a lot of commotion 'round here, ya know."

"I'm sorry, but I don't think that's any of your business."

"So be it. We're all 'ere if ya need us. If you feel up to it, me and Shante are going out to get drinks tonight."

"No thanks."

Just then, Shante walked into the restroom. Our eyes floated over each other momentarily, and when she said good morning, I rolled my eyes and looked away. Shante went into one of the stalls, and I went back to brushing my teeth. Maybe I shouldn't have been so mean, but I was tired. My eyes stared back at me before the mirror, and I looked like death. I needed more sleep, but every time I closed my eyes, I would think about all the people who had betrayed my trust. As much as my heart hurt, I felt betrayed by it for making me wonder what Angelo might be doing. I wondered how he was feeling after the terrible championship loss. Each time he got sacked, I cringed as if I could feel his pain. Eventually, I turned off the TV and went to bed. The next morning I found out that we had lost the game.

The walk across campus to the cafeteria only took five minutes, but as slow as I was walking it felt like a half hour. I grabbed some hot food off the bar, a second cup of coffee from the machine, and took a seat near the window. I could see the sun rising behind the Washington Monument and the Capitol at a distance. The view of Washington was always beautiful. I recalled the day that Angelo and I went to visit all the historical landmarks. Angelo was everywhere it seemed.

For a moment, I thought about transferring to a school back

home, but I knew going back home would make me feel like I was running away from my problems instead of facing them head on. If I went back home I would never become my own person.

"You mind if I sit here?"

I looked up from my half-eaten plate to see a tall, skinny girl wearing blue jeans and an oversized colorful sweater. She was wearing her hair in a wavy bun.

"I'd rather eat alone, Shante."

"I'm really sorry, Germaine."

"How many times are you going to say that? All of you are sorry. Just sorry, no-good people."

"I didn't have a chance to say anything to you, Germaine. You were running out of the hotel."

"Shante, let's be honest for a change. You wouldn't have told me whether I was running out of the hotel or walking. Your and Lisa's loyalty has always been to your sorority. If Donna had found out you told me, you would've been kicked out the sorority for breaking the code."

"That's not true. Listen, you and Lisa are good friends of mine and I really hate that we're not together anymore. The three of us were so close, and I miss that."

"Friends? What's that?" I rolled my eyes, stood up, and walked away.

Shante caught up to me as I was leaving the cafeteria. I couldn't believe she was hot on my heels begging for my forgiveness when she should've thought about that at first.

"I know it hurts, Germaine," Shante said, keeping up the fast pace with my walk. I felt anxious to get back to my room and slam the door.

"The first cut is always the deepest."

"What're you talking about?"

"Ace was your first love, and when you love someone for the first time and they hurt you, it cuts deep. Like a knife to the heart. Trust me, I've been there."

"Shante, have you forgotten that you hurt me too?"

"We're all standing in the circle of your pain, but at the core, you're most hurt at Ace."

"Whatever you say, Oprah Winfrey."

"None of us intentionally hurt you. I know Ace wasn't right for what he did, but I think he really loved you, Germaine. Before any of that happened, I saw a change in him. He was starting to mature. I could tell he loved you, because I saw him turn down girls at parties and he even stopped hanging out with his frat brothers as much. And Lisa, you know she took her anxiety medicine that night, and unbeknown to us, she had a few drinks too. Lisa never wanted Ace. Just think about it."

"Are you through justifying everyone's behavior, including your own?"

"I'm trying to get you to see the whole picture."

"Shante, I see the whole picture every night when I close my eyes, and it never changes."

"Well, I've said my peace. I'll leave you alone for a while."

"You do that."

STIRRING THE POT

"What're you trying to say, Doctor?" I wanted to make sure my ears heard him correctly.

"The same thing I've been saying all week, Ms. Dupree-Landry. The reason you missed your period is because you're going to be a Mom." Dr. Martin said to me, as I sat on the exam room bed.

"No, this has to be a mistake!"

Dr. Martin heaved a long frustrating sigh, as he looked up at me from his clipboard.

"The test is 99.9 percent accurate, and you've taken three already."

"But you don't understand. My parents will be very disappointed in me. I'm supposed to be a lawyer."

"You still can be whoever you want to be, it may just take a while. Now, here are your prenatal vitamins, and I'd like to see you back in four weeks to see how you're doing," Dr. Martin said, trying to hurry me out of his office. I'd come to visit him at the *Columbia Hospital for Women* three times this week hoping for a different answer.

As soon as I stepped outside of the hospital, I puked by the curb near my car.

"Miss, are you okay?" asked a passerby who was walking along L Street.

"Yes, I'll be fine," I nodded, as I wiped my mouth. My hands trembled as I fumbled through my purse for my car keys. Once I got inside, I buckled my seatbelt with a shaky hand. My forehead was sweating and my heart was pounding a mile a minute. I caught a glance at myself before the rearview mirror.

"Oh God, Lisa, what have you done, girl?" I burst into tears, as I pulled out of my parking space.

BEEEEP'

"HEY, WATCH WHERE YOU'RE GOING, YOU FREAKIN' IDIOT!" the driver of another car shouted and honked his horn. He swerved around me. I was so distraught that I didn't look in my sideview mirror to make sure no cars were coming before I pulled out of my parking space.

All I could think about was that I was pregnant, and the baby was Ace's. How on earth was Germaine going to forgive me after this? What were my parents going to think? I couldn't possibly have this baby and finish school. I couldn't be a Pink Lady with a baby bump either. The timing of this whole situation was off. Sure I wanted to be a mother, but not while I was in college. Not when I had the potential to become a top lawyer. Not when I wasn't married. What was I going to do? Who was I going to tell?

MENDING A BROKEN HEART

I had Phyllis Hyman's *Living All Alone* in constant rotation in my CD player. Each night Phyllis's lyrics spoke to my heart. She sang about trusting someone you loved, but being played for a fool. Being somebody's baby one minute and the next being all alone. Phyllis understood me and what I was going through. I couldn't write, and I barely ate or slept. I was like a deer who'd been struck by a car, and I wished someone would just shoot me to put me out of my misery.

While I lay back on my twin-sized bed staring blankly at the ceiling, I heard a knock on my door. It was Saturday, and I didn't know who it could be. It was a little after seven in the evening and normally when we had room inspections it was in the morning, so I didn't think it was the RA. I approached the door and looked through the peephole. I was surprised to see Shante and Kendra standing on the other side. I inhaled deeply and then exhaled before opening the door.

"What?" I murmured.

"Germaine, I'm not going to keep apologizing to you. As your friend, I won't allow you to stay in this room another night crying over Ace," Shante stated.

"Dat's right! It's high time ya get out 'ere and stop playing dat depressing music. Ya coming with us!"

"You both are crazy. I'm staying right here in this room." I attempted to crawl back in bed.

"Oh no you don't!" Shante grabbed me by the arms. "You're gonna get dressed and come with us. Kendra, find her something to wear."

"Found it!" Kendra grabbed a pair of jeans and a cowl neck sweater out of my closet. I couldn't believe they were taking over my personal space. Before I realized it, I was dressed and headed out to Kendra's car.

"Ya gonna like dis place, I promise." Kendra sped off, as if she was in a hurry. She had said it was a surprise and that I was going to love it. She was nearly running every red light causing Shante and I to grip the cushion of our seats. I didn't mind the fact that she thought enough about me to get me out of the dorm room, but I prayed silently to myself that we would make it safely to wherever she was taking us.

We ended up at a spoken word event in Columbia Heights at a lounge called The Whatnot. It was dark inside as I closely followed Kendra and Shante, who seemed more familiar with the lounge spot than I was.

We walked into a room that was slightly dim. There were round tables with red tablecloths and candles as centerpieces. The tables were filled with people, and I didn't think there were any more seats until the waiter motioned Kendra from across the room. He directed us to an empty table in the corner by the stage. I believe Kendra had reserved the table just for us. As we took our seats, a young man with locks and a linen dashiki had stepped to the microphone.

"This one is called, *Water Flower*," The poet spoke softly into the mike. He had a smooth voice that sounded relaxing and soothing. As he recited his poem, I loved all of the imagery and symbolism that he expressed. He was able to paint a picture that gave us all a visual of what he was talking about.

She lay naked and exposed to the sun
Her bruises were seen by everyone
I pulled her up from the pot, and gazed at her roots
She was still attached to men who were dead fruits
I said to her, 'Water flower, where are your wings
build up your strength and let go of these things!
I drenched her with raindrops of pure Jamaican love
The kind of romance she'd always dreamt of
I watched her grow with my seed and give birth to a king
My beautiful water flower became my everything.

At the end of his performance, everyone cheered, and then the MC announced the show would break for fifteen minutes. We ordered drinks and appetizers, and then the second part of the show began.

"Are there any other poets in the house tonight who would like to share?" the MC asked the audience.

"Go ahead Germaine, you can do it," Shante gave me a nudge.

"I can't."

"My friend 'ere has a poem to share!"

"We have a volunteer poet tonight everybody," the MC said. He walked over and extended his hand, as the lighting crew hovered the spotlight over me.

"But I have no idea what to say," I whispered to him, as he quickly escorted me towards the stage.

"You can do it. Speak from your heart," he said, with a cordial smile. "What's your name?"

"Germaine Landry."

"Ladies and gentlemen we have a virgin on the mike tonight, her name is Germaine Landry, so let's give her some encouragement."

The audience stood up and applauded. My hands were shaking as I approached the standing microphone in the middle of the stage. The bass player began to slowly drum his fingers against the strings. I could see the audience gradually bopping their heads to the beat, as they waited for me to start. Strangely, I thought of Angelo who once told me, *you have the power to make people believe what you say, but you have to believe it yourself.*

"I'm-I'm-I'm new here," I stuttered nervously, as I wiped my sweaty palms on the front of my jeans.

"That's all right sistah girl!" A young lady who looked about my age, shouted from the audience.

"This poem is called *Lost Without You.*"

When we fell in love
you trapped me in the webs of your heart
I became tangled in every emotion
I was sprung from the start
For your every whisper made promises I thought you'd keep
They festered into lies that only made me weep
I battle with my heart because it loves you still
I'm lost without your love and it gives me chills
If I take you back, would it be a lie to myself?
I'm so lost without your love, I don't want nobody else
If I fall for your fancies, will I suffer with regrets?
I feel lost without your love, but I can't go back to your mess.

"Thank you for listening," I concluded, and took a bow. The audience clapped and cheered.

"Give it up again for Ms. Germaine Landry!" the MC shouted. He gave me a hug before I exited the stage.

"I told you you could do it."

"Thanks."

"Good job, Germaine!" Shante and Kendra hugged me when I returned to our table.

"Thank you, guys. I really appreciate you both bringing me here. This is just what I needed."

I felt so scared at first when I recited my poem, but afterwards I felt relieved. I knew I could probably do it again someday. . .

DAMAGED GOODS

As a result of the recent allegations about me using steroids, and gambling on games, the media put a lot of pressure on Rockford's Athletic Department. This forced Dean Patterson to hold a press conference in Rockford's media room. She told Coach Jacobs and I to make sure we cleared Rockford's *good* name. The media were like vultures, who wasted no time to come after me as their prey.

". . . and is it also true that you have used performance enhancing drugs as well?" asked another reporter.

I paused before I answered the next question. In my brief moment of silence, cameras flashed to capture my every movement, even a twitch in my nose. They were trying to break me, but I was already broken just like Germaine had said. I pondered over whether I should tell the truth now or continue to live one big lie.

I glanced at the audience and spotted my parents holding hands. They never held hands in public. It was a façade. I looked to my left at Coach Jacobs, who was wearing a black Rockford cap with the school name written in purple script across the front. He tightened his lips and gave me a threatening look that said, *you better not tell the truth.* Coach Jacobs knew I used steroids. He was the one who introduced me to the narcs dressed in fancy suits so nobody ever knew they were dealers. He wanted to win football games to keep his job, and I wanted to win to please my Dad.

"Yes, I've used performance enhancing drugs," I replied, and the entire room gasped in shock.

"How is it that your urine test before this press conference came back clean?"

"Another student took my urine test for me."

"Mr. Pearson, if you took a urine test right now, are you saying it would come back positive?"

"That's what I'm saying. It may even come back positive for marijuana too. I used it because it was the only way I could free myself from pressures like this."

"What do you mean, Mr. Pearson?"

"Every one of you guys put me here. We were all selfish in this game of football, right Coach Jacobs? You said those drugs would help my performance, remember?"

"He's lying! I don't know what he's talking about!" Coach Jacobs rushed off the platform, and hurried out of the media room.

"As long as I won football games everyone did whatever it took to make me happy and keep me out of trouble, right Dad? Tell the media how you paid Mario to take those urine tests for me, and how you paid for Donna not to press charges against me. Let's not forget that whenever my grades dropped you bought my professors a new car," I said, letting the floodgates open.

"Hey Dean Patterson, tell everyone the real reason why you didn't suspend me for choking Donna at the sorority party. It wasn't because it didn't happen on school campus, was it? Oh noooo, the reason you suspended my girl and not me was because I helped Rockford to get another TV deal. So, you see everyone, I'm just a commodity."

The room suddenly became chaotic, as my parents zipped out of the room like the speed of lightning.

I tapped my hand on the microphone to get everyone's attention and to calm the room.

"Before I leave here today, I would like to apologize to my teammates and to the students here at Rockford who supported me over the years. You guys deserve a true champion, and I'm sorry I wasn't that champion to you. To all the kids and the people here in the DMV community, and Baltimore, I apologize for letting you guys down. I don't take what happened lightly, and I hope to become a better person after this. Thank you all for being supportive fans."

CAUGHT UP

I didn't tell my sorority sisters that I was pregnant, and especially not Shante who was friends with Germaine again. I didn't want Germaine to find out. Donna had officially made me President of the Pink Ladies at our Christmas party last night, and there was no way I was going to ruin my family legacy.

Speaking of Donna, she asked if I could be in her wedding to Marcus Johnson. I declined and told her I had an internship this summer and I wouldn't be able to get away. Besides, I haven't forgiven her for setting me up with Marcus and Ace. It was her fault that I was pregnant in the first place.

Everyone was surprised by Donna's sudden engagement to Marcus, but I wasn't. I saw firsthand how quickly Donna's feelings for Marcus changed when she saw him meeting with NFL scouts recently. I heard she even proposed to him.

As the new President of the Pink Ladies, I was determined to do things differently around here. No more schemes and running games on people. I was going to enforce a rule that no one is to sleep with another sister's man or a relative's man. We were going to get back to being the traditional, classy sorority that my mother and grandmother were once a part of. They were women who carried themselves with dignity, respect, and pride. Right now, our reputation on campus was that we were the Pink "sluts." All of that was going to change.

I was sleeping like a rock until I heard someone banging on my dorm room door like there was a fire. I opened one eye and glanced at the clock on my nightstand; it read 3 o'clock in the afternoon, and I couldn't believe I had slept that long. I must've still been tired from the Christmas party last night. I looked through the peephole and it was Ace, and there was some other guy with him who was dark-skinned with a bald head. I assumed he finally got my message. I opened the door and right away he shoved me aside and barged right in, while his friend waited in the hallway.

"Tramp! You trying to set me up!" he shouted, reeking of alcohol.

"I'm not trying to set you up. You better calm down before I call security!"

"You know that's not my baby!"

"Look, I don't want to accept this no more than you do," I said, panting out of breath. His belligerent demeanor scared me, and reminded me of someone I didn't want to remember.

He laughed, as he wobbled his head uncontrollably from side to side, and then flopped down in the chair to my desk. He nearly knocked over everything that was sitting on top. He smelled awful and looked like a mess. His curly hair had grown wild over his head, and looked like it hadn't touched a comb in weeks since his press conference. He'd grown a beard that looked shabby and unkempt, and his eyes looked dark like he hadn't slept in days. He had definitely hit rock bottom. A part of me actually felt sorry for him. He'd been suspended indefinitely, and kicked out of the Bulldogs fraternity.

I sat down on my bed, but kept my eyes on him to make sure he wasn't going to try anything foolish.

"Lisa, you know Marcus hit that first. Did you call him?"

"No I didn't."

"I get it, you want the baby to be mine, but not Marcus's? Why is that? So you can mess up my chances of getting back with your cousin? I mean, your half-sister, since that's what you guys told Dean Patterson when we met."

"We have to deal with this situation and figure things out."

"Deal with it? That's not my baby. I was strapped. The only girl I never wore a condom with was Germaine. My mother always told me not to trust a big butt and a smile."

"It's not Marcus's baby. You're talking crazy, Ace! You were drunk, so how do you even know for sure that you wore protection?"

"Lisa, you put the condom on me! It was my emergency condom and the only one that I always kept in my wallet. When I woke up the next morning, it was gone. Not to mention that Germaine walked into the room, so we stopped. Call Marcus and tell him that he got you pregnant."

When Ace stood up from the chair his knees slightly buckled, and then he zigzagged his way out the door. I sure hoped that his friend was the designated driver.

When Ace left, I lay across my bed and wept. Everything in my life up until this moment had been filled with fun and excitement. Now the enormity of the responsibility I had before me felt like weights in the middle of my chest. I tried not to believe that Ace was telling the truth, but the more I thought about that night, the more I realized he could be right.

How could I ever explain to my unborn child, yet alone my parents, that I had slept with two men? What would they think of me? And if Marcus was the father, my parents would never approve of him. He was too immature.

Once I gathered myself together, I called Marcus to break the news.

"Lisa, you trippin'! Everybody knows you get around. You better scratch my name off your list."

"I don't have a list! I was only with you and Ace recently, and it's not his."

"I don't need this right now!"

"Me either!"

He heaved a long sigh. "What're you gonna do?"

"I guess we don't really have a choice, do we?"

"Let me know how much this is gonna cost me, and I'll get you the money to handle it."

"Fine." I slowly hung up the phone. I still felt uneasy about my decision, but I didn't know what else to do.

WHO AM I?

I had no idea of who I was as a man. My life had been defined by my parents, and I had played it out how they wanted me to, until it ruined me. I yearned for mental escape from my emotional pain, so I started drinking and smoking more often. After a while, that wasn't enough so I went after something stronger from the street pharmacists.

I spent my weekends back in Baltimore, hanging out with my man Woody. He was a friend I'd known since high school, and he was just as bad off as me. Woody had lost a good paying job when they started downsizing. Shortly afterwards, he caught his girlfriend with another man. We were two miserable guys who buried ourselves in drugs, booze, and partying. I could feel myself spiraling downhill quickly, and I didn't care anymore.

My last words to the press about me getting my life together were as promising as a politician vowing not to increase taxes. It felt right to say it in that moment, but once I realized how hard it was going to be, I gave up in trying.

This Sunday morning was no different from any other morning after a party. Woody and I had just left West Baltimore around 7:00 a.m. I woke up unable to recall where I was or whose house I had passed out in. Woody had to drive my truck for me like always until I sobered up. I was always worse off than he.

Woody drove us to a bagel shop on Light Street, and when I stepped out of the truck the cold air cut into my cheeks like a knife, and took my high and my breath away. I stepped over clunky pieces of snow and ice that were leftover from a storm days ago. I anxiously opened the door to go inside the bagel shop for heat. I rubbed my hands together and welcomed the warmth from the shop. The aroma of fresh bagels and hot roasting coffee beans whiffed across the bridge of my frosty red nose.

"Can I help you?" the short Asian man looked at us suspiciously. It was 7 o'clock in the morning, and he was probably thinking that two black dudes walking into a bagel shop wearing all black could only have one thing in mind this time of morning.

"Two coffees, one black and one with . . . Ace, how do you take yours?" Woody looked over his shoulder at me.

"Two creams, two sugars," I said, before staggering over to one of the tables against the wall. I flopped down in the wooden chair with the round back. There was a big mirror on the wall and I caught a glimpse of my reflection. My eyes were dark, and I was in desperate need of a haircut and a shave. I was underarm funky, and couldn't remember how long I'd been wearing my sweatpants and hoodie under my coat. Living pillar to post for nearly a month and a half, I must've looked homeless.

Woody joined me at the table with two coffees and bagels. He took off his hood, exposing his bald head to the warm air. Woody had kept his head shaved bald since I'd known him. He had one of those perfect head shapes and the chicks used to love that he was dark-skinned with a bald head. Today, they'd probably think he was a bum off the streets with his dirty clothes. He had dark circles under his eyes, his lips were chapped and dry, and his body reeked a funk of cigarettes, beer, and something stale.

"Say man, we got some queers up in this piece. Take a look!" Woody pointed. I wiped the sleep out of my eyes, I couldn't tell who they were at first glance, and I really didn't care. It wasn't my business.

"I should go over there and toss my coffee in their faces," Woody scrawled. He was always bullying people even when we were in high school, he would pick on the social misfits and the nerds.

The two men stood up from the table, and headed in our

direction since we were sitting near the exit. The closer they got, the more I recognized one of their faces, and when he laughed so loud and boisterously, I knew who he was. I peeked at his short stature and stocky build. He was wearing those infamous beige khakis, shiny black shoes, and an Oxford-style shirt with an argyle vest under his coat. I knew exactly who he was, but I didn't know his friend that he was now holding hands with.

"You all right, Ace?" Woody tapped my hand. "You look like you just seen a ghost, man."

"Yeah, I'm all right." I said, then quickly ducked my head in the fold of my arm as the couple passed me by. I didn't want them to see me.

"I got bubble guts!" I blurted out to Woody, and then rushed to the restroom holding my stomach. I suddenly felt ill from the shock of what I'd seen.

As soon as I opened the restroom door, I hurled everywhere, and missed my aim for the toilet. When my stomach finally stopped upchucking everything I'd eaten and drank since yesterday, I felt empty and weak. I washed my hands and rinsed my mouth at the sink. Someone wasn't going to be happy to clean up my mess that's for sure.

"You alright? Check your boots and make sure no toilet tissue is stuck at the bottom," Woody joked, when I returned to the table.

"I need to go. Are you ready?"

"Yeah, let's bounce up outta here, bro."

I was sober enough now to drive on my own, although I felt very weak on the stomach. I dropped Woody off at his cousin's house near Druid Park, and then I drove to my parents' house.

I rushed inside like someone had been chasing after me. I found my parents sitting at the dining room table eating bagels and drinking coffee.

"Boy, how did you get keys to my house?" Dad looked up in surprise."

"It don't matter. Step outside so we can talk," I demanded,

nodding my head toward the door.

"You hear the way this boy is talking to me? He acts like I'm the one who ruined his life when he did it to himself."

Dad wiped his mouth with a napkin and stood up quickly from the table.

"Now I got no problem stepping outside, but you're not gonna stand here and buck at me like I'm not your father."

"Save that macho talk for somebody that'll believe it, chump!"

"Angelo! What's the matter with you?"

"Nadine, I told you this boy is on drugs. Look at his nose, it's red as a cherry, and he smells like the streets!"

"Ralph, please go easy on him."

"Let's go outside boy, and you better not tell me something that's gonna cost me money, that's for sure."

I wasted no time to beat him outside, and I cut right to the chase.

"I saw you." I pointed my finger at his face.

"Come again?"

"I saw you at the bagel shop. Are you gay?"

He snatched me by the coat collar, and pulled me down to his dark, round face.

"You better watch your mouth."

"Get offa me, man!" I shoved him. "After all of these years you've been living a double life."

"Don't speak what you don't know."

"I know what I saw."

"No you don't! You were hallucinating. I told you to get help. You're sick, son. Let us call a rehab center for you," He said, his tone suddenly sounded sympathetic. For a moment, I actually questioned if I was hallucinating.

"Now wait a minute, don't try to twist this on me! You were kissing another man. How long have you been gay?"

"I'm not gay! Can't you see I'm a man? I don't switch when I walk, wear makeup or talk that woman's jive."

"You're in denial."

"Shut up!" Dad tried to grab me by my throat, but I pushed his hands away.

156

"Don't touch me. Don't you EVER touch me again!"

"You keep your voice down."

"Why? If you were living truthfully there wouldn't be anything for you to feel embarrassed about. This all makes sense now."

"What're you talking about?"

"When I got locked up, you said you read about me in the papers at a bagel shop with your *friend*. I thought you were just talking about a buddy, but it wasn't the first time you mentioned going to the bagel shop. Was that guy your lover?"

"I've heard enough. Give me the spare key that you got to my house. Give it to me now! I told Nadine not to give you any spares, but she did it anyway. Give me the keys!"

I tossed the keys at him, and they almost hit his face.

"You're a closet queen."

"You got some nerve to judge me, but look at you. You're a mess!"

"Well, if I'm so *screwed* up, it's because *you* and *Mother* messed me up!" I clenched my fist and swung at the air out of anger. I needed to hit somebody or something to let out my frustrations. I needed to find something quick and just break it.

"You messed up yourself, boy."

"No," I cried, as my lips quivered and my eyes swelled with tears. "I don't know who I am because of trying to live *your* dreams and *her* dreams and not mine! I treated women bad and betrayed my friends. I'm this good-looking dude on the outside, but man I'm ugly on the inside. Just like you!"

"You didn't get that from me."

"Oh yeah I did. This family is good at putting on airs, but crack the shell and watch what comes out."

"You don't know what you're talking about."

"I know plenty, and you're bisexual. The real reason you got my mother pregnant so fast and married her was to win back your parents. They disowned you because you had a lover in the military and that's why you got kicked out. I remember those photos you showed me as a kid when you were in the military. You looked quite affectionate toward that Martin fella, and nearly cried when you told me he was your *friend*. Was that Martin with you at the bagel shop?"

He heaved a deep sigh, and slowly walked away and sat down on the front steps. His chin dropped to his chest.

"I'm not the only one who was forced to live a lie," I continued, standing over my dad, as he started crying and howling like a little girl. It was an emotion that I'd never seen from him before. He had always been mean, controlling, and condescending, but it was all a front.

"Wipe them crocodile tears and go tell Mother the truth or I will!" I walked by him, bumping into his legs and not caring, as I went back in the house.

I could hear my mother crying. I peeped around the corner and saw her in the living room. She was sitting in a chair by the fireplace.

"Everything will be all right. Please don't cry, Mother." I kneeled down in front of her, took her hands into mine.

"I'm a horrible mother and a terrible wife."

"Don't say that, Mother. That's not true. You did your best."

"How could I not see that your father was gay?"

"Neither one of us knew. Dad hid his secret well."

"All those late business meetings, going camping, and making long trips to the bagel shop in the city. He never once invited me. Twenty-two years of marriage and now this?"

As I tried to console my mother, I didn't hear my dad when he walked through the door. By the look on my mother's face, I instinctively looked over my shoulder. My father was standing in the corridor. His eyes stared at my mother's sobbing face.

"I'm sorry, Nadine," he mumbled, and shifted his gaze toward me. "I'm sorry too, son. I loved you both. I always wanted what was best for us. I really did." He slowly climbed the stairs. I heard a door slam, and a few minutes later we heard:

POW!

I'M DROWNING

Donny Hathaway's *This Christmas* was playing from my boombox while me, Shante, and Kendra were having drinks in my dorm room. We were cracking jokes and exchanging girlie gossip about people on campus. I had warmed up to Kendra over the past few weeks, and although she loved to talk, she was kind, caring, and funny. The three of us had also visited The Whatnot Lounge again for poetry nights, and I would share my poems. Last week, I noticed a flyer of The Whatnot posted in the library, and it featured my name. I felt excited to see my popularity growing so fast.

"Listen guys, I hate to hurry you off, but I'm leaving early in the morning before the bad ice storm," I said to Shante and Kendra, noticing it was almost eleven o'clock. They'd been good company this evening, but I needed to get my rest so I could make the drive to Charlotte in the morning. It was my fault I had to drive instead of fly. I'd waited too late to reserve a flight, and now all the flights headed South were booked.

"Okay, Germaine. Kendra and I need to get going anyway. We have red-eye flights tonight," Shante said, giving me a hug.

"Have a merry Christmas ladies," I said, walking them to the door.

"You too, and a happy Kwanza my sistah!"

I packed away my things to take down to the car, so I wouldn't have to do it in the morning. My father had bought me a Lexus as a way to show that he was sorry. We had talked at length about what happened in the past, and I was slowly allowing time to heal my heart. My stepmother Lolita had even called me to apologize about the way she had treated me. I could tell my father put her up to it, because it sounded disingenuous. She also tried to encourage me and Lisa to kiss and make-up. "You're sisters for goodness sake," She had said. Lisa and I have seen each other since she slept with my boyfriend, and we do speak now, but I wasn't about to invite her to my room to be social with my friends. I wasn't ready for all of that yet. Anyway, at least this road trip would give me a chance to finish working through my pain, and give me an opportunity to see what my new whip could do.

I packed the spacious trunk with my bags of laundry and bedspreads. This way, I could wash them for free once I got home. I left one quilt in my room to get me through the night, and stuffed the others in my trunk. Lord knows all the rolls of quarters I had to use on my quilts at the school's laundry room. I could wash them at home and they would last me a while.

Winter break was six weeks, and I was already missing my girls, Shante and Kendra. They had told me their plans for winter break, and how they were going to spend time with their boyfriends. I didn't have anyone special to spend the holidays with, and I wasn't sure how I would spend my break. Besides the usual routine of going to church events, and having Christmas dinner with my family, I'd probably binge watch repeat episodes of *The Fresh Prince, Beverly Hills 90210,* and *Saved by the Bell. I could finish up my manuscript,* I thought to myself. Thanks to Shante and Kendra my enthusiasm to write came back, and my grades improved. I knew grandma and my dad were going to be proud once my report came in the mail.

When I closed the hood of my car, I jumped in shock at the man before me.

"Oh my God!" I gasped. My heart began to race.

"I didn't mean to scare you." The bass of his voice vibrated through the darkness, and he removed his coat hood from his head.

"Angelo? How dare you scare me like that!"

"I'm sorry."

"Well, what do you want?"

"Help me, please."

"Call Lisa to help you."

"I'm here because I need *you*."

I sucked my teeth and walked back toward the dorm.

"Please don't walk away!"

"Angelo, don't do this now. I'm just getting back to a good place in my life."

"My dad died!"

I turned around abruptly. "What did you just say?"

"My dad . . . he's gone."

"I'm so sorry to hear about your dad, Angelo, but—"

He threw his arms around me and squeezed me tight.

"I need somebody to talk to right now. I'm afraid of what I may do to myself."

"Angelo, don't talk like that."

"I'm looking up from the bottom Germaine, and this may be it for me. On my way here, I thought about letting go of the steering wheel in the middle of the highway."

Angelo was scaring me. I'd never seen him like this. I knew I couldn't turn my back on him. If he took his own life, I wouldn't be able to live with myself.

Angelo sat down next to me on my bed and explained what had happened to his dad and why. I could see the pain and agony all over his face, and hear the sorrow and frustration in his voice. I couldn't believe his father would take his own life. I felt so sorry for Angelo. I took hold of his hand, and clutched it gently.

"Have you guys started making arrangements?"

"It'll be after the holidays."

"How is your mother taking it?"

"Like a two-edged sword. I'm trying to comfort her as best I can, but I need help myself. I feel awful about the way I spoke to my father before he took his life. I shouldn't have done that. He was my father no matter what, and I should've shown him respect."

I searched quickly for the right words to say. Although I wasn't sure, I said, "Maybe you were caught up in the moment, and we all say things we don't mean when we're hurt."

"My dad made his mistakes, but I know he loved us."

"I'm sure he did. Is there anything I can do?"

He looked up at me, his eyes that normally sparkled with excitement were filled with grief.

"Come to the funeral. I don't think I can handle it alone." He brought my hand to his mouth and softly placed a warm kiss in the middle of my palm.

Suddenly, we heard a loud BOOM from outside, and what sounded like a bowling ball rolling down an air duct. I trembled for a moment, and watched the fluorescent ceiling light flicker, and then it blew out. Thankfully, my desk lamp was still on, and I could still hear the music playing softly from my boombox.

"I should go before it gets worse."

"You can wait awhile and see if it stops. I thought the storm was going to be tomorrow evening, but from the looks of things, the weatherman was wrong."

"Well, I hope I'm not a bother."

My eyes gazed over him. I didn't respond to him about being a bother. It was obvious that this wasn't how I planned my evening, but he was in trouble. Angelo really looked bad, and I could tell he needed help. I thought about the time my grandma took in a homeless man for a few days, and the church helped him to find a job. If she could help a stranger than surely, I could help a friend.

"Would you like to use our shower?" I offered as tactfully as I could. He looked like he was letting himself go. His clothes were uncoordinated, he smelled like the musk from outdoors, and he needed a haircut. The Angelo I knew was meticulous about his looks. He would change his outfits two or three times until he settled on the perfect attire. He was also never seen without a haircut or shave.

"A shower?"

"We're friends, right? Friends care about each other. It's why you came. Besides, there are only a few people still here, and it's dark. No one will know it's you." I offered him my toiletries bag, and he followed me cautiously down the dark hallway. Only one light was on in the restroom, the storm had blown out the others, but it was still enough light for Angelo to shower up. While I waited for him to finish, I took his clothes down the hall to the laundry room and washed them. I was glad it was working, but the dryer wasn't, so I took his clothes back to my room and laid them on my radiator.

When I walked back to the restroom down the hall, Angelo was just stepping out of the shower, as a trail of steam followed behind him. I wrapped a new towel around his waist, and offered him a stick of deodorant, Nair shaving cream, and a razor. He used the deodorant, and then shaved off his cave-manish beard at the sink. Then he took my hair mousse and rubbed it through his hair. When he was finished, he looked and smelled like a baby doll, but at least he was fresh.

"Thank you," Angelo said to me, once we went back to my room. I handed him a T-shirt, and an old pair of his boxers that I found in my drawer.

As I changed into my night clothes, Angelo's eyes studied my every move. He was sitting on the edge of my bed wearing my TLC T-shirt, *Ain't Too Proud to Beg*. It was so small that it raised above his navel. I laughed because he looked like a grown man wearing a baby shirt. Angelo knew what I was laughing about.

"Yeah, it's too small and too tight," he chuckled. As he stretched his arms to come out of it, I could see that all of his muscles were still intact. I tried not to stare, but he looked sexy.

Angelo's smile instantly disappeared, and his eyes filled with tears. His shoulders started to jerk up and down, and he began to cry uncontrollably. I couldn't think of anything else to say that would comfort him, so I sat next to him and gently stroked his back.

He whimpered. "My life is screwed up right now without my father. I'm so used to him telling me what to do that I don't know how to do things for myself."

"In time you will figure it out on your own. You will get

through this. Pain doesn't last always." I gave him a big hug, ran my fingers through his hair, and kissed his cheek. He nestled his head against my bosom. He needed a friend.

"I love you, Germaine. I appreciate you doing all of this for me."

"I love you too, Angelo, but what you did still hurts sometimes."

"I'm sorry," he gently kissed my lips. "I never meant to hurt you Germaine. I'm broken, just like you said."

"Now that you can see it, what're you going to do about it?"

"My mother said I should go away for a while."

"I don't normally agree with your mother, but she's right."

"Will you wait for me?" His eyes pleaded, as P.M. Dawn's *Die Without You* played softly in the background from my boombox. I couldn't think of how to answer, but an indescribable feeling came over me. Before I realized it, I kissed him. I didn't know if I kissed him because I felt sorry for him or because I still loved him.

He laid me down on the bed and kissed me with an uncontrollable thirst and a hunger for more. I became overwhelmed with compassion for him, as we removed what little clothing we had on. My body quickly flooded with warmth, as his naked body pressed against mine.

Our foreplay worked up an unbearable heat that forced our energies to the next level. Slowly, our bodies blended together as if we were made to fall into one another. We rocked a harmonious rhythm, and made love face-to-face, from behind, and from the side; this way and that way. I tugged at the curls of his hair as a wonderful bliss tensed our bodies with pleasure. We could feel ecstasy approaching like a ticking time bomb. The anticipation made us pull each other in as close as we could until our bodies locked in tight, and then jolted. My love came down in pulsating waves, as my moans escaped from deep within my soul.

We caught a second wind and made love again. By the third time we had worked up a thin film of sweat, pleasuring each other as our bodies clapped at a rapid speed and reached new heights. By the fourth go around, we had exhausted ourselves, and our bodies sunk into each other's souls within minutes. We had no more energy or loving to give. We could barely move. We ended up falling asleep in each other's arms.

The sun sneezed its rays of warmth through the curtains the next morning. I could sense motion in the room. When I opened my eyes, I saw Angelo sitting on the edge of the bed. He was fully dressed and staring at me. He smiled, and then leaned in slowly to kiss my lips. His eyes gave me the once over as he rose from the bed and made his way toward the door.

He stopped and looked over his shoulder at me, before twisting the doorknob. Our eyes fixed in on each other and froze for a moment. I knew what his thoughts were and what he was feeling in this moment. I didn't want to say goodbye and neither did he. It seemed like a mutual feeling. He let go of my gaze, and walked out of the room. All I could do was hope that one day we would be together again.

TOO LATE

I didn't want to leave Germaine, but I had to. I was ready to get my life together. I called my mother as soon as I got to my apartment, and I told her to register me for the Hope House Rehab Center in upstate New York. My new goal was to complete rehab, then return to DC to be with Germaine and attend Corcoran School of Art.

I started packing my bags immediately, and when I was almost finished, I heard a loud knock at my door. It sounded like someone pounding with their fists rather than a casual knock. I wasn't sure if it was the landlord coming to collect rent money that was overdue.

Before I could get to the door, I heard a loud thump, and the entire door popped off its hinges and crashed to the floor. Before me stood five huge guys the size of WWE wrestlers, all wearing what looked like black leather motorcycle outfits. The ringleader had a mohawk and arms like Popeye. They were inked in skulls with some kind of gang symbol with dice underneath. I could smell a shakedown, and this was going to happen whether I wanted it to or not. One by one they started to trash my place. I grabbed one of them and pushed him into the wall, and another guy I punched in the face. I threw a punch at the ringleader with the mohawk, but his face felt like stone. He belted out a loud devious laugh.

"This kid thinks he's got one up on me? Come on, let's show him!"

I tried to run back down the hallway with the aim of jumping out of my bedroom window, but they grabbed me and started punching me with their fists. I fought back and threw punches of my own.

"You're a wise guy, eh?" The ringleader griped, as the other four grabbed me and stood me up straight like a bowling pin. Mohawk aimed his fist at my face, and I tried to duck, but my timing was off. His punch crashed into the side of my jaw as if he'd thrown his entire body weight into it. I heard and felt my jaw crack, followed by my mouth filling with a pool of blood. My knees buckled from the impact, and I collapsed to the floor.

"Chump!" The youngest looking guy in the bunch kicked me in the stomach to finish me off. A sudden gush of pain jolted throughout my entire body.

"Let's go!" The ringleader shouted to his guys.

"But Victor said to whack him," the chunky one in the bunch said.

"Victor said that? I thought he said to teach the kid a lesson."

"Yeah he did, but he also said to whack him."

"Fine!" The ringleader shrugged his shoulders. My life meant nothing to him. He quickly withdrew what looked like a pistol from his pants leg.

"Noooo!" I groaned from the floor. "Pleeeease don't kill me! I'll get Victor his money!" I held up my hands weakly.

"Too late, kid."

I heard a loud pop. I saw a flicker of light, and then darkness, as life left me. . .

THE COLDEST WINTER EVER

Christmas and New Year's came and went. I had tried calling Angelo, and I even went by his house, but I never got an answer. I had no idea where Angelo was. I didn't even attend his father's funeral because I didn't know when or where it was being held. I assumed he finally went away to get help for his addictions, and I thought that maybe his mother had taken the trip with him. It was important that I reach him, he needed to know that I was pregnant.

After my unsuccessful attempts to reach Angelo, I broke down and told my family that I was expecting. My dad was furious. "We're going to Baltimore and we're going to straighten this out with Angelo's folks!" My father had yelled over the phone when I called to break the news a week ago. Now we're heading to Baltimore. I'd never seen him get to DC so fast from Richmond.

During the ride to Baltimore, my father lectured me about the possibility of me losing my scholarship, not graduating, and ruining my life. You know, all of the clichéd things that a parent says to their daughter when she's pregnant, and not married. I know I should've been angry with myself, maybe even sad or a little afraid, but I didn't have any of those emotions. I actually felt happy that a piece of Angelo was growing inside of me. I could finally have someone who would always be with me.

I didn't know how things would turn out between me and Angelo, especially since we hadn't talked since that night, but I knew somehow, I always wanted him to be a part of my life. If Angelo had gone away to get himself clean and to fix his life, I knew that I would take him back when he returned. We could be a family.

***

We stood on the front steps of Angelo's house for at least ten minutes. I felt a few drops of rain plump down in the middle of my head. I was ready to leave until the door finally opened. Mrs. Pearson appeared in the doorway wearing a pink robe with matching slippers. She looked like she'd been crying. I assumed she was still sad about Mr. Pearson's passing. It wasn't easy for me to see her again, but under the circumstances, I prayed she would show sympathy toward me since her husband had died.

"Hello, Mrs. Pearson."

She glared at me and then gawked her eyes at my father.

"I'm Germaine Landry, remember me?"

"What do you want?" she scoffed, tightening her robe around her thin waistline.

"I've been trying to reach Angelo. You see, Mrs. Pearson, I'm. . . I'm expecting his baby."

"Haven't you heard?" Her eyes zeroed in on me.

"Heard what?"

"Angelo is dead!"

Angelo is dead. Her voice rang through my head. Suddenly I felt nauseous.

"D-d-d-ead?"

"DEAD!" She shrieked. "I suppose you'll be hearing about it soon. I thought he'd gone off somewhere to binge, but his neighbor found his body. Now get off of my doorstep before I call the police."

"Just a minute, Mrs. Pearson. My daughter is still pregnant by your son, and we demand a—"

Mrs. Pearson slammed the door shut, and didn't let my father finish speaking.

"Come on, Germaine. Don't worry, everything will be okay." Dad placed his arm around my shoulders, and escorted me back to the car.

I cried like waters from a broken levee as my chest shook forcefully up and down. It was the "ugly" cry where snot dripped from my nose, and my face turned beet red. My mascara ran down my cheeks, and my lipstick was smeared. I imagined I must've looked like a heartbroken clown, but I didn't care. Every other emotion I felt before arriving was pushed from my very being. I felt like someone had yanked the cord out of the socket, and zapped out all of the power I had within me. Angelo was gone! I was speechless. My father tried to share consoling words to me, but his voice was just a blanket of sound in the background, buried behind my sorrow.

When my dad pulled into the campus parking lot, I didn't want to get out. I sat in the passenger seat and sulked. How was I supposed to move on after this? I needed answers. Did Angelo kill himself? Did he overdose? What happened? I was waiting for someone to jump out of the bushes and tell me this was a bad Bulldogs prank.

"I'm so sorry, Germaine."

"Everyone I love dies," I mumbled, wiped the snot from my nose with a tissue.

"It may feel that way sweetheart, but your family is still here for you. Me, grandma, your stepmother, and Lisa."

"Oh Daddy!" I threw myself into his arms. "What am I going to do?"

"You're going to keep living. I know it hurts, but you need to pull yourself together for the baby's sake."

"Do you need me to come inside your dorm for a while?"

"No. I need to be alone."

"I'll walk you inside."

"No Dad! Please don't. It'll draw too much attention."

He heaved a long sigh, not knowing what else to say I guess.

"Call me if you need anything, all right?"

"I will."

"Listen Germaine, maybe you ought to let your sister know what happened. You could use some support right now."

"I'm not ready to talk about it, but if you want to tell her you can."

"I will. I'll pray for you baby girl. You will get through this."

***

The next morning, someone knocked on my door. I could barely get out of bed. I had cried so much that I didn't have any energy left. I looked through the peephole and it was Lisa, Shante, and Kendra standing on the other side. I slowly opened the door. Their eyes were filled with tears.

"I'm sorry, Sis!" Lisa cried, and wrapped her arms around me. Reluctantly, I hugged her back. We did a group hug, and then they followed me over to my bed where I sat down. Immediately the floodgates opened again. We were all crying.

"I'm sorry, Germaine," Shante said. "I heard the news this morning on TV, and I rushed out to grab the newspaper. "I'm not sure if you want to see this, but Angelo is on the cover of the sports section," she mentioned. My eyes quickly scanned the headline of the paper. It had a picture of Angelo on the cover cheering as he celebrated a touchdown, but the headline read:

ROCKFORD UNIVERSITY
FOOTBALL STAR, ANGELO "ACE" PEARSON
FOUND DEAD

"I just can't believe this," I moaned, and continued to read the article. "This says, he was found in his apartment with a gunshot wound to the head. Who would kill Angelo and why?"

"We don't know, but our prayers are with you my sistah," Kendra said, as she handed me a cup of hot tea she'd bought.

"Thank you Kendra."

I heard another knock on my door, and Lisa got up to answer it. It was the RA with two policemen.

"We need you ladies to clear the room. The police needs to talk to Germaine right now!" The RA said, in a tone that sounded accusatory instead of sympathetic.

"Germaine, you don't have to talk to them without a lawyer present," Lisa stated.

"It's okay."

"Well call us when they leave."

The officers started questioning me about Angelo and my

relationship. They wanted to know where I was on the night he was killed. The interrogation lasted an hour, and I felt even worse after they left.

Rockford became chaotic that day, as the news about Angelo traveled across campus in a matter of minutes. So many people came by my dorm to see me. There were news reporters, students offering their condolences, and Coach Jacobs who brought me flowers.

After a while, it became overwhelming. Dean Patterson had to provide security for me, and prevent anyone else from knocking on my door.

Later that evening, students held a candlelight vigil outside of Angelo's old apartment on Connecticut Avenue. The sidewalks and the streets were filled with so many people that they were blocking traffic. The police had to redirect the cars to turn down alternate streets. Amongst the crowd of mourners was Marcus. He was crying harder than the Bulldogs and his football teammates.

"I'm sorry." Marcus's voice cracked, as he hugged me. I was surprised to see him expressing sympathy, but each Bulldog shared their condolences with me. They were all really broken up. A part of me wanted to turn them away since I knew how much they resented me, but I was broken just like them and I needed the sympathy.

"It's our fault!" PeeWee cried. "We-we-we shouldn't have kicked Ace out the frat."

Each person spoke in the center of the gathering about how kind and giving Ace was. How devoted he used to be to his fraternity, football team, and Rockford University as a whole. There was an outpour of sentimental expressions, and I only wished that Angelo was alive to see it, but it all came too late.

WHERE HAVE ALL THE FLOWERS GONE?

After all the flowers, sympathy cards, phone calls, and other condolences, I was still left with a broken heart, and the mystery of Angelo's death. I was starting to wonder if God allowed me into this world to only experience joy for a little while and then cover my life with misery.

As much as Grandma told me not to question God, I did. I asked why take the life of a young man with so much potential? Although Angelo cheated on me, I still loved him and I forgave him, so I wondered why Angelo still had to die. Did his sins outweigh all the good? I was filled with questions that only God knew the answer to, and I believed he would answer me in his own due time.

I packed away all the sympathy cards, news articles, and other sentiments about Angelo in my memory box along with the rest of our memorabilia, but I still felt a part of him remained with me.

At night when I lay down, I would wrap his jersey around me and fall asleep. It still smelled of sweat with a mixture of his sandalwood scented cologne. It made me feel like he was with me through the night. In the mornings, I would pray that God ease my grief a little more each day.

Shante and Kendra often kept me company, but while they joked and laughed to try to cheer me up, I kept a poker face. Often times, I couldn't wait for them to leave so I could be by myself. Perhaps I felt like no one understood my grief, and for me there was nothing to be happy about. Everything I loved had gone.

One morning I woke up feeling sick on the stomach. I realized it wasn't something I ate, but it was morning sickness. I was quickly reminded that I was still carrying Angelo's baby, and I was due for my next check-up with the doctor soon.

When I returned from the restroom, I was almost blinded by the sunlight spilling throughout my dorm room. On the ledge of my window was a bird. It wasn't a gray or brown pigeon that one would normally see in the city, but it was an all white dove.

My eyes watched, and waited to see if it would fly away, but it didn't. I slowly approached the window and discreetly lifted it to open halfway. I noticed the dove had a stout body, slender bill, and a short neck. Its eyes darted rapidly as it gazed at me, and I thought it was going to take off out of fear. Instead, the dove stepped its pinkish feet ever so gently onto my hand.

"Do you want to come inside, little buddy?" I asked, gently stroking the soft smooth coat of its round head. I noticed it had something shiny in its mouth.

"Can I see?" I gently touched its beak, and the dove let go of a small shiny number 19 pendant. It was Angelo's jersey number.

"Oh God!" I dropped to my knees. "Thank you for letting me know Angelo's with you."

The dove immediately flew back out the window, flapping its majestic wings high up towards the heavenly skies.

Seeing the dove that day gave me hope. I didn't know what was to come of my life or my child's, but I knew by God's grace and tender mercies that I would make it. I would be OK . . .

PART II

TODAY – 2015

"And that was a very difficult time for me," I was saying to Angelica, as we were packing away some of our old belongings in the attic.

"Even though I never got a chance to meet my father, I always feel sad when I think about him," Angelica lamented, as she set aside the newspaper article about Angelo's death. She knew all about her dad, but she still liked to see pictures and go through my old things whenever we went up to the attic. Each time, I would share more with her about Angelo. I refused to throw away my old college journals and memorabilia about Angelo, even when my fiancé asked me to.

"Look, I found another poem. I don't think I've seen this one before."

"Which one is that?"

"This one is written in shorthand. It was inside one of your journals. Can I read it?"

"Sure, Angel. Go ahead and read it," I said. We always called her by her nickname.

I sat down on the wooden floor of the attic, and shifted my body close to her, so I could follow along as she read it.

I refuse to remember you
as ashes buried in the grave.
You were once a living soul
filled with promise and brighter days.

How could you leave me all alone
to walk on this planet Earth?
How could you leave me all alone
to carry your child and give birth?
O' how great is this sadness,
I have a hollow soul.
We were meant to be together
until our younger days turned old.
Forever is a fairytale
when there is only today.
Yesterday was a long time ago, I wish you would've
stayed.

"Mom, this is really sad. You guys really loved each other."

"Yeah, we did. That kind of love never goes away."

"That's how I feel about Cory."

"Yeah well, you and Cory have a ways to go." I stood up and dusted off my crop pants, and made a mental note to mop up here later.

"So, you never did tell me whatever happened to Marcus, my dad's best friend."

"He went on to play for the New York Giants. He came to my baby shower during his pre-season game against the Redskins. I never asked for any help, but he wrote me a check for $10,000."

"Just $10,000?"

"What do you mean? *Just* $10,000, girl? That was a lot of money back then. It helped me to buy a lot of things that you needed, and I had enough left to pay for a few of my classes."

"Well in that case, that was nice of him," she said. "Whatever happened to your friend Kendra?" she asked, holding up a picture of me, her, and Shante hanging out on campus.

"Kendra became a nurse and went back to Jamaica when her parents got sick. We lost touch over the years."

"Aw that's too bad."

"She was a good friend, but life goes on, you know?"

"Life does move on, but did you?"

"What do you mean?"

"In your journals you never mentioned dating anybody after my dad died, and I don't see any pictures in here of you with anybody else."

"I kept my focus on school while Grandma took care of you in Charlotte."

"There's one thing I never understood, Mom."

"What's that?"

"Why wasn't there a funeral for my Dad? He was a famous local athlete, right?"

"Your paternal grandmother told the Press they had a private ceremony, so the students from Rockford had a memorial service for him off-campus. They decorated a hall with pictures and memorabilia, Mayor Marion Barry spoke, and different people shared thoughts about him. It was a nice service."

"From the news article, it looks like there were a lot of people there."

"It was standing room only, and some people couldn't get in so they stood outside."

"I still think it's messed up that my grandmother didn't invite you to the private service though, and I still don't understand why she never accepted me."

"Well, like I told you before, I used to write letters to her, but when they all came back, I stopped writing. I figured she knew about you, since it looked like the envelopes had been opened. The rest was up to her."

"She would've been the closest person to tell me more about my dad. Like what he was like as a kid and stuff like that."

"I know. I wish things were different, but you've turned out just fine without her."

"Sure did!" she winked her eye.

"Well, we better get these boxes downstairs. I need to come back up here to mop, and then get cleaned up."

"Where're you going?"

"Preston is coming over later for dinner."

She sucked her teeth and rolled her eyes to the ceiling, as she grabbed three boxes to take downstairs.

"I know you don't like Preston, but that's because you keep comparing him to your father. They're complete opposites, you know."

"Is that why you want to marry him?"

"No. I just think it's time I give a commitment a chance. Don't you?" I asked, lifting the last box to take downstairs since Angel had grabbed the others.

"I think you should commit to someone who's right for you."

"Angel, you never liked Preston, and that's okay. You're entitled to feel that way, but you can't decide whether he's right for me. I know what's best for me."

"Whatever you say, Mom."

We set the boxes by the front door. Our spring cleaning was long overdue. It was Angel's spring break from the University of Maryland-College Park (UMUC). I was glad she made time to finally help me around the house instead of hanging out with her boyfriend, Cory every day.

"There's the Goodwill truck." Angel pointed through our glass door.

Angel insisted on helping the guys load up the truck with our old things, despite them offering to help. She'd always been a tomboy since she was a little girl. I'd dress her up in cute skirts and shoes, and she would still go outside and play on the basketball court. The boys wondered who the cute girl was in the pretty dress shooting jumpers.

Her Aunt Lisa even tried to get her into ballet and dance, but to no avail, Angel hated dance. Even though she was nominated in high school as the prettiest girl in the whole school, she rocked sneakers in every senior picture, including the prom! I eventually accepted that my daughter wasn't going to be a "girlie" girl.

"Looks like we're all done, I'm gonna go shoot some hoops outside," Angel said, grabbing her basketball that was always somewhere nearby.

After I finished cleaning the attic, I showered and got dressed. I was starving! I went into the kitchen to make a sandwich, and caught a glimpse at Angel shooting 3-pointers, as I stood at the kitchen window. We had a court out back that I'd purchased for her when she was in high school. I knew she loved to play basketball more than any other sport she'd played. She had earned a full basketball scholarship to UMUC. Although many schools wanted to recruit Angel, I suggested she stay close to home. It was just the two of us, and I wasn't ready to be by myself. I imagine that's how my grandma felt when I had left Charlotte to come to DC.

"Whew! It's kind of warm out there. I need something to drink," Angel said, reaching in the fridge for a bottled water. She gulped down a few swallows and then sat at the counter at the island. She pulled her honey colored hair back in a ponytail and began to press various buttons on her phone. I assumed she was on social media or probably texting Cory.

"I was just making a sandwich. Want one?" I offered.

"Sure, Mom," she replied without looking up. I swear these kids are going to have serious neck problems as much as they use their mobile gadgets these days.

"You know, Angel, I'm very proud of you," I mentioned, as I prepared our favorite sandwiches—tuna on rye bread.

"Are you just saying that because I just helped those guys tote big boxes onto a truck?"

"Of course not, don't be silly. It's just that after looking through all of our old things, it helped me to see how far we've come and just how much you've grown up. I mean, you're a junior now, and an All-American. You've got the WNBA scouting you. It seems like yesterday when your great-grandma and I were just changing your diapers."

"Oh Mom, don't make me cry." Angel tried not to blush, as her hazel eyes crinkled at the corners, and her dimples pierced like two tiny dots in her cheeks.

I opened the door to our giant monolith refrigerator. It was filled with our favorites, including a variety of cheeses, grapes, yogurts, and traces of Preston that he always left behind. I had to shift his cases of beer out the way to get to the jar of pickles. It was the last touch to the tuna sandwiches. Angel and I never ate a sandwich without pickles.

"Mmm, I remember Great-Grandma would make sandwiches like this," Angel said, after biting into her sandwich.

"And I remember how she reminded us to say our prayer before we ate."

"Oops, my bad." Angel bowed her head, and we prayed together.

"I miss your Great-Grandma too. She was a woman of wisdom and always helpful. I'm glad she went away peacefully in her sleep."

"Are you selling our house because she died here?"

"Of course not. Preston is tired of commuting from DC to Bethesda whenever he stays the night. He also thinks it'll be a good idea to create new memories someplace else."

Angel twisted her lips and rolled her eyes.

"What now, Angel?"

"Why does everything have to be about what Preston wants? He never considers how you feel."

"Of course he does."

"Not anymore. It seems like ever since you two got engaged, he's been changing things. He never had a problem coming out here to Bethesda before."

"Listen baby, everything will work out fine and that's all you need to be concerned about. We won't leave you out during the selling process, and that's a promise. I'll share the proceeds with you, okay?"

"Are you sure you don't want to ask Preston if that's okay?"

"Excuse me?"

The sound of the doorbell interrupted our conversation.

"Expecting someone?"

"Yep! That's Cory. We're going to Shadowland."

"What kind of place is that?"

"It's a spot where you can play laser tag. I'll text you when we get there. . . ." She hurried off.

"Tell Cory to drive carefully!"

SHANTE FRANKLIN

Monday morning came too quickly, and I found myself slumped at my desk eyeing a stack of what appeared to be unfiled paperwork. In a law office like Lisa's, this would be a sign of success, but as a social worker at Eliot-Hine Junior High School, it was merely another sign of me being overworked. I found myself retyping the last sentence of my latest report over and over again. I paused and took a sip of my coffee, but I couldn't bring my mind to focus. I picked up the phone and dialed Germaine.

"Washington Post, this is Germaine Landry."

"Good morning."

"Hey Shante, to what do I owe this early morning phone call?" She sounded chipper, but for me, my coffee hadn't kicked in yet.

"I'm calling to see if you scheduled us to get fitted for our dresses yet?"

"I'm not quite sure I even like those colors anymore."

"Germaine!"

"Whaaat?"

"You said that last week. Now look, you're getting married in three months. You're behind with your planning, girl."

"I know. It's not all my fault. Besides, things have been so busy. I have a deadline to meet for my latest novel, and I've been prepping myself to go to Paris next week so I can cover President Obama's press conference with the French president," Germaine said, spilling out a list of excuses.

"Germaine, are you getting cold feet?" I asked out of concern. This was Germaine's second marriage proposal within a five-year period. The first guy, Gary, seemed like a perfect match for Germaine. He was a school teacher who also loved to write. I'd personally introduced them to each other during my job's holiday party. They clicked instantly, and he grew to love Germaine and Angel. They dated for two years, got engaged, and two weeks before the wedding, Germaine called things off because she was afraid. We were all blown! Gary was so heartbroken that he moved back to his hometown in Seattle.

"Can we not talk about this right now? I'm at work." Germaine reminded me. She was right, I shouldn't have called her at work, but she had been avoiding my text messages.

"Fine, call me when you get home, please."

"Okay, I will."

As soon as I hung up with Germaine, I checked my voicemail. It was a message from Lisa. She was talking to my VM as if she actually had me on the line. She went on and on about her latest date with some guy who was a dentist with his own practice. While Lisa was desperately seeking a husband, her half-sister was pushing away all the good men. I swear, sometimes both of them drove me crazy! After all of these years, I wondered how I still ended up in the middle of their drama.

LISA THE DIVA

When it came to divorce, I loved going for the jugular vein of no-good, back-stabbing, cheating men. The case of McCall vs. McCall was no different. It was a high-profile case, and my firm represented Mrs. McCall. She was the wife of a former congressman from the state of Maryland. When the judge ruled in favor of Mrs. McCall, I nearly fell backward from my chair with excitement. Mrs. McCall cried after I settled her case, because she was still in love and didn't want things to end, but I laughed all the way to the bank! After working for months on the case, today it was finally settled. After celebrating the win over lunch with my partners, I headed home early for the day.

When I pulled into the driveway of my Potomac, Maryland home, my jovial spirit immediately flew off to Mars somewhere. I noticed the landscape had not been touched. The shrubs weren't trimmed, new mulch hadn't been put down, and my request for perennials hadn't been planted. Everything that was supposed to be green looked dry and withered. I could just imagine if Grandma Roberts were still alive, she would faint at the sight of my yard. I shook my head feeling disgusted as I drove into the garage to park my white Jaguar.

'BUUUURNP BUUURNP'

Just as I was about to press the remote key to close my garage door, I spotted a big truck with the words *Mac Daddy Landscaping* from my rear-view mirror.

"How you doing Ms. Lisa, with your fine self?"

I stepped out of the car and walked over to Mr. Houston, the guy I'd just hired to do landscape work. He had been passing out flyers downtown about a week ago, and begged me to let him provide landscape services to my yard.

"You're late, Mr. Houston."

"Just call me Quinton, baby boo."

"I prefer Mr. Houston, and you need to refer to me as Ms. Dupree-Landry. Only my friends call me by first name."

"That's cool. I got it. We got stuck on another job, but we'll get started right away."

"Typical black business owner."

He laughed it off, wiped the sweat from his bald head, and propped his chiseled arm on the railing of my front steps. I couldn't believe he wasn't taking me seriously, and just laughed at me. Despite how sexy his smooth dark chocolate body looked, I told myself, *snap out of it, Lisa, and check this guy!* I changed the channel of my thoughts and gave him my, 'the nerve of you' stare, with my eyes winced on him and lips buttoned tight.

"Mr. Houston, you have some nerve showing up at my house late! I paid a good deposit for you to fix up my yard. I'm sure when you take a look around this neighborhood, no one would dare give a company with a name like Mac Daddy Landscaping the time of day, but I did. Figured I'd give a *brotha* a chance since that was your whole spill to me."

"Are you through?"

"Yes, I am *through*."

"Good. My crew and I will get started, and when we're done you can pay me."

"I will pay you upon satisfactory completion of the work."

"So be it."

He whistled for his crew to bring the supplies from his truck, and as he walked away I overheard him mumble to one of his workers, "Say man, let's make this quick before this bourgeois broad work my last nerve."

"Excuse me! What did you say?" I questioned him, as I set my briefcase down, and rushed over to him as he stood in my front yard assessing everything. "That was unprofessional, Mr. Houston!"

"Look, maybe you had a rough day, but I always keep my

word with clients. We never expected you to be home at two in the afternoon, anyway. You wouldn't have ever known we were late, and the job would've been complete without you nagging."

He made a valid point, but I had already gotten my emotions worked up and couldn't let him win.

"Would you have called me bourgeois if I was one of my white neighbors?"

"Come again?"

"You heard me. I'm standing right here in your face and you are *not* hard of hearing. You black men are all the same. You think all successful black women are snobs because we won't allow men like you to short-change us. Well, I'll tell you one thing buster, the difference between us and white women is that they get respect automatically, but we have to demand it. Why is that?"

"Are you going to let me do my job or what?"

"You do that! From now on, remember that just because we share the same ancestors doesn't give you the right to walk over me. Do we understand each other?" I pointed my finger at his nose.

"You're right," he replied firmly, quickly grabbing my pointing finger, and pushing it to my side.

"But I expect for you to talk to me like a man, and not roll your neck and bark orders, know what I'm saying? How do you think this makes me look in front of my crew? Don't matter much if you're black or white. Respect me and I will respect you. Do *you* understand?"

"Agreed." I threw up my nose and walked inside my house. I swear I love a man who won't let me run all over him.

I peeped through the blinds, and watched Quinton's big, strong muscular arms work up and down as he dug up holes in the ground to plant my perennials. They were beautiful evergreen rock jasmine that bore rosette leaves in small clusters. They looked good against my stone wall garden, and I began to think to myself, *maybe I should've been nice to him. Sometimes, I can be a little too hard-nosed.*

***

The doorbell rang two hours later, while I was reading over a transcript from another case I had been working on. I removed my glasses and set them down on my coffee table. I reached in my purse for my soft white musk, and sprayed two pumps over my body, before rushing to answer the door.

"Everything is done," Mr. Houston said, stoically. I stepped outside and glanced at my front yard. It was absolutely beautiful!

"Un-be-liev-able!"

"We're professionals, not hoodrats and thugs."

"Listen, I'm sorry about earlier. I guess I overreacted and—"

"Just pay me what you owe me."

"You really don't have to be so short with me, you know," I said, handing him my credit card. He swiped it using Square on his phone.

"Thank you. Your receipt will go to your email address." He quickly walked away.

I watched Quinton load up everything onto his truck, and I truly felt bad. I walked over to him, forgetting that I was barefoot and left my heels inside, but I couldn't let this chocolate pie get away from me.

"Quinton, I'm really sorry."

"Oh, so now you want to call me by my first name?"

"I was wrong, Quinton, okay? So how about I buy you a drink or something?"

"I don't drink."

"Really?" I asked surprised, as I ran my fingers through the curls of my hair, trying to quickly think of another way to land him in my bed.

"Well, how about dinner? It's on me."

"I don't eat out, but if you cook, I'll bring the dessert."

"How about this Friday?"

He looked like he was in brief thought for a moment.

"Okay," he nodded. "I'll see you on Friday at seven, but if I'm a little late don't be mad."

"Just make sure you show up and won't stand me up."

GOING THROUGH THE MOTIONS

I was clock-watching in my living room after dinner. Eight o'clock went by, nine, ten, and I decided to go to bed just when I heard keys outside of my front door.

"Oh hey, sorry I'm late. I had a lot of photos to get out for the Press, and more to do tomorrow. Thought you'd be asleep by now," Preston said, eyes widening behind his dark-framed specs. He looked surprised to see me standing in the doorway with my arms crossed, and feet knocking against the floor impatiently. I was leaving for Paris tomorrow, and I was hoping to spend quality time with him and Angel before my trip.

"You should've called."

"My phone battery died."

"Again?"

"Germaine, I really don't need to hear your complaining tonight," he said, as he hung up his jacket in the hallway coat closet.

"Angel and I had to eat dinner by ourselves again."

"Sorry." He leaned down and gave me a hard quick kiss with no tongue, and then turned toward the stairs.

"Is that all you have to say?" I followed him up the stairs.

"What else do you want from me, Germaine?"

"We were supposed to have dinner and go over our wedding plans. You also missed the realtor who stopped by to discuss the sale of the house. My bride's maids are all wondering what they're supposed to wear, and your groomsmen said they've been calling you for days and not getting a response. I've been delaying the caterers about the menu too, and Lord knows if Shante calls me one more time asking questions, I'm just going to tell her that it's *you* who is stalling, not me."

"I'm tired from work and the long ride out here. Can we discuss this some other time?"

"Fine Preston. Whatever you say!"

I didn't sleep well last night, and I woke up early because I had a flight to catch. I went to the kitchen where Preston was drinking coffee and reading the paper at the island countertop.

"Good morning," I lamented, still upset about Preston coming home late again. This was the third week in a row, and he always had an excuse. A lame excuse at that!

"Good morning," Preston responded without looking up from the newspaper. "Damn it! They printed the wrong photo!"

I walked over to the Keurig to make my own coffee. "You know, Preston, you could've made some coffee for me. That would've been nice."

He looked up at me and rolled his eyes.

"It's easy to make coffee, Preston," I hinted, pouring the coffee into my favorite mug from Howard University. I'd purchased it during grad school. After four and a half years of undergrad at Rockford, I had wanted a change.

"Are we really arguing about coffee? I'm more concerned about this photo."

"I see."

"Germaine, sometimes you need to let go. I had to work. Don't punish me for that, and now I'm going to have work longer hours this week to make sure no more mistakes like this happens again."

"I have let go. It's just rude not to make coffee for me."

"I guess something is wrong with your own hands now?"

"I thought we weren't going to argue."

He heaved a long sigh.

"Are you still taking me to the airport?"

"Airport?"

"I'm going to Paris or have you forgotten about that too?"

He puffed his cheeks and jutted his lips to deflate an air of frustration. I didn't know what was happening between us lately, but there was too much tension considering we were supposed to be getting married soon. Something was pulling us apart, and I could feel it.

Angel walked into the kitchen, as I was glaring at Preston waiting for him to let me know if he would take me to the airport.

"Good morning." Angel smiled, kissed my cheek, said nothing to Preston. He had always hoped for a small act of kindness from Angel, but he never got it.

"Well good morning to you too," Preston snapped at Angel, but Angel ignored him.

"Mom, I'm taking the leftovers for lunch today. I really appreciate the *time* you put into it, and I don't want it to go to *waste*. I can heat it up at the campus cafeteria," Angel said, giving Preston a snide look.

"Thanks Angel."

Preston tossed the newspaper on the counter. "I don't need this crap." His lean body headed toward the stairs.

"Guess that means I'll have to call Uber?" I shouted, but Preston didn't respond.

"Preston's not giving you a ride to the airport?"

"Angel, I'll work it out. I'm a grown woman."

"He's a scrub!"

"Angel, don't say that."

"But he—"

"Angel, please! I can handle myself. I'm not going to force Preston to do what he doesn't want to do. I'll deal with him when I come back."

"If I didn't have school I would drive you to the airport myself."

"I know you would sweetie," I said, giving her a hug goodbye as she headed off to school. "I'll see you in two weeks when I get back. Your Aunt Lisa will be by here on Friday to take you to New York to go shopping."

"Mom, I seriously can't take him anymore."

"Don't worry. Go on to school and we'll talk more when I get back, okay?"

"Okay. Love you."

"Love you more."

***

When Angel left for school, I put in a pickup request with Uber, and when the car arrived, Preston didn't even have the common courtesy to help me take my luggage out to the car. The Uber driver had to assist me.

SHANTE'S "ME TIME"

I took a few days off work to decompress. I decided to pamper myself at the spa, hair salon, and I even went out to the movies by myself. No children, no husband, and a good break from my two BFFs, well kind of. I haven't talked to them, but both of them have been texting or leaving messages. Germaine texted me about how wonderful Paris was. She's hired a tour guide named Nathan, who speaks English and French. Every picture she's texted looks absolutely gorgeous, including her hotel. I'm so jealous! And Lisa, she's been leaving me long VM messages about another new guy she met named Quinton. The dentist fella didn't work out, but I was surprised when she told me Quinton was a landscape professional and not a doctor or lawyer. She always preferred blue collar men. He was also six years her junior. She sounded like a giddy teenager as she spoke about him. I sure hope it's the start of something new that will lead to a commitment. None of the men Lisa dated ever lasted a year. I couldn't understand why she never wanted more for herself.

After my few days of self-indulgence, I spent the weekend hanging out with my daughters, Brittany and Brianna. We went shopping, bowling, and then to the National Harbor for lunch. Afterward, we stopped at Rita's for ice cream.

My girls loved hanging out with me. I was never one of those parents where my children felt they couldn't talk to me. Both my husband and I tried to be as open as we could with them. Brianna was really quiet for some strange reason, though, and she hadn't said much since we'd been hanging out.

"Honey, are you okay?"

"Don't be a snitch, Bree," Brittany said to her younger sister, looking at her from the corner of her eye, as she spooned a big chunk of watermelon ice cream into her mouth. The two of them were only a few years apart. Brittany was seventeen and Brianna was fourteen.

"Never mind, Mom." Brianna replied, after catching Brittany's intimidating facial expression.

"Girls, we don't keep secrets, remember?"

"It's not *our* secret. It's somebody else's."

"Who?"

"Well, Brittany said for us not to say anything, but—"

"Spit it out, girl!"

"We saw Mr. Preston with another woman."

"Preston? Your Aunt Germaine's fiancé?" My heart sped up a few beats. "Well, what exactly did you see?"

"They were kissing."

"Did you see him too, Brittany?"

She nodded her head a slow yes.

"Where were you guys?"

"We were leaving the skating rink, and they were in the parking lot," Brianna explained.

"And did he see you guys?"

"No."

"How long ago was this?"

"Last week," Brittany declared.

"Thank you girls for telling me the truth. Your Aunt Germaine and I will have a lot to talk about when she gets back."

I was furious! I had some choice words I wanted to blurt out, but not in front of my girls. I know Germaine is going to be so heartbroken when I tell her. I'd have to break it to her gently. I feel so bad for rushing her to the altar now. How could Preston cheat on Germaine? She did everything for him. She was even about to sell her house.

DATING YOUNG

I couldn't believe I was spending another Saturday afternoon with Quinton Houston when I should've been working on my next case. It was another big one—the firm would earn another six figures if we won this case, but Quinton reminded me that it was the weekend, and that I needed to leave work at the office. I'd let Quinton talk me into joining him at East Potomac Park to see the cherry blossom trees.

The mall was packed with tourists from all over the world. At first, I was feeling awkward about being surrounded by so many people along the Potomac tidal basin. Sometimes crowds of people made me feel like I would have another panic attack. When Quinton took hold of my hand, however, I started to feel like it was just the two of us.

We explored the cherry blossom trees that were lined outside of the tidal basin. They looked like tiny pink cotton balls, and they were beautiful. My Grandma Roberts helped me appreciate flowers, which is why I went all out for her funeral to make sure she had the best of everything, even though it had upset Germaine. She had accused me of taking over. Anyway, despite the beauty of nature, it was still spring, and my eyes were starting to itch so bad that I thought I was going to scratch them off my face.

"I thought you said you didn't have allergies." Quinton looked at me concerned as we paused in the middle of the sidewalk, and people brushed by us as if we weren't standing there.

"I don't. I mean, I didn't." I twitched my nose and tried to hold back whatever was tickling inside my nostrils. 'HIIII-CHOO!' I turned my head just in time, so I wouldn't give Quinton a face shower.

"Aw, look at you, your nose is turning red, and your eyes are puffy. I think we should go, babe," he suggested.

"Go where?"

"I'll think of something. I don't want you to start looking like Will Smith in the movie, *Hitch*."

I laughed. "Maybe you're right. Let's go."

I climbed into Quinton's black Bronco as he guided my hand, and shut the door closed behind me.

"So, did you say you were divorced or separated?" Quinton asked, as he climbed in on the driver's side.

"Neither. Why?"

"Your last name is hyphenated."

"Everyone always asks that question. The short version is, I have my maternal grandmother's maiden name, Dupree. She wanted all the women in the family to keep the family name so that when we pledged for the Pink Ladies Sorority, they would know we were her family, and part of a legacy. My mother and all of my aunts hyphenated their names after they married, and they're all Pink Ladies. Keeping my grandmother's name helped me to become a Pink Lady too. I'm now a chairwoman for the organization, with a seat on the board."

"Wow, ya'll take the sorority thing pretty serious I see."

"We do."

"So what will you do once you get married?"

"I'll still keep Dupree, but drop Landry."

"That's gotta be disrespectful to the men in your family."

"It's not. They all know it's part of the package deal."

"You're one of those liberated independent type chicks, huh?"

"If you say so, but I don't see why men can't change their last names."

"Because we're the head of the household. God put us in charge."

"Oh, and I see you're one of those pig-headed men who probably thinks a woman's place is in the kitchen."

"I don't think that, but I do feel like a woman should want

to carry her husband's last name."

I sneezed again.

"This is so embarrassing. Do you have any tissue?" I asked, opening the glove compartment.

"Hey! Don't go in there! Close that back!"

I puckered my brow. "Why, do you have something to hide?"

"No, but I got some personal stuff up in that joint that I ain't ready to talk about yet."

My eyes caught sight of a pink paper from the DC Superior Court Family Division. Naturally, I grabbed it, and immediately read the subpoena.

"Oh boy." Quinton puffed his cheeks and blew out hot air.

"You're being sued for child support?"

"Why're you sweating that? Can't you see that paper is six months old?"

"It doesn't matter! You never told me you had a kid, and what kind of father are you that you have to be subpoenaed for child support?"

"I'll explain everything to you later."

"Oh no! You can just take me home!"

Suddenly, I felt the Bronco stall, and the next thing I knew we were coasting down the 395 highway. Quinton managed to get off at the next exit near the Southwest waterfront, and I panicked. I couldn't believe the truck had just broken down.

"This is ridiculous, I'm calling Lyft!" I pulled out my cell from my Kate Spade handbag, as we stepped out of the truck.

"No, don't do that, I can call one of my homies to come get us." Quinton tried to take my phone away.

"Don't touch me!"

"Lisa, come on don't be that way, babe."

I ignored Quinton and entered the street address into the Lyft app, which was Maine Street SW, and indicated I wanted to be picked up there ASAP.

"I can't believe you just gonna roll out on a brother like that." Quinton said, shaking his head in disbelief. He started pacing the sidewalk back and forth, while I stood with my arms crossed and stared at his broken down truck. On the outside, it looked very nice. It was all waxed up with shiny rims, and it had a nice sound system, but obviously, he hadn't taken care of the most important part of the vehicle.

Quinton approached me and gently rested his big hands on my forearms. I knew he was embarrassed, but so was I.

"I'm sorry, Lisa. I forgot to change the oil. This is a busy time for landscape work, and I got caught up."

"Ya think!"

"I also should've told you I got three children."

"Three? I only saw one name on that subpoena."

"Quinton and Quintina are twins. They're freshman at UDC, and my little shorty, Quincy is five. The papers you saw were for Quincy."

"Do they all have the same mother?"

He belted out a loud laugh. "Well, of course the twins have the same mother, Lisa."

"You know what I mean."

"My ex-wife Davita is the twins' mother."

"Ex-wife? I never knew you were married. Oh my gosh, where are the cameras? Is somebody pranking me?" I checked the bushes behind us.

"Lisa, it's not a joke. I married young, and neither of us were ready, but I was trying to do the right thing for the twins, know what I'm saying?"

"This is so crazy. I can't believe this," I said, rubbing the side of my temples in frustration.

Quinton removed his cell from the holder clip on his pants. He proceeded to show me the pictures of his children on his phone. All of them were a spitting image of him—dark chocolate complexions with beautiful big dark eyes.

"I never had trouble with my ex-wife Davita, but Quincy's mother . . . whew! She's a piece of work!" He exclaimed, and I could tell he detested her. "She does everything she can to try to get back at me for breaking up with her. I never missed a child support payment, and she was held in contempt for lying."

I gave him a suspicious stare.

"Now, would I lie to a lawyer?"

"You weren't exactly forthcoming, Quinton, so I consider that the same thing."

"Well, that's my truth, Lisa. I never lied to you. That court paper is six months old."

My eyes bucked at the next row of pictures I came across on his phone.

"Oh my!"

"Wassup?" he tried to look over my shoulder, but I turned away from him.

"Why do you have naked pictures of women on your phone?"

"Huh?" His eyes stood still like a billboard poster.

"You heard me."

"There's a good explanation for that too."

"I'm listening."

"Some are clients and others are women who got crushes on me. Don't mean much though."

"If they didn't mean anything then why do you still have their pictures?"

"Lisa, I'm a grown man. I like looking at beautiful women, shoot. You should send me a naked picture of you too."

I rolled my eyes and tossed the phone back at him.

"Why do I always find out the truth from you no-good men *after* I give you the cookie? You men are all the same. You hide the truth until you hit it."

"I was honest with you Lisa. What more do you want?"

"You only told me the truth because you had no choice. I see this kind of thing all the time in court, you know."

"Look, I don't like arguing. I did that with Quincy's Mom. I'm not going to keep explaining myself like I'm on trial. You know what's up so you can either deal with it or move on."

There it was. That was the immature side to Quinton that had been waiting to break out. The six year age difference between us was showing its ugly head. All along he'd been trying to act like he was so smooth and mature, as if he had everything under control. I was glad the Lyft car pulled up just in time, because I was ready to leave.

"Well, here's my ride. I hope you find a way home, Quinton."

"You just gonna roll out on a brother?"

"Quinton, I'm the victim here. Not you. You said I can deal with it or move on so I'm moving on."

He threw up his hands, not knowing what else to say.

"And do me a favor, kid."

"Kid? So I'm a kid now? You weren't calling me that last night when I was in your bed."

"Yeah well, lose my number. It was a fun *ride* Quinton, but here's where I'm getting off."

"So it's like that?"

I climbed into the car, and the Lyft driver drove off. I dared to look back. Looking back at Quinton standing there by himself would only make me have second thoughts. I kept looking ahead, and I was about to plan ahead too. I dialed the name of a stock broker I'd met at a professional's conference a few months ago.

"Hello Jeffrey, this is Lisa Dupree-Landry, remember me?"

"How can I forget? I'm glad you finally decided to call."

The rest of that conversation was history. We booked a date to get together next week.

I didn't have time for games, and if Quinton wanted to play them, he'd have to play them with somebody else, because I wasn't the one.

PARIS

My tour guide, Nathan, and I had just left one of the cafes on Rue Monsieur Le Prince, where I had some of the most delicious and robust coffee. The pastries were good too. The croissants were light, flaky, and buttery. I knew I would never taste another croissant like it back in the States.

Rue Monsieur Le Prince was a busy boulevard graced with cafes, restaurants, and small shops. It was similar to DuPont Circle back in DC because of all the roundabout streets. The only difference was less traffic congestion in Paris.

"Let's head over to Luxembourg Park," Nathan suggested, and we walked across the street to the park.

Luxembourg Park was surrounded by an iron-gate fence, but there was a main entrance that we walked through. Beyond the gates was a world of its own. The park looked like a palace garden. It was huge, with several bike trails and walk paths. There were plenty of park benches, and I loved the variety of flowers, shrubs, and trees.

We walked around the park, and I snapped pictures of everything I could with my camera or shot video since it was multifaceted. That's when I stumbled upon the famous Fontaine Médicis. The fountain was like a hidden treasure inside the park. You could easily walk past it and not notice because of the cemented wall and tall trees that surrounded it.

"This was built sometime between 1623 and 1630," Nathan explained the fountain. I liked how he never sounded like a textbook while he showed me around Paris. He said just enough for me to get the point and move on.

"Wait, I remember the story behind these Greek statues," I pointed out to Nathan. "The statue of the man staring down at the couple below is Polyphemus. He was jealous of Acis being with Galatea, and that's Acis and Galatea below him. He tries to kill Acis, and that's the boulder in his hand, and when he does kill Acis, Galatea makes him an immortal river like herself. That explains the water basin below."

"You got it! I'm quite impressed."

"Well, what can I say? I'm a hopeless romantic, and I studied Greek mythology in school. Do you ever wish you could make someone you love immortal and nothing ever happens to them?"

"I actually believe true love lives on forever," Nathan said. "Even if someone you love dies, that doesn't mean your heart stops loving them."

"I know exactly what you mean."

"You know, we've been walking around a lot. There's a gentleman by the name of Pierre Garcon who does free portraits on Thursdays. He's right over there," Nathan pointed out a man wearing blue jeans, boots, and a black T-shirt. He looked like a quintessential artist with the matching black French beret on his head from what I could tell from a distance.

"It'll give you a chance to rest your feet, and you'll get a nice portrait picture done in return."

"Hmm... I don't know."

"Oh come on, this guy is the best. Everyone who comes to this park has had their portrait done by him before, including me."

"Well, if you say so. I'll give him a try."

Nathan gave me an admiring, but cordial smile. He was tall, with reddish brown hair and freckles. He was kind of lanky looking and reminded me of Shaggy from *Scooby Doo*.

"I'll be right back. I'll go see if he can paint you next."

I watched Nathan approach Pierre Garcon at a distance. From where I was sitting on the bench, I could see Pierre from the side. He was painting a portrait of a little girl. Her parents stood aside, while she sat in the chair. They were in awe as a replica of their daughter was painted on the canvas. Other people started to gather around him, and watch in amazement as he painted.

I decided not to smother the guy. I walked around and snapped a few random photos at scenes of nature that caught my eye in the park, in particular, the rows of lavender color hydrangea plants that smelled like jasmine. They were surrounded by a field of plush green grass that flattened in waves as a light breeze flowed over the field. The park was filled was so much beauty that I couldn't possibly snap a picture of everything, so I started filming video. I couldn't wait to show Angel, and my friends back at home. My coworkers already envied me for being rewarded by this special press assignment in Paris. They all wanted to go, but my boss admired my writing and interviewing skills. She trusted me with this assignment better than anyone else. I felt honored. I was determined to make her proud.

"Germaine!" I heard Nathan shout for me. I was now on the other side of the park. I thought I had more time to record. It seemed like Pierre was going to be a while. Guess I was wrong.

I strolled back over to the other side of the park, and walked over to Pierre. He had his back turned to me while he was mixing colors. I sat down in the chair in front of him. When he turned around to face me, I couldn't believe my eyes.

I opened my mouth to speak but no words would come out. Suddenly, I felt lightheaded and thought I was going to faint. Our eyes locked in on each other for a moment, but he quickly looked away. I watched his peachy-tanned skin flush red, and his forehead started to sweat.

My heart pounded with an alarm of emotion that felt too big to put into words. I wondered for a moment if I was dreaming. I rubbed my eyes and blinked twice, and even shook my head, but this was real!

He no longer had the stocky build of a football player, but he was slimmer, toned, and all his curly hair that I used to run my fingers through was tucked under his hat, with a few loops sticking out of the corners. He had a five o'clock shadow for a beard, and his eyes were the genetic code that made me recognize him. They were still charmingly handsome and hazel like a translucent jewel.

"Do you know this gentleman, Germaine?" Nathan asked, breaking my ghostly stare.

I nodded my head a slow yes. Time had suddenly stood still, and I felt like I was in a dream. I stood up slowly from the chair, as my knees buckled from nervousness. I needed to touch him. I needed to feel him to make sure he was real. I gradually stretched out my hand, and tenderly stroked the side of his cheek. The soft hairs along his jawline prickled my fingertips, and his eyes swayed with mine, and I knew. I knew he was Angelo "Ace" Pearson. I'd gazed into those eyes too many times not to know it was him.

My mouth moved to speak, but my mind couldn't formulate any more words. After all these years, I had tried to settle my soul and make it understand that Angelo was gone forever, but now he was sitting right before my face. I wasn't dreaming. I didn't know if I wanted to shout for joy or cry. I didn't know if I wanted to be angry or bitter for having been a single mother for almost twenty-one years, when all along my daughter's father was alive. My mind was swimming with so many thoughts at once that I didn't realize Angelo stopped looking at me. He had turned away and began to pack up his supplies.

"An-an-angelo!" I managed to say.

"Je'm'appelle Pierre Garcon!" he shouted, angrily. He stood up abruptly, and stormed off, hauling his supplies in a big tote bag, and easel in a case. I was left with my mouth gaped open feeling confused.

"Germaine! Germaine!" Nathan had to shake me out of my daze.

"It's him. I can't believe it's him."

"Germaine, why is Pierre leaving?"

"His name is not Pierre. It's Angelo Pearson," I snapped out of my daze. "Nathan, we have to follow him!" I quickly snatched up my purse and bags.

"Germaine. We simply cannot do that. Can you tell me what's going on?"

I stood up and gave chase to Angelo before he got too far away. When Angelo looked over his shoulder and saw me running after him, he took off running. I tried to catch him, but he got away. He still had the speed of a football player that was for sure.

I must've looked crazy chasing after a grown man, but I didn't care. As I huffed and puffed, and wiped the sweat from my brow, Nathan finally caught up to me.

"For the love of God, Germaine. Please tell me what is going on."

"Nathan, I promise you I'm not going crazy. I know Pierre. I mean, Angelo." I reached inside my purse and showed him a picture of Angelo on my mobile phone. It was a picture from college that we'd taken together on campus.

"They do favor," Nathan admitted. "Come, let's go have a seat over here on the bench."

Nathan and I sat down, and I gave him the short version of my history with Angelo, but enough so that he could understand why I felt the way I did.

"Incredible story, but—"

"Nathan, you've got to help me find out where Angelo lives. It's important that he and I talk."

"I'm sorry, Germaine. All I know is that he owns a shop just down the block that's called . . . oh my!" He paused and covered his mouth with his hand.

"What is it?"

"His shop is called, *Germaine Beaux-Arts*. You're telling the truth. Seems like he named the shop after you!"

BACK DOWN MEMORY LANE

It had been years since I'd seen Germaine, and she had grown into a beautiful woman. I wondered what had brought her to Paris. I was so scared that I thought maybe she'd been sent by someone to spy on me, so as soon as I got back to my condo, I called Detective Bailer in the US.

"She's clean as a whistle," Detective Bailer said to me over the phone. "It's okay, Angelo, like I told you before, Victor and that whole mob is gone now. Nobody's spying on you. You can even come back to the States if you want." He'd been telling me that for eleven years now, but I'd decided to stay in Paris.

"Do you need to know anything else?"

"No thanks. I'm okay."

"Still keeping your nose clean?"

"Twenty years clean as of last week."

"Your memory is fully recovered?"

"Memory is good now."

"What about your paranoia? That obviously still needs work if you're calling me."

"Well, when God saved me after being shot in the head, that didn't mean I would walk away perfect."

"You got that right. You're a miracle. That's for sure!"

"Thanks for checking her out for me."

"Take care and let me know if you need anything else."

When I hung up the phone, my mind suddenly flooded with memories of Germaine Landry. I never expected to run into her here. I felt like I wanted a do-over from what had happened earlier today. She must've thought I was crazy not to remember her. I wondered where she was staying and how long she was going to be in Paris. I wanted to see her and tell her that time hadn't changed the way I felt about her in my heart. I needed to find her, and soon.

PIERRE GARCON

The next morning, I walked back to Luxembourg Park to see if I could find Germaine or the tourist guy who was with her, but I couldn't find them anywhere. I decided I'd check back again later, I had to open my store and set up shop. Fridays were busy business days for me since everyone got paid. I'd named my art store after Germaine so I would always feel like she was with me; the same reason for the tattoo on my chest with her name inside a heart.

I wasn't doing any free paintings today, so I got dressed in my black Brooks Brothers suit, royal blue shirt and tie, and my pointy-toe Salvatore Ferragamo dress shoes. Sometimes I met some really aristocratic buyers, and I couldn't be wearing blue jeans and T-shirts when my customers were buying paintings worth ten thousand dollars or more. I learned quickly that Paris was all about appearances. After all, it was a place of fashion and wealth.

As I was setting up some of my newer pieces on the wall, the doors chimed to let me know I had a customer. I turned around and it was the tour guide fella from yesterday. I never paid those guys much attention, but I was kind of glad he walked into my store. I figured he may know where Germaine was staying since he was with her yesterday.

"Bonjour." We both spoke at the same time, and then he started expressing interest in one of my pieces and asked how much it would cost. I explained the price and told him I would give him a discount on the frame. Just as I was about to inquire about Germaine, she walked in. She was wearing a sky blue linen pants suit, and carried a small leather briefcase. She looked all business as if she were coming to meet a client. As she walked towards me, the curls of her hair bounced with so much luster and body it looked like she could audition for a hair product commercial.

Nathan excused himself and said he would be right back. I didn't have to guess that he wasn't really interested in buying anything, he'd set up this indirect meeting for Germaine, and I was glad.

Germaine stood right in front of me. There was nowhere for me to go, except to the back. Seeing her again made me feel a mix of emotions that I couldn't explain. A part of me wanted to grab her and kiss her, and tell her all the things I'd been through; while the other part of me felt a need to hold back, and proceed with caution.

"Listen, I'm sorry I startled you yesterday," she stated, removing her sunshades. Her eyes were still big and beautiful, with thick long lashes.

"I know you're not Pierre Garcon. You're Angelo Pearson. You may be Pierre to the people here in Paris, but I know you. Some people in life you never forget."

Suddenly, I felt overwhelmed. All of my confidence in meeting Germaine went out the window. I felt scared. It was an emotion that I hated having since I'd been shot. One minute I'd feel like the confident Angelo that I used to be, but whenever I felt nervous, I wanted to crawl back into my shell. I stepped back away from her and walked behind the counter near the register. My bottle of anxiety pills were under the counter, but I didn't want to pop one of them in front of her. Maybe I wasn't ready like I thought I was.

For years, I had rehearsed what I would say if I ran into someone from my past, but I couldn't remember the words I was supposed to say because I gave up on the chances of something like this ever happening.

"Je mi'apple Pierre Garcon, ma'dame."

"Okay, fine. Your name is Pierre Garcon, so be it!" She slung her hands wildly in the air out of frustration. "Did you know we thought you were dead? But here you are living out your dreams." Her eyes glanced around the room.

"Did something happen to you?"

I dropped my chin to my chest. I felt afraid and ashamed for not being ready for this reality.

"Yesterday was a long time ago, but I have never forgotten it. You meant the world to me, Angelo. I cried so many nights and I was depressed for months believing that you were gone forever. I remembered everything about us and our experiences together—good and bad. I'm just sorry that you don't remember." Her head hung low as she turned around and slowly walked out of the store.

Come on, I have to snap out of this. I can't just let Germaine walk out of my life again. This is the moment I've dreamed of!

I rushed outside just as Nathan had whistled for a taxi for Germaine.

"Je me souviens de toi!"

Germaine looked over her shoulder at me, and then asked Nathan, "What did he say?"

"He said he remembers you!"

Germaine turned around, and we rushed into each other's arms.

"You know I could never forget you, Germaine with a G," I kissed her forehead.

"Oh my God! It *is* you!" she cried, as liquid quickly filled her eyes and tears spilled down her cheeks.

"I missed you so much, Germaine!"

"I missed you too!"

"You still look beautiful," I stepped back and stared her up and down. She was still slim, but popping in all the right places.

"You still look handsome yourself, and it looks like you lost a lot of weight."

"I always had to bulk up for football, but this is my true size."

"It fits you. You don't look like a bulky body builder, but more like a well-toned model."

"Thanks. Would you like some coffee? I have a kitchenette in the back of the store."

"Sure. I see you remembered your English." She hit me playfully. "You had me looking like a fool!"

"Sorry. I didn't mean to."

"Pardon me, but should I return by a certain time?" Nathan asked.

"Yes, maybe in an hour because I have to set up for the Press," Germaine said to him.

I put the *Out to lunch* sign on the door, and Germaine and I headed toward the back. Although it wasn't even near lunch time yet, customers were going to have to wait. This was important.

"I'm so sorry for acting that way. I was just shocked to see you," I apologized to Germaine. She took a seat at the small round table where I normally ate my lunch. I gave her a cup of coffee with two creams and two sugars the way we always liked it.

"I kept wondering, why is he saying his name is Pierre Garcon?"

I laughed lightly. "There's a long story behind that, but what brings you here to Paris?"

She swayed her pointy finger. "Oh no! You don't get off the hook that easy, buddy. You tell me why *you* are here in Paris while everyone else back in DC thinks you're dead!"

"We're gonna need more coffee."

"Well start brewing, because I got one hour to listen and I'm all ears."

I explained to Germaine that I had owed Victor money, and because I didn't pay him, they beat me up and shot me in the head. An elderly couple in my building had called 9-1-1 after hearing the gunshot from my apartment. It turned out that the couple was the same elderly couple I'd seen in Victor's diner my junior year in college. "Remember I told you, you would reap what you sow, now I'm praying that God saves your life!" The elderly woman, Martha had said to me, as they rolled me into the ambulance.

Anyway, the cops came by the hospital to investigate what happened to me, and the word quickly got back to Victor that I didn't die from the gunshot.

Victor had his guys dress in disguise as police officers, and visit me at the hospital. The plan was to finish me off, but a nurse tipped the real police when she noticed the guys looked suspicious. I was transferred to another hospital and the U.S. Marshall provided witness security until the trial.

I testified against Victor and his crew for attempted murder. I would not have snitched if they hadn't tried to kill me, but my loyalty had reached its limits.

After the trial, I was placed in a temporary Witness Protection Program for ten years, until I turned 32. By then, I'd have a choice to come back and reclaim my identity if Victor and his crew no longer existed. My mother felt that Paris would be a good safe location for me to start my life again.

I had survived the shooting, but suffered with amnesia on and off for a few years. For a while, I actually *did* believe I was Pierre Garcon, a name the FBI had given me. Eventually, all the real memories came back in time, but I still have to deal with a paranoid personality disorder.

I left out no details while telling Germaine all of this. If anyone deserved to know about me, she did. Not to mention, if I wanted to keep my memories real and not imagined, my therapist once said that telling the truth was always helpful.

"Oh my gosh, I'm so sorry that happened to you." Germaine gently gripped my hand, and then turned it loose. Her touch woke up a familiar sensation that I hadn't felt in a while.

"Are you ok now?"

"I'm okay now, so what about you? How has life been treating you?"

"Great, no complaints. I'm a reporter now, and a novelist. In fact, I'm here for a press conference with President Obama and President Francois Hollande."

"Wow! That's amazing Germaine! You always were determined to reach your goals even back in college. I'm happy for you."

"Thanks."

"How long will you be here in Paris?" I asked, standing up to get us more coffee.

"Until tomorrow."

"You're leaving so soon?"

"Well yeah, I've been here for almost two weeks now. Part of it was vacation so I could check things out, and the other part business."

"Dag man, I wish I'd known."

She started laughing.

"What's so funny?"

"You still have your Baltimore-DC accent."

"It comes out every once in awhile."

"Should I call you Pierre or Angelo?"

"Here in Paris, I'm Pierre, but you can call me Angelo."

"What will happen if you came back to the States?"

"My legal paperwork can be changed since I'm not in the program anymore. The only challenge will be explaining why I was ever in a Witness Protection Program, and why my death was fake. That's why I stayed here for all of these years. I didn't feel like dealing with the media after the way they treated me in college."

"Your secret is safe with me. I know you don't want that kind of attention."

"I appreciate that. My mother wouldn't want the past to come back up either."

"How is your mother?"

"She's good now, but when I first came to Paris it was difficult for her to let me go, especially after my dad died."

"I can only imagine."

"She moved into a mansion in Georgetown after she sold Iron Motors."

"Good for her, so you're allowed to keep in touch?"

"Now we can keep in touch, but in the beginning I couldn't talk to anyone in the US for ten years, except the FBI."

"Have you visited her?"

"I haven't been back to the US since I came here in 1994. My family has been out here a few times after the program ended, but it's been a while since they last visited. My mother, stepfather, and my younger half-brother, Chris that is."

"You have a brother now?"

"Yeah, my mom and my stepfather had a son. He plays football at Ohio State. Looking to go pro. He likes how everyone compares him to me, but I told him to be himself."

"Your family sounds stable now. I'm happy to hear some good news out of this."

"Are you married?"

"Whoa! That came from left field." She laughed, and then sipped more of her coffee. "No, I'm not married. Are you?"

"Nope. I'm not married and I don't have any kids."

"Why not?"

"I should be asking you that."

Suddenly, we were interrupted by someone ringing the store's doorbell.

Germaine looked at her watch. "That must be Nathan. We need to get going."

"I'd like to see you again before you leave." I walked her outside.

"I think that's a good idea. There's something very important that I always wanted to tell you."

"Maybe I can take you out to dinner tonight?"

"I was hoping I could get to visit you at your place."

"Well uhm . . ."

"If it's a bad idea I understand. I shouldn't just invite myself anyway."

"It's not a bad idea at all. You can come over to my place."

"Are you sure?"

"I'm sure. You can come over to my place, and I'll cook dinner." I jotted down my address on the back of one of my business cards.

"Okay, I'll see you around seven?"

"Sure, that sounds good."

JUST LIKE OLD TIMES

Johnny Boy, my Rottweiler, followed me over to the dining table. He was hoping to catch a few vittles that fell from the plates. When I got tired of him sniffing and begging behind me, I tossed him a few pieces of lamb.

I setup the dining table with a white linen tablecloth and lit two candles. I had purposely placed my dining table by the window so I could always get a nice view of the Eiffel Tower at a distance. It was a view I fell in love with when I first got the condo.

It seemed like yesterday when I crammed everything I owned into one suitcase, then stayed with my grandparents while I continued to recover. After rehab, both physically and mentally, my grandparents bought me a condo so I could start a new life on my own.

When I first moved to Paris, guests used to be an intrusion on my privacy, and only led to nosy questions I didn't like to answer. It's why I lived alone and why I wasn't married by now, because I found it difficult to trust anyone.

I kept my new girlfriend Lenora around because I was getting older and a little lonely, but she was tired of just hanging with me. She kind of forced my hand to a commitment recently. If I said no, I knew she would stop giving me sex, and I didn't want that. I cared about Lenora, which is why I told her the truth that I was having dinner with my ex-girlfriend. It was a mistake to tell Lenora, because she kept calling me.

"Nothing will happen. We're two old friends," I kept telling her, but who was I kidding? If Germaine really wanted me, I knew I wouldn't put up a fight. I loved Germaine with everything within me, and I would give my life for her the same way she tried to save mine.

Over the years, I tried to find a replacement, but no one could replace Germaine. My therapist once said I needed to let go so I could find love again, but that kind of love only came once in a lifetime as far as I was concerned.

I was so nervous about Germaine coming over that I took two showers because I kept sweating so hard. I felt I had to impress Germaine and prove to her that I was a changed man. I wasn't the same Angelo that I was in college. I wasn't a Bulldog anymore, and no one here called me Ace. I came to hate that nickname because it reminded me of the dog I used to be.

My doorbell rang, and it was Germaine. She greeted me in her familiar smooth and articulate voice. I invited her in, and she took a seat on my purple leather sofa.

"Nice place, very Rockford-like with the color scheme."

"Well, you know, I had to represent." I chuckled. "Would you like a glass of Bordeaux?"

"Wine sounds good, that press meeting was stressful."

"At least it's over with now."

"You know, I've been thinking a lot about what you told me earlier today. I can't get over what you've been through."

"I certainly didn't mean to overwhelm you." I handed her the glass of wine, and motioned my hand for her to join me at the dining table.

"I'm not overwhelmed. I've been processing everything in my head, and imagining what I would've done in your situation."

"It was a lot to go through. I can't lie about that."

I set her plate of lamb chops with a fresh mint sauce before her, and served it with creamy mash potatoes, and spinach.

"This looks good. Did you order dinner?"

"Aw come on. Cut me some slack. I cooked this myself."

"Get out of here! You're the same guy who burned my Ramen Noodles when I was sick."

I burst out laughing. "Yep, they were so mushy I had to run out and get you some Hot and Sour soup from Hunan China."

"Seems like you've learned a lot in Paris."

"I have actually. I took culinary classes and became a short order cook. After that, I took visual art so I could perfect my craft."

"You're multi-talented, Angelo, and this is delicious."

"I'm glad you like it."

"How long have you had the art shop, it's really nice."

"It's been about ten years. I teach the kids art lessons on the weekends, and sell my pieces during the week."

"That's kind of you."

"You inspired me, so I named the shop after you."

"I appreciate that, but you did the work."

"I just wish my Dad could see that I did OK without football. I loved the game, but I really couldn't see myself playing for the rest of my life. This is much more satisfying."

"I'm proud of you." She briefly resting her hand on top of mine.

"That means alot coming from you."

After dinner, we had a small slice of chocolate cake for dessert, and made our way to the sofa. We continued to talk, as Will Downing's classic, *Love's the Place to Be,* riffed softly in the background from my iPod. We stretched out our legs and got cozy. Germaine updated me on what was happening back in the States. I also told her a lot more about my experience in Paris.

"This feels just like old times when we used to talk on the phone for hours," I mentioned.

"It seemed like we never ran out of subjects to talk about, and I was always the first to fall asleep."

"I would just listen to you sleep. You had the cutest snore. It sounded like a whisper."

"Those were the good ole days."

"Yeah, I really miss that."

"Did you miss me?"

"Of course." My eyes gazed into hers.

"How come you never came back for me, especially after the program ended?"

"I figured you had moved on with your life. I didn't know if my heart could take you being with somebody else. Before I knew it, too much time had passed. I've been living with those regrets for a while now."

My phone started vibrating again, interrupting the conversation. It had been vibrating since dinner.

"You should get that. It must be important."

"Nah, I'm good." I peeped at the phone on the clip of my pants. It was Lenora calling again. I powered off my phone, despite having a passing thought that it was a bad idea.

"It was so hard for me when I thought you had died. I was depressed for months."

"I'm really sorry you had to go through that. I was miserable too. I could only imagine what you were going through as well. That's why I asked Ms. Martha, while at the hospital, to send you a dove. She liked to train birds, so I asked her if she could train a dove to fly to your dorm room, and I gave her my jersey number pendant. I gave her the location of your window. Told her it was the one behind the tallest tree, with pink curtains. I was leaving for Paris, and I wanted to send you something special to remember me by."

"Oh Angelo! Are you serious?" Germaine became overwhelmed with emotion. I cuddled her in my arms, wiped her tears with the tips of my fingers.

"I thought it was God answering my prayers, but all along it was you?"

"It was me, but no doubt it had God's influence. I'm glad to hear that you received it, because I wasn't sure if you did. I couldn't talk to Ms. Martha after I left the hospital and entered the program. They whisked me off on a plane so fast that I felt like I was getting kicked out of the country."

"Wow!"

"Anyway, you said you had something important to tell me. What was it?"

"Well," she slowly sat up, and turned around to face me. "Do you remember our last night together? That stormy icy night in my dorm room when we made love?"

"Absolutely."

"Well," Germaine paused, and took hold of my hand, and intertwined her fingers between mine. "We made a baby that night."

"WHAT?" I shifted my weight on the seat, and Germaine's head slipped from my arm.

"We have a daughter. She's twenty, and she'll be twenty-one in September of this year. Her name is Angelica."

"Wait a minute! Are you saying I'm a father?" I rose quickly from the sofa.

"Yes. Your mother never told you?"

"No!"

"Not even after you learned that you could come home?"

"Germaine, I swear to you, I never knew I had a child."

"My father and I went to your house, and told your mother the news. I wrote letters to her and sent pictures of Angelica, and she sent them all back to me. Maybe she didn't want you to know."

"This is blowing me right now." I started pacing the room.

"I know it's a lot for you to take in, but I'm telling you the truth."

"I believe you Germaine. You've always been the only woman I ever trusted. It's just that . . ."

"What?"

"I guess I feel cheated," I admitted. "What's worse is that you had my baby by yourself. This wouldn't have happened if I didn't agree to the program."

"Please don't blame yourself, Angelo," she stood up and gently stroked my shoulders. She then reached into her purse, and pulled out her mobile phone. She showed me pictures of Angelica. In one of the photos, she was wearing a white basketball uniform with jersey number 19 written in red. It was the same number I wore when I played football. It almost creeped me out how much she favored me. Even her deep dimples and regal nose were like mine.

"We call her Angel."

"Wow! She's so beautiful. I can't believe I'm a father. I have

216

a daughter?" I was flabbergasted. I slowly sat back down on the sofa, staring at the picture of Angel on the phone.

I felt Germaine gently rub my back. "I'm sorry you had to find out like this."

"First I missed my mother's wedding, then my brother's birth, and now my own daughter? I feel so left behind."

"I can't say that I understand how you feel, but I do understand how Angel feels about her Grandmother. She too feels left behind, and neglected by your side of the family."

"I'm sorry for that."

"Don't apologize for them. The good news is, Angel knows all about you. She's very proud to be your daughter, believe me. That's why she watches your old football games on YouTube, and vintage footage of your interviews. She keeps pictures of you in her phone too."

"I see she's wearing my jersey number."

"She's proud of it."

"All that's fine but, she doesn't need a daddy now."

"Angelo, you can't change the past; all you can do is fix the present. Angel is going to be so happy when I tell her you're alive. I've shared everything with her. It's like you're alive in her heart."

I zoomed in on the picture of Angel with my finger. I studied her beautiful features closely, and imagined what it must have been like to raise her.

"We did this, huh?" I cracked a half smile.

"Yes, *we* did, and Grandma helped me to raise her while I finished school."

"At least we made her in a bed, and not on the football field."

"Or in the library. Even Angel couldn't believe that."

"Wait, you told our daughter about that?"

"She thought her Mama was a nerd. I had to let her know I wasn't."

"Oh you were a nerd, Germaine, but a freak on the side." I reminded her, and she hit me playfully with her fist. I set the phone down and eased back on the sofa, tried to digest what I was just told.

Suddenly our eyes locked in on each other, and a feeling of nostalgia came over me. I cupped Germaine's cheeks with my hands, and slowly leaned in and placed my lips against hers. They felt warm and soft as I continued to kiss her tenderly the way she had always liked to be kissed. I could feel her flinch as if she wanted to push me away, but as my tongue slithered its way inside the heat of her mouth, I felt her arms wrap around me. As her tongue danced with mine, I could feel her breath quickening, as she got into it.

I lay her back down on the sofa, and place a trail of warm kisses along the nap of her neck and down to her breasts. Her body felt so warm and so soft, as I kissed her delicately from her midsection to her navel. She moaned in anticipated, and I always loved hearing how much I pleased her. Knowing she was the mother of my child, and the woman I had always loved, made my nature rise. I desperately wanted to explore her world and become familiar with all of her territory again.

Germaine gently sucked down on my bottom lip, and then trailed the tip of her tongue from my mouth to my earlobe. My weak spot. *She remembered,* I thought to myself. I felt my entire face flush red, and in a minute I was going to peel her clothes off and explore her nakedness.

DING DONG.

Damn! I said to myself.

"Are you expecting someone?" Germaine quickly sat up on the sofa and immediately started buttoning up her blouse.

"Not really."

I fastened my pants, shirt, and slipped on my shoes before I made my way to the door. I looked through the peephole and it was Lenora standing on the other side.

"Bonjour."

"Est-elle toujours là?" Lenora asked bitterly if Germaine was still in my house.

"Oui."

"Je veux rencontrer la fille qui a toujours votre cœur." She crossed her arms, and demanded to meet the girl who still had my heart. I nodded, and let her inside. I knew I didn't have to,

but I figured she would cause a scene if I didn't.

"Germaine, this is Lenora, Lenora this is Germaine." They both gave each other an awkward stare. Lenora stepped in further. Her eyes floated over Germaine in judgment, as her big designer bag dangled from her skinny arm. Lenora's eyes darted around the room, catching sight of the empty bottles of wine, glasses, and Germaine's high heels loosely scattered underneath my living room table. She sharply turned her head towards me. Her green eyes narrowed on me, turning rigid and cold.

"Tu es un menteur et un tricheur putain! C'est fini!" Lenora called me a liar and a cheater, and then smacked me across the face. She stormed out the door with her straight bleach-blonde hair flying in the air.

"Angelo, I didn't know you had a girlfriend. I didn't mean to cause any trouble. I just wanted you to know about your daughter."

"Finish telling me about Angel." I steered Germaine back toward the sofa.

"No, I think I should go." Germaine snatched her purse and phone from the table.

"But Germaine, we were having a good time."

"I know. Maybe *too* good of a time. Look, I guess I shouldn't be too upset about Lenora, because I'm engaged to be married in three months."

"WHAT?"

"I'm sorry, Angelo," Germaine gently stroked the side of my face. "We both should've said something sooner."

"I'm sorry too," I muttered, shoulders sunk in disappointment.

"I hope you'll find the courage to come back to the States. Angel would love to meet you. As long as there's still time, it's never too late."

"Please don't go, Germaine."

"I can't stay, Angelo. This was nice, but I have a plane to catch early in the morning."

"Please stay. I'll drop you off at the airport in the morning."

"But I just told you I'm engaged."

"That's his problem."

"Excuse me?"

"Do you love him?"

"Do you love Lenora?"

"No. She was a filler for good company. Now are you in love with your fiancé?"

Germaine huffed, and looked off in deep thought. I glanced down at her hand and didn't even see a ring on her finger.

"Times up. If you love him you wouldn't have to think about it, and you definitely wouldn't have been kissing on me."

"It was a mistake."

"Was it?" I put my arms up on each side of her, to close her in against the door.

"Wha-wha-what do you want me to say, Angelo?" She stuttered, her knees buckling just like she'd done years ago when I first met her. She couldn't resist me if she tried.

"It's not about what I want you to say, but how do you feel? Tell me what your heart is saying to you right now?"

"It's saying that I still love you." Her eyes swayed with mine.

"Do you really love me?"

"Yes Angelo. I really love you."

"I love you too." I kissed her lips, and pinned her arms against the door.

"Angelo," she panted, as I kissed her neck and tender spots.

"Angelo, please stop. We can't do this, it's not right." She pushed me back.

"You just said you still love me."

"I do, but is that enough to make you come back to the States?"

"All I know is right now, in this moment, I want to make love you to you."

"And then what?"

"We can go with the flow."

"Is that all you want from me?"

"You know it's not."

"What do you want from me?"

"What do you want for yourself, Germaine?"

"What should I tell my fiancé?"

"Tell him the truth."

"What truth is that?"

"You don't love him. You love me."

She shook her head. "I need to sort some things out. I need time. I don't want us to move too fast."

I threw up my hands. "No problem."

"I'll have Angel to call you so you guys can get to know one another."

"I'll walk you out to your rental car."

"It was good seeing you again, Angelo."

"Same to you. Call me and let me know you made it back safely."

"I will."

I planted a kiss on her cheek, and closed the car door. I watched her drive off until the car faded away into the distance.

BFFs

"Close your mouth before a fly gets in it," Germaine said to me, while we were sitting on a bench in Lincoln Park. She'd been really busy at work since her return from Paris, and we hadn't talked in weeks. I couldn't take it anymore, I told her to meet me for lunch.

I was stunned by her latest news. She had just told me about her entire trip to Paris, including how she ran into Angelo Pearson! He was *not* dead! I couldn't believe it! I thought I was going to faint. By the same token, I couldn't shut my mouth because Germaine was bubbly and giddy when she spoke about him.

"Well, have you told Angel?"

"Yes, and she and Angelo have been talking on the phone and texting almost every day since I've been back. You would think they were long lost friends."

"This is really good news, Germaine, but what does this all mean for *you*?"

"I don't know. Angelo and I have been talking every day since I've been back too. I'm afraid of what my phone bill is going to look like next month."

"Let me get this straight," I crossed my arms. "You haven't been busy with just work, you've been busy with Angelo."

She blushed. "Kind of."

"What about Preston?"

"What about him?"

"Well, excuuuse me! Are you guys together anymore?"

"Nope. I suspected something was up with Preston. While I was in Paris, he never returned my phone calls. I asked Angel and Cory to follow him to work, and report back to me when I got home. They showed me pictures of him with another woman. She wasn't just a friend. In quite a few pictures they were kissing. So you know what I did?"

"What?"

"I told him he could come and get his things from my house. Not one time did he question why. When he showed up at the door, Angel tossed his bags outside. He said to me, 'I guess this means I should collect my ring.' I handed it back to him inside the box. He said, 'I have a new lady and this ring will fit her perfectly.' I said, 'Good for her. Perhaps it may mean something that it never meant to me.' Then he said, the reason we broke up was because I was too uptight and always complaining. Can you believe that crap?"

"WOOOW! What a complete jerk!"

"After all the things I did for him."

"You know, while you were away, Brittany and Brianna told me they saw Preston too. That's why I've been trying to get a moment with you so I could tell you."

"I believe you. You know, I put up with a lot from Preston. I was even going to marry him despite how my own daughter felt about him."

"Why?"

"I don't know. I guess after that breakup with Gary, I didn't want to look like a failure again. I also felt like I should marry Preston because time was of essence. I'll be 41 this year. When Angel graduates next year, and goes off to play professional basketball, I'll be by myself. Who will I have, then?"

"Germaine, just because you break up with someone doesn't mean you're a failure. It just means that relationship didn't work out, and there are lots of women over 40 who aren't married and they're living happily. I would never want to see you settle for less than what you deserve."

"Shante, you're my best friend. You know good and well that I haven't had any success with men."

"Maybe it's because your heart never let go of Angelo. I mean, I haven't seen you smile like this in a long time. What's happening with you two?"

"I don't know yet, but I love the way things are going. It's like we've started all over again."

"You're still in love, I can see it in your eyes."

"It's that obvious, huh?"

"Yes, it is, but that's not a bad thing."

"I know. I just hope he'll come visit us soon. Angel's championship game is coming up. It would be nice if he was here to see her play too."

"Maybe then you guys can talk about your relationship and where things are headed."

"There you go!"

"What? I'm not pressuring you. I've learned my lesson now. Whatever decision you make, you know I'll be here to support you."

"Thanks for understanding, Shante."

"I'll always have ya back girl!"

We gave each other a hug, and then parted ways.

STILL WATERS RUN DEEP

I was gathering my clothes for the folks from the cleaners to pick up, when suddenly Quinton's Washington Wizards cap fell from the top of my closet. It was the third time this week that something had happened to remind me of Quinton Houston.

Yesterday, when I turned on the TV, *The First 48* was on. Quinton and I used to watch the show together. This morning, when I went to make breakfast and opened my cabinet, I discovered a bottle of Island spice on the shelf. Quinton was half-Jamaican and loved to spice up his food.

Even though Quinton and I dated for such a short time, each day was packed with adventure and excitement. Tonight, Quinton would have to disappear from my mind though, because I was going out with Wesley, a chiropractor. After four weeks without any loving, my back needed to be cracked.

After the staff from the cleaners came to pick up my clothes, I headed to Bethesda so I could pick up Angel. It was our monthly ritual to get pampered together, and go shopping on my dime. I loved to spoil her rotten. The word *no* wasn't in my vocabulary for Angel, except this thing about her wanting to play professional basketball. She was too smart to spend the rest of her life bouncing a ball. I was hoping she would do something with her intellectual talents. The girl was a math wizard. She majored in accounting, but this basketball thing had taken over. I couldn't believe Germaine was okay with it. If she were my daughter, I'd steer her in another direction quick!

I pulled into the driveway of Germaine's country-style home with the walk-around porch. The house had very nice curb-appeal, and it looked like a modern-day American ranch, with pillars made of mixed gray stone to match the gray painted house, and white trimmings. It was too secluded for my taste, however. Although I lived in the 'burbs' myself, my neighbors didn't live a half-mile down the road like Germaine's did. I believe that's how Germaine preferred it, since she had it built back in 2000.

She had moved Grandma Roberts from Charlotte to live with her. Grandma Roberts wasn't as mobile as she used to be during that time because of dementia. She also had trouble remembering things, and had almost set her Charlotte home on fire. If it wasn't for a neighbor who saw and smelled smoke, Grandma Roberts wouldn't have made it to Maryland. The neighbor called Germaine and that's when Germaine moved her to Maryland. Germaine lived in a condo at the time, but two years after that is when she had the house built.

I sure miss Grandma Roberts. She was a sweet person who gave everybody her last. She could cook too. She made the best juicy fried chicken and buttermilk biscuits that I'd ever tasted. She also loved beautiful gardening, and planted the prettiest flowers. She always treated me like I was her own.

When I stepped out of the car, I could hear the bouncing of a ball, and I knew to walk to the back of the house. I spotted Angel and Cory playing basketball.

"Hey Auntie, wassup?" Angel asked, while simultaneously driving the ball to the basket for a lay-up. "Yeah baby! That's game!"

"Angel, I hope you're gonna take a shower before we go."

"Of course. I wasn't expecting you so soon that's all."

"Well, it's the weekend, and I didn't know if I would run into highway traffic."

"How're you doing, Aunt Lisa?"

"Cory, how many times have I told you that until you marry my niece, I am Ms. Dupree-Landry to you?"

"My bad," he laughed, revealing a mouth full of braces. He was tall and skinny, with reddish curly hair. He was cute in his own way, but he wasn't good enough for Angel. Not to me anyway. Jocks were playboys who lived on a wing and a prayer that they'd make it to the league.

"Guess I'll see you later, babes." Cory, a power forward for Georgetown, leaned down and kissed Angel on the lips. *Yuk!* I said to myself.

"Hello, Germaine," I said when Angel and I walked through the door. Germaine was sitting in the living room in front of the fireplace, reading *A River Moves Forward*.

"Hey," she replied, barely looking up.

"How long are we going to keep doing this, Germaine?"

"Do what, Lisa?"

I walked over and snatched the book from her hands.

"You're always throwing shade at me every time Angel and I hang out together."

"Lisa, give me my book back!"

I tossed it back at her, and she quickly flipped the page back to where she'd left off.

"You know what, Germaine, you have no right to keep hating me the way you do."

"I don't hate you, Lisa, and I'm not throwing shade. You always walk in with it."

"Really? How is that?" I slung my long wavy hair over my shoulder.

"There it is, right there."

"Are you saying I'm shallow? Come on, Germaine, spit it out."

"You're interrupting me from reading my book."

"No, let's just cut to the chase!"

"Fine. Go ahead."

"I think you're jealous of my relationship with Angel."

Germaine belted out a loud sarcastic laugh. "I'm not jealous. Far from it! Hah-ha-hah!"

"Germaine, I can hear the venom in your voice every time I come over to get her. You're jealous because I can show Angel things that you can't. With me, she sees what success looks like. After all, I was listed number five in the top family law firms in the *Washingtonian Magazine*. I have a house with a pool, a Jaguar, and I shop with a black card, okay? And guess what? Men are practically drooling over me. In fact, I'm dating a doctor tonight, so BOOM!"

"Are you through? *Half*-sister?"

"I'm done, girl. The mike is yours." I took a seat in the chair across from her and crossed my legs.

"First of all—" Germaine snapped her finger and rolled her neck "—having material possessions does *not* make you better than me or anyone else. I'm not jealous of you. Look around, I'm doing just fine too. If I wanted what you have I could get it. I just choose to save money for a rainy day. Second, *my* daughter Angel is her own person. She doesn't need *you* trying to change her or *buy* her love. Every time you prance through my front door, you remind me of how I *don't* want Angel to be!"

"And that's why you hate me, huh? Have you ever tried to understand my point of view on anything? Have you ever tried to see the least bit of good in me and what I've done for Angel? No you haven't, because you hate me and everything I stand for."

"I don't hate you as a person, Lisa. I just hate your *ways* because you will always try to upstage me, even at Grandma's funeral."

"Look, I've apologized for that, when are you going to forgive me? All I've ever tried to be was a sister to you, Germaine. A caring sister! I thought hiring a caterer for the repast would relieve the stress on both of us," I cried, feeling myself becoming unusually emotional.

"If you think that throwing me under a bus every chance you get is a caring act, then you need a reality check!"

"I never threw you under a bus."

"Sure you did! Let's start with the funeral. Did you know I had people from the church who had offered to cook for Grandma's funeral? But you went behind my back and hired caterers. They really wanted to prepare something so they could feel a part of it as her friend. You also took over the programs and had them redesigned, and then had the audacity to hand them out to people as if the ones I had printed weren't good enough. Should I continue? Because I have a list of all the things you've done to me over the years. And, let's not forget that you slept with my man just so you could become president of a sorority."

"I'm sorry! Can't you say you're sorry too, Germaine?" I wiped my tears.

"Why should I be sorry?"

"You should be sorry for not walking with us!"

"What? What're you talking about?" Germaine glared at me with a look of confusion.

"If you came with us, it wouldn't have happened!" I cried, and I could see it all like it was happening yesterday. The occasional flashbacks that kept happening at the most inconvenient times, like now. My therapist said it would until I talked about it more often and openly.

Germaine gave me a puzzled look. "What're you talking about, Lisa?"

"Germaine, I know I said you were jealous of me, but I guess . . . I guess I've always been jealous of you."

"I don't understand. All our lives you were the favored one. The golden child who could do no wrong. Why would you be jealous of me?"

"Because your grandpa always made me do it, but not you."

"Do what? What're you talking about, Lisa?"

"What do you think happened during those walks? Why do you think it took us so long to come back from the park? Huh?"

Germaine's mouth dropped. "Now Lisa, be careful of what you're saying."

"I know exactly what the hell I'm saying, Germaine. Now you be quiet and listen! All those summers we spent together were miserable! You know why I hated coming to Charlotte? It was because of what your grandpa made me do to him. The only reason I went to his funeral was to make sure the bastard was dead!"

"Oh my God I'm so sorry, Lisa. I never knew."

"I hated you, Germaine. I always wanted to know why he picked me and not you."

"I never knew grandpa would do something like that," she said, gazing at the look of distress in my eyes. "Does Dad know?"

"He knows now. My therapist said I should tell him and my mother, so I told them about a month ago. Dad said he thinks your grandpa made me do that to him out of revenge for what he did to Aunt Vera."

"That's just crazy!"

"He was a sick bastard!"

"I honestly didn't know. I never saw that side to him before."

"You don't know what I've been through, Germaine. I wasn't just molested, but I also had an abortion in college."

"NO WAY!" She shook her head in disbelief.

"It's true. I got pregnant that night you caught Angelo and I together, but I had also slept with Marcus that night too. I couldn't live with not knowing for sure who the father was, and I didn't want to hurt *you* if it was Angelo's. Later on when you had Angel, I saw that God made a way for you to care for your child, and maybe he would've made a way for me too if I had kept mine, but I didn't. I aborted my child! What kind of person am I?"

Germaine walked over and hugged me.

"Lisa. I'm sure God forgives you, but you have to forgive yourself. It's not too late for you to have a family of your own."

"I hope not."

"I'm sorry that happened to you, Aunt Lisa," Angel peeped her head around the corner. She'd showered up and gotten dressed. I motioned for her to come on into the living room to join us.

"I'll be fine, baby. Don't you worry your pretty self." I stroked the side of her cheek with my hand.

"What you overheard stays here," Germaine said to Angel.

"Of course, Mom. This is family business."

"Lisa, I'm sorry for isolating you." Germaine took hold of my hand.

"I didn't make it easy for you not to, and I apologize."

"Aunt Lisa, do you think my Mom can come with us to the spa? We never invite her to the places we go to."

Angel was right. I'd never even thought to invite my own sister, and maybe that's why she never invited me places with her either. This had to change. We needed to break the cycle of hate.

"Well—" I glanced at Germaine "—if she's not too busy reading her book. I'd love for my *sister* to join us."

Germaine smiled. "I'd love to come."

PART III

TIME CHANGES THINGS

My clean bill of health from my physical exam was just part of the process of getting my passport to travel back to the United States. US federal agents had to communicate with the authorities here in Paris about my history before they would allow me to leave the country. Two months later, I had a passport with my name, Angelo Pearson. I was now headed back home to see my daughter, along with hopes of rekindling my relationship with Germaine.

As the cab driver drove me from Dulles International Airport to my mother's mansion in Georgetown, I felt queasy. As I gazed out the backseat window, it seemed as though everything had moved on in my absence. Nothing looked the same, not even the people. I was starting to feel like a tortoise, and I wanted to pull my head back inside my shell, but I knew I needed to face my fears. I needed to move on and not be afraid to embrace change. I removed my cellphone from the clip on my pocket, and flipped to the picture of my beautiful daughter, Angel. I had to do this for her.

"Here we are, Mr. Pearson, this is Volta Place," the cab driver said, as he followed the long swervy driveway right up to the front entrance of my parent's mansion. It was a colonial style mansion with pillars, and surrounded by a huge, green landscape, with a water fountain in the center of the driveway. Tall oak trees grew behind the house, and gave off just enough shade so natural sunlight could reflect the house. The windows were big and wide with elegant drapery. I saw a shadow of someone walking through the living room toward the door.

"Thanks, my man." I tipped the driver after grabbing my luggage out the trunk.

"Angelo? Angelo is that you?" I could hear my mother calling for me before she could get the door unlocked. I made sure she was going to be home today by checking with my stepfather a day before my flight. I told him I wanted to surprise her.

When she opened the door, she looked up at me with a ghostly stare. It was the same look that Germaine had when she saw me for the first time in Paris. I knew my mother had cosmetic work done to her face. Her lips were fattened, jawline a little higher, and she had dyed her hair auburn brown. Mother never wanted to age, and always complained about her wrinkles when we talked. Her skin looked as smooth as a baby's bottom. I'm sure she continued her regimen of weekly facial treatments with trips to the spa. Nonetheless, she was still beautiful, and I missed her.

"It's so good to see you! I missed you, my darling!" She rushed into my arms and squeezed me tight. I could feel her chest shiver against mine, as she started to cry for the missed time. I gently stroked her hair, and then kissed her forehead.

"I missed you too, Mother."

"Chris! You will never guess who is here!" Mother shouted, and my stepfather came walking down the stairs. His hair was gray-white around the top of his balding mottled scalp. His ears looked bigger, his Jewish nose a little longer, and his stomach was round and hung over his belt buckle.

"Well, well, well, look what the wind blew in!" He stretched out his big arms and we hugged each other. "You finally decided to come home, I see!" He winked his eye. This surprise would stay our secret.

"Yeah, I was hoping it wouldn't be too much if I crashed here during my visit."

"Listen to him, Chris; he sounds as if we're his buddies. Of course you can stay here, honey. You can stay as long as you like. We're just so happy that you're here."

While my stepfather carried my lighter bags to the guest room upstairs, my mother showed me around the mansion. After a tour, the three of us ate an early lunch. I felt jet lag coming on, so I went up to the guest room to take a nap.

I woke up at three in the afternoon. I had received text messages from Angel and Germaine asking if I'd arrived. I'd forgotten to let them know. I texted them back, and they invited me to dinner at seven. I got up and took a shower; then dressed in a pair of slacks and shirt. I was in the habit of dressing up since living in Paris, but decided to ditch the necktie. I didn't want to appear overly dressed.

"Where're you off to, honey?" Mother asked. I was checking myself out before the mirror, and noticed my barber did a great job cutting and shaping up my hair.

"Just going to visit some friends. Is it all right if I borrow the car?"

"You don't still have a license do you? I certainly wouldn't want you to get pulled over. The cops aren't as friendly these days."

"I don't think they ever were," I smirked, recalling the time they nearly beat me to death at Anacostia Park.

"I can have Sara call a Cadillac service for you," she said, referring to her help. "Just let me know when you're ready."

"Mother," I called her before she walked out of the guest room. "We need to talk. Please come in and have a seat for a minute."

"Sure darling. What's on your mind?"

"Does the name Germaine Landry sound familiar to you?"

She looked like she was in thought for a moment and was trying to remember.

"I don't recall. Why do you ask, son?"

"I brought her to the house to meet you when I was in college. You guys didn't hit it off too well."

"The girls you used to date never met my expectations."

"Mother, I really loved Germaine. I still do. She's part of the reason I'm here."

"Oh!"

"Mother, why didn't you tell me I had a child?"

"I know no such a thing!" She stood up suddenly and turned her back to me, glared out the huge window.

"I deserved the right to know. Germaine was pregnant, Mother. She came to you, and you turned her away. How could you deny me that right?"

She turned around and hugged me. Basically, she threw herself into my arms.

"I thought I was doing the right thing, baby."

I stepped back. I saw through her façade of emotion. She wasn't the victim here. I was.

"How could you possibly think that was the right thing to do?"

"You were in trouble, Angelo. You were on drugs and suicidal. What could you have done with a baby at that time?"

"When I sobered up you could've told me. That was over twenty years ago, Mother!"

"Darling, I'm sorry. You're right and I don't want to fight with you. As a mother, I thought I was doing the right thing."

"You should've at least acknowledged Germaine and Angel. They never asked you for money or anything. They only wanted to be a part of the family. I think at that time it probably would've done you all some good considering everything that happened. You could've leaned on each other."

"Please forgive me, Angelo. We've been through enough already. I don't want to talk about the past. I'm a different woman now."

I pushed her hands away as she tried to embrace me.

"I need time, Mother."

"I understand. When you go to Germaine, tell her that I'm sorry."

"It's better if you tell her yourself."

"Very well, then. Why don't you invite her to dinner?"

"You do it, Mother. I'll leave you with her phone number. It'll be your first step in apologizing."

***

When the Cadillac arrived, I asked the driver to take me to Baltimore since I wasn't expected to have dinner with Germaine and Angel until later in the evening.

"You can park right here on the corner," I said to the driver, and he pulled up to the curb, and parked a few doors down from my old house. I spotted a family walking out of the house. They were all dressed up nicely and carrying bibles. It was the middle of the week, so I assumed they had some kind of bible study service to attend. I watched the couple and their three children climb into their minivan and drive off before I approached the house.

I stepped out of the Cadillac, and walked up to the house. Everything still looked the same. I stared at the front porch steps and felt myself getting choked up. My father had cried on these same steps before he went inside the house and took his own life. For years I blamed myself for his death, but my therapist convinced me that it wasn't my fault. I went around the back and reviewed the yard, remembering the days my father and I played catch or went for a swim in the pool.

After playing outside, my mother would be in the kitchen cooking one of her favorite French cuisines that her mother had passed down to her. Our favorite dish was Hachis Parmentier, which was a French version of the English shepherd's pie. I missed those good times. I picked up a few acorns from the ground that had fallen from the tree, and I placed them in my pockets as I headed back to the car. If I never came back here again, I'd get to keep them as a memory.

"Please take me to Rockford," I said to the driver.

Once we were back in DC, I saw a lot of old houses had been made into condominiums. Corner stores that were once carryouts were now coffee shops. I didn't see too many black faces, even in the rough areas of Northwest. There was nothing around to remind me of what used to be. The IBEX night club was gone and so was Victor's Italian diner. All of the black-owned clothing stores and beauty shops had been replaced with professional office buildings and upscale retailers. I couldn't believe my eyes. As people walked about their daily routines, they seem to be in a natural flow of things, and I was on the outside looking in. I felt like a guest in a community that I'd grown up in.

"This is Rockford University, Mr. Pearson," the driver said. Rockford was the only piece of history left that I recognized in this part of Northwest.

I stepped out of the Cadillac and walked toward the multi-purpose stadium. The gate had been left open, so I walked right onto the field. I closed my eyes and I could see and hear the crowds the way they use to cheer for me when I scored a touchdown. I felt on top of the world each time I had scored.

I could feel my body warming with excitement as if it was happening all over again. I envisioned the TV reporters rushing to me after the games for interviews, and fans wanting my autograph. When I opened my eyes, it was like turning off a dream and facing reality. I suddenly thought about what could've been. These past couple of months had made me realize how precious time was, and that once it was gone, you could never get it back. I just hope my brother Chris would make all the right moves and not screw up things for himself the way I did.

"Ace, yo Ace, is that you?" I heard a loud man's voice call. I looked over my shoulder and saw a man about my height, dark-skinned with a big potbelly rushing toward me. I started to run, since I wasn't ready for anyone to know that I was home yet.

"Who wants to know?"

The man rushed up to me wearing a Rockford University shirt, black pants, sneakers, and glasses. I noticed there was a whistle hanging from his neck. I wondered if he was one of my old trainers.

"It's me!" He stretched out his arms. The closer he got to me, the more I began to recognize him.

"Marcus? Marcus Johnson? Man, get outta here!" We embraced.

"I can't believe it's you! I thought I was seeing a vision or something! Your mother told everybody you were dead!"

"Yeah, I know."

"Well I'm happy to see it wasn't true. Where you been, homey?" Marcus asked, all smiles, and I noticed he was gray at the temples and going bald on top.

"I've been traveling that's all, but look at you!" I playfully hit him on the belly, trying to skip talking about my story.

"That's what you call good lovin, know what I'm saying?"

"Donna can cook? I didn't think she had that in her."

"Donna? Man, we never got married. Donna was a gold-digger, but now she's fallen on hard times the last I heard. She moved back to Florida with her family, and never did become the dancer she always wanted to be. I moved on and found me a beautiful wife. Her name is Robin, and we have three children. Matter of fact, I'm about to be a grandfather."

"That's wonderful, man. So, what're you doing here?" I nodded toward the university building.

"I'm the assistant football coach. After I retired from the New York Giants I came back home. It's my way of giving back."

"I thought you'd be living in Hawaii with a mansion and a yacht."

"We got a mansion in the suburbs of Baltimore, but this is what makes me happy, bro, giving back. God has blessed me, and so I'm blessing others."

"So you're a Christian man now, huh?"

"All day every day. It's the best thing that ever happened to me."

"Good for you. So, how's your family?"

"My mom is good. She married a cat that's half her age, but she's happy. I bought them a house in Atlanta, but Gregory . . ." He lowered his eyes. "He died last year."

"Aw man! Not Gregory!"

"Yeah, it's a shame. He thought he could ride both sides of the fence. He lived off my money when he didn't turn pro, but he still wanted to be a thug and live that life. Some guys robbed and shot him at a nightclub."

"I'm really sorry to hear that. How have you been holding up?"

"By the grace of God. I'm blessed by the best."

I laughed. I couldn't believe Marcus was a Christian.

"What about the brothers? What's been up with those dudes?"

"Tony's a fashion editor for some kind of clothing magazine back in New York. PeeWee finally stopped stuttering. He's a news anchor out in Dallas. Eric dropped out after he lost his football scholarship. His grades dropped really low. He took it really hard when you...died. I heard he's a barber now with grown children. What about you, Ace? I can't believe I'm standing here talking to you. Feels like I'm talking to a dead man."

"I'm very much alive, but anyway, I got a daughter I need to meet. Her name is Angelica. We call her "Angel." I whipped out my phone and showed him a picture.

"Yeah, she's all grown up now." He nodded his head. "Where did you travel to? You must've been locked up or something since you're just getting to meet your own daughter. Why would your mother say you were dead? Ya'll were pretty close."

I could tell Marcus was anxious to know, but I wasn't ready to go there yet.

"I wasn't locked up, but I'm glad to be home."

"Well, she's a pretty girl, Ace, you did good." Marcus playfully hit my shoulder. "I heard she's playing good basketball too. You better watch her, Ace. You don't want a Bulldog coming after her. You know how we were."

"Man, they don't want it. I got that heat for any joker that tries, believe that."

"You look good, though, Ace. Older, and a little gray, but still a good-looking cat. You lost some weight though, bro. You had a body like The Rock back in the day."

"That was steroids, man. Now I just got natural body muscle."

"Yeah, you still got it." Marcus threw a playful jab at my stomach.

"You all cleaned up man, that's good cuz' you know that dude Woody you was running with back in the day overdosed out there in them streets."

"Really?"

"Yep. I'm glad to see you got yourself together Ace."

"Me too," I sighed, thinking about Woody. I felt bad that our old lifestyle had taken him away. It could've easily been me.

"Listen Marcus, I gotta split, but give me your number and maybe we can grab a beer before I leave town again."

"Sounds good. You got some explaining to do, bro," he said, and then told me his number.

As I was keying in his number on my phone, guilt suddenly came over me. After all of this time I still felt bad about how I did Marcus years ago. He was my best friend, and the brother I never had back then.

"Listen Marcus, I never got a chance to say I was sorry, but I am."

"I owe you an apology too, Ace. Donna and I never should've done what we did to you and Germaine. You loved that girl, and we were just jealous. We was young and stupid back then, Ace. I'm sorry, and I put that on everything."

"I accept your apology, but I think if that stuff didn't happen, I would've still been a cocky son of a—."

"Don't say that!" Marcus cut me off. I just laughed at him. It was hard to believe he had changed.

"I'll be in touch, Marcus." We embraced like soldiers.

"Cool. It'll be like old times, Ace."

"I look forward to catching up, and Marcus?"

"What's up bro?"

"Just call me Angelo. Ace died a long time ago."

"You got it!"

LETTING GO

We lost the case. My partners were upset with me for not going for the jugular vein, and not getting Mrs. Shorter full custody of her children with alimony. I decided to allow our associate attorney to represent Mrs. Shorter, who was a lying gold-digger, and her seventy-year-old husband was just as sweet and honest as he could be. He wasn't abusive or neglectful of their small children like his wife had claimed. Mr. Shorter wouldn't hurt a fly, but his wife was ready to hurt his pockets. She probably felt it was taking him too long to die. I couldn't let the courts strip this old man of everything he owned, and his children. As attorneys, we were good at exaggerating the facts and fabricating the truth, but when Mr. Shorter cried on the stand, I felt myself getting choked up. I couldn't defend Mrs. Shorter and her lies any longer. I took a seat and allowed one of the associate attorneys to do the interrogating, and she bombed. I was happy Mr. Shorter got to keep his kids and his money.

I just couldn't see myself taking advantage of the old man anymore. I wanted to at first, but what I felt initially was bigger than Mr. Shorter. I didn't want to pay men back for what had happened to me in my past. I wanted to be fair and do what I felt was honest and just. Although my partners were upset with me, I knew they would eventually get over it in time.

Back at home that evening, I called Quinton and asked him to come over for dinner. We really needed to talk.

"Did you get lost?"

"Nope," he sneered, brushing right by me, all cleaned up and smelling good. I quickly forgave him for being thirty-minutes late.

"What's wrong with you?"

"Do you really have to ask that?"

"I'm sorry Quinton."

"It took you two months to tell me that? Why now? Your chiropractor boyfriend can't break your back no more?"

"How do you know about him?"

"You posted his pictures on Facebook and tagged me in it."

I admired his jealousy. I didn't know he still cared.

"What do you want, Lisa? Because right now you're the immature one."

"Would you like a drink?"

"You know I don't drink." He snatched me by the arm. "If this is a booty call, let's just do what we need to do."

I set the glass on the counter, and quickly hurried up the stairs. I was already wearing a robe with a teddy underneath, so I slipped off the robe, and crawled into bed. I could hear Quinton running up the stairs to come get me. Capture me. Make me his. I lay across the bed and waited for him to come and take me. Quinton burst the door wide open, and immediately started yanking off his clothes, while staring at me with a fiery desire in his eyes.

That's when I saw the flashback of the old man standing in the doorway. My fantasy was immediately shot. I couldn't move. I couldn't budge. I lay back on the bed, and I just let Quinton take me, like so many men before him had taken me. It was untamed and aggressive, the way I had always liked it until now.

When it was over, I didn't feel satisfied like I used to. Instead, I felt used and tossed aside like an old pair of sneakers. When Quinton rolled off of me, I pulled my legs up to my chin and sat with my back against the bedpost. I wanted more for myself. I was tired of auditioning men in my bedroom and expecting a commitment out of them. I deserved better.

"Are you okay?" Quinton asked, sliding his arms around me.

"Quinton, I'm not a cougar, and I don't want to be treated like a sex object anymore."

"I never felt that way about you, Lisa, *you* did. I just gave you what I thought you always wanted."

"I'm forty-two years old, and I'm tired of this endless cycle."

"What're you talking about?"

"I want more. I want us to give things another try."

"Feels good to hear you say that. Are you sure this time?"

"I'm positive." I took hold of his hand, smiled.

"Cool. From now on, I'll be upfront with you."

"Good, because after I tell you what happened to me when I was little, maybe you'll understand why I act the way I do sometimes. Maybe you can help me to be more kind and understanding of other people."

"We can help each other. I'm not perfect either, but together, we can bring out the best in each other."

I gazed into his big handsome eyes that always looked like he was taking in the world around him, and I felt compelled to say something I'd never said to any man before.

"I love you, Quinton."

"Wow, now that part I didn't think you would say, but since we're being honest, our time apart made me realize that I love you too."

I blushed. It felt good to hear him say those words and mean it.

I'd never opened up to share my life with any man the way I did with Quinton that night. Despite him being six years younger than I was, he was kind, gentle, and a good listener. He showed compassion for what happened to me when I was young, and shared a few heartbreaking stories of his own.

At the end of the night, we shared some good stories too, and had a few laughs. I didn't know what the future had in store for us, but I knew I wanted Quinton to be in it.

HOME

I blew hot air into my hands to check my breath, then popped a breath mint into my mouth before ringing Germaine's doorbell. The door opened and there she was welcoming me with opening arms. We hugged each other, and then I handed her two dozen red roses. I planted a kiss on her forehead, although I wanted to kiss those luscious lips. I didn't want to come across that aggressive. I had to pick my timing.

She thanked me for the roses and invited me in. She offered me a seat in her living room while she went to place the roses in a vase.

"Oh, I will be right back, I left something in the car." I rushed out to the Cadillac and returned.

"What's that?" Germaine asked about the heavy wrapped square-shaped box I carried inside.

"It's a gift for Angel."

"It looks heavy. You have me curious as to what's inside."

"Yeah, customs gave me a hard time with bringing it back here to the States, but I hope she'll like it." Germaine directed me as to where I could set it, and I propped it against the wall by the fireplace.

"Would you like something to drink?"

"Sure."

While Germaine went into the kitchen, my eyes observed the country-style ambiance. There were wood beams across the high ceiling, and throw rugs placed in front of the coffee table and fireplace. From a distance, I could see the den where there were wood book shelves that matched the wood in the living room. All of the furniture looked antique but expensive. It reminded me of a log cabin with the brick fireplace and reading chair, it felt cozy.

"Here you are," Germaine handed me a glass of iced cold

lemonade. Our eyes flirted with each other for a moment, and then she bashfully looked away, grinning. Almost every song from the 90s was running through my head— Jodeci's *Stay,* Boyz II Men, *Please Don't Go*, but especially P.M. Dawn's *Die Without You*. It was our favorite song. I would play it so much at the frat house that the fellas hid the CD from me for a month!

"You have a really nice house."

"You really like it?

"Absolutely. Most houses are so modern that they look like museums. It's nice to see a house with so much personality. It fits you. I can tell you're a southerner."

"You know, Preston always thought it was too far away and secluded. He never liked it out here."

"He probably didn't appreciate nature, but I like being away from it all. I loved all of the winding roads lined with trees on my way here, and you don't have to worry about nosy neighbors either."

"I appreciate that. So, how was your flight in?"

"Long and tiring. I took a three hour nap."

"I'm sure your parents were happy to see you."

"They were. It felt good to see them too. Speaking of which, my mother wants us to have dinner."

"Oh no! I'm not subjecting myself to *that* again!"

"Well, I can't say that I blame you, but I had a long talk with my mother. I told her how I felt about you, and how I felt about her *not* telling me I was a father."

"How did that go?" Germaine crossed her arms and gave me a skeptical stare.

"I'm not quite sure yet, but I did get it off my chest."

"Well, I'm not interested in having dinner with her."

"She plans to call you, so if you still feel that way just let her know."

"You gave her my number?"

"It's not like that. I told her if she wants to make things right with you, she needs to make the first move."

"Aw, thank you," She gave me a hug. "I'm glad to see that you finally stood up to her."

Suddenly, we heard the sound of keys and the front door screeching.

"Oh, that must be Angel. She went to the Whole Foods to grab dessert for us to eat after dinner."

A tall young lady who looked like she was around 5'8, walked in wearing shorts, sneakers, and a T-shirt with singer Chris Brown's face airbrushed on the front.

"Hello." We both spoke. Our hazel eyes met each other for the first time.

"You must be Angel. It's so good to finally meet you in person." We hugged, and I wasn't sure if she could feel how hard my heart was pounding with nervousness. I didn't know what she would think of me.

"Nice to meet you too. You look much taller in person."

"This is such a special moment for me. You guys have to forgive me for tearing up like this," Germaine wiped a small tear from her eye.

"It's okay, Mom."

I felt a little emotional myself, but held it together. I didn't want to cry in front of my daughter.

"Angel, I made a gift for you."

"Oh, you didn't have to."

"I know, but I wanted to. I'm so sorry that I couldn't be here to see you win the championship game against Connecticut. My passport application got held up."

"Dad, you don't have to keep apologizing," she reminded me. Hearing her call me "Dad" warmed my heart each time she said it, even when she typed it in her text messages to me. It still felt surreal.

Angel sat next to me on the sofa, and opened the gift. Instantly, her mouth dropped open.

"Wow, this is beautiful!"

"You really like it?"

"I love it! Look, Mom, isn't this beautiful?"

"WOW! Angelo, you did a great job painting Angel's portrait. This looks incredible!"

"I'm glad you ladies love it."

"I want to hang this in our hallway. Can we Mom?"

"Sure, we can keep decorating as much as we like, since I don't plan to sell this house anymore. We'll have to find the right hanging tools though, it looks so heavy."

"The pieces are in the box," I said to Germaine.

"Cool. Well, shall we eat? I don't want dinner to get cold."

"You don't have to tell me twice. I'm starving!" I rubbed my tummy.

After we had dinner and dessert, we snapped a few selfie pics with our phones, and even did a quick video of us together. We then went into the entertainment room, and watched a Kevin Hart movie. We cracked up laughing!

As it started getting late, my driver rang the doorbell.

"Mr. Pearson, I hate to be rude, but my shift is ending," he said.

"Whelp! I better get going," I said to Germaine and Angel.

"Aw come on Dad, stick around. This is fun!"

"I don't want to wear out my welcome." My eyes shifted from Angel to Germaine.

"Angelo, please stay," Germaine expressed caringly.

"Are you sure? I forgot my toothbrush, my clothes, and—"

"We have toothbrushes for guests, and we can take you to get your clothes tomorrow."

"To get my clothes?" I looked at her puzzled.

"Yes, you can get your things and come back here. Stay with us. Right Angel?"

"Exactly. Stay with us Dad, come on," Angel motioned her hand for me to follow her back to the entertainment room. I wasn't going to give them any other reason to say no.

I told my driver he was free to go, and I followed them back to the room. I flopped back down on the sofa between them, and wrapped my arms around them. I felt like a father. I felt like this was home. This was the life I had been waiting to live.

FORGIVENESS IS FREE

My stomach would not stop gurgling the entire ride to Angelo's parent's house in DC. Angel seemed more excited than nervous like I was. I'd only agreed to have dinner with Angelo's parents because of Angel. While she and Angelo joked around on the way there, I glared out the Cadillac window wondering what I was going to say or not say to Angelo's mother, Mrs. Levitz. I had rehearsed certain words in my mind, and I had even jotted down my thoughts in my journal before arriving, but some things you just couldn't plan; you just had to let the chips fall where they may.

"Why hello there, you must be Angel, it's so nice to meet you." Mrs. Levitz hugged her. She spoke to Angel as if she was a little girl instead of a young lady turning twenty-one in four months. Mr. Levitz introduced himself and gave Angel a hug as well.

"Germaine, it's been a long time." Mrs. Levitz squeezed my hands. I was glad she opted out of giving me a hug. I didn't want to be phony. This woman hurt me in more ways than one.

We had small talk for a few minutes in the living room, and then Angelo's parents gave us a tour of the mansion. Mrs. Levitz still loved to rub people's nose in the fact that she was rich. As we walked the hallways, she was quick to point out vases she'd purchased in Italy or throw rugs she'd bought in Japan, even telling us how expensive they were. When we finished looking around, we were invited to the dining room for dinner finally. I was glad, because I felt like I had gone on a museum tour. Now I see what Angelo meant by my house feeling cozy.

Mr. and Mrs. Levitz were filled with questions for Angel mostly. Angel talked to them about basketball, Cory, places she'd traveled to, and whatever other topics came up that were all surface topics, or as we called them in journalism, "safe" subjects. I could tell Mrs. Levitz was kind of avoiding eye-contact with me, but it didn't matter. I was going to tell her how I felt before the night was through. It was one thing to hurt me, but a whole other thing to hurt my child by acting like she didn't exist.

"Dinner was delicious, Mother. I can't tell you how much I missed your cooking," Angelo smiled, and then wiped his mouth with a napkin. Even though he had stood up to his mother by speaking up for me, I always hated how he changed his mannerisms around her. Perhaps it was the French custom.

"Yes, that beef short ribs were the bomb!" Angel added.

"Angel, how about you and your father join me in the entertainment room to catch the NBA finals," Mr. Levitz suggested.

"Sounds good to me! I think the Warriors will beat the Cavs."

"The way things are looking, you could be right, Angel."

"Germaine, we won't be too far away. You and Mother can join us when you're done," Angelo kissed my cheek, and left to join his father and Angel.

When everyone else left the dinner table, it felt awkward sitting there alone with Mrs. Levitz. I didn't know if I should rush to finish my meal and light into her like a firecracker or try to strike up a conversation first. Neither one of us said anything to each other for a few minutes nor gave each other eye contact, but then I decided to break the ice and cut to the chase. I wasn't the same shy girl in college who was afraid to speak up for herself.

As I reflected on the past, I felt my anger swelling up from the pit of my stomach and my breath felt shallow. I was surprised at how raw my feelings still were, and the pain still felt brand new. I remembered how every returned letter looked when they came back to me, and how each year I had to procrastinate with my daughter instead of telling her the truth that her own grandmother didn't want her. It was bad enough we had no explanation for her father's death back then.

***

"You know Mrs. Levitz, I never imagined that dinner would be this nice at your home."

"Oh really?" she glared at me, with a condescending look on her face.

"Yes, you were very rude to me during my last visit."

"Germaine, it does no one any good to hold on to the past," she smiled without showing her teeth.

"It's hard to let go when you're not given a reason to."

"As a parent it was my responsibility to protect my son. It's no different than you protecting Angel, I am sure."

"Protect your son? You never even gave me a chance to prove to you what I was about. You dismissed me with your preconceived notions!"

"My Angelo was a humdinger, and he still is," she chuckled. "Honey, he brought so many girls by the house and they all wanted him for his good looks and money. I had to challenge you to see which side of the playing field you were on, but you held your own I will admit. You were the first girl to stand your ground with me, and I respect you for that. I do."

"I know Angelo. I loved him for the person he was on the inside, and you had no right to treat another human being so cruel, Mrs. Levitz."

"Please call me Nadine, you don't have to be so formal," she said cordially. I didn't understand why she was trying to be so nice to me, and why she was downplaying what she had done.

"Were you looking out for Angelo by not telling him he had a daughter after all of these years too? My goodness! I didn't even know that he was still alive! You could've told me! How could you deny his daughter a relationship with her father? How could you deny her a relationship with you too?"

"That was so very long ago."

"It doesn't matter. It still hurts."

"I'm sorry I hurt you. Really I am, but there is nothing we can do about what happened yesterday."

"Do you even realize how disingenuous you sound?"

She slowly stood up from the head of the table and walked

down to me as I sat on the far end. She took hold of my hand, and I snatched it back.

"Please Germaine," she grabbed my hand even more gently, as she looked into my eyes. I refused to cry. As angry as I was, I was not going to give her the satisfaction of seeing my tears. I swallowed hard and blinked back the liquid forming in my eyes.

"Back then," Mrs. Levitz began. "I couldn't tell anyone my son was alive. It was for his protection, and it hurt me for years to live like my own son didn't exist. Can you imagine if you had to do that with your daughter? Can you?"

"You are not the victim here. We all thought Angelo was dead. You didn't just lose a son, but I lost a boyfriend. I lost the father of my child. After the program ended, you could've told Angelo at that time. Angel was still young, she could've built a strong relationship with her father. There was enough time for them to do that. You took those years away from Angel and Angelo, and all you have to say is that we can't change what happened yesterday?"

"You're right. That was unfair and selfish of me. Again I'm sorry. How can we move forward?"

"We can't. I feel like you're being very dismissive right now. For once, can you show a little bit of sympathy. Just a little bit?"

She heaved a long deep sigh, and I let go of her hand.

"Angelo loves you, Germaine. When he admitted that the only reason he came back home was because of you and Angel, it hurt me. I didn't tell him, because Angelo doesn't like to see me upset, and I wanted to keep the peace. I've always been the main woman in his life, and when you stepped in I admit that I felt threatened. I have to ask you, do you still love him as much as he loves you?"

"I do love him. I love him with every breath in me."

"Does he know it?"

"I believe he does."

"Then I hope you'll give him a reason to stay here, because my heart cannot take him leaving *us* again. You both have my blessings. From now on, I will show you the kindness and respect that you deserve."

"I would like that."

"Would you like to help me take the guys some dessert? I baked a cake, and it's in the kitchen."

My heart felt reluctant at first, but I remembered what Grandma told me about forgiveness. She said, '*when ya forgive child, it frees ya soul. It's not always about the other person, it's about you.*' I didn't want to hold on to the pain anymore. I wanted to feel free.

"Sure, I'll help you." I followed Mrs. Levitz into the kitchen.

"I hear you're still a writer," she mentioned.

"I am."

"I've been looking for a co-author to help me to write my memoir, but I think I found her."

"Who?"

She turned to me and puckered her brow.

"Oh I couldn't. I mean . . ."

"Sure you can. I think we're long overdue in getting to know each other. Besides, I read about you recently, and I admire your credentials. You're a best-selling author, and you're nominated for a Pulitzer Prize for your recent article about President Obama and President Hollande of France."

I couldn't help but smile. I was surprised by her research about me, and that she took the time to look me up.

"Perhaps we can work together on your memoir, Mrs. Levitz. I mean, Nadine."

"I'd like that very much, Germaine."

ALL WE HAVE IS TODAY

"You still love Angelo, so just ask him to move back here to the States," Shante said, when we returned to my house. We'd just come from shopping. It was the first time in years that I, she and Lisa had gone shopping together. They had brought up the subject of Angelo on the way back home.

"You know Germaine is always dragging her feet," Lisa said. "Girl, you're not gonna get too many chances like this."

"I'm not draggin' my feet."

"Then what's the problem?" Lisa questioned.

"You know what they say, Germaine, time tells no lies about what a heart can feel," Shante mentioned.

"I've never heard of that."

"You know Shante probably just made it up, but you're making excuses, Sis."

"I'm not making up any excuse."

"I get it. You want to test the waters again and see if it's still good, right?" Shante asked with a flirty grin.

"For your information I already know it's still good, thank you."

"Well excuse me. When did this happen?"

"All last night."

"Ooooo!" Shante shook her head in surprise.

"So now what? You're a couple again?" Lisa asked.

"We haven't had a chance to talk about it. As you can see he's still outside playing ball with Angel. They've been out there since we left hours ago."

"Well, he's leaving tomorrow, you know." Shante reminded me.

"I don't want to put any pressure on him. He still has a business in Paris."

"Angelo is not Preston. I'm sure if he sacrificed flying across country, he doesn't mind closing his shop and moving here."

"Shante is right, Germaine. Angelo loves you and you love him. I can tell by the way you guys look at each other. Besides, why waste time guessing what he's going to do or not do? Just tell him you love him and you want him to stay. That's what I told Quinton."

"WHAAAAAT?" Shante and I shouted in surprise.

"I don't have time to waste, all we have is today."

"You're right Lisa," I nodded.

"Well, Sis, Shante and I need to run, but I hope you'll make a decision that's best for you," Lisa hugged me.

"Okay. I will."

"Love you, Sis."

"Love you too, Lisa. See you later, Shante."

As evening approached, I was putting away the leftovers from dinner while Angelo was in the living room browsing through my family photo albums. Angel got cleaned up and went to the movies with Cory.

Angelo was leaving tomorrow, and I couldn't imagine my life without him here. These past few weeks of quality time together helped me to see that I still loved him. Last night he made passionate love to me, and feelings that never went away have only intensified. I felt the same way in Paris, but even more so now. Lisa and Shante were right, Angelo was not Preston. Work didn't come first for him. If it did, he wouldn't have left Paris in the first place. I didn't have to force myself to love him so we would "look" right to other people. I didn't have any reservations in my heart like I had with Gary. I could be open. I could be Germaine.

After I put the leftover food away from dinner, I walked into the living room where Angelo was sitting on the sofa still looking through one of the photo albums. He was staring at pictures of me and Angel through the years. His eyes lit up when I walked into the living room. He set the photo album aside and stood up slowly from the sofa as I approached him.

"Angelo, I have something to tell you."

"Sure, what's on your mind?"

"I love you, and I don't know if that's enough to make you stay, but the thought of you leaving makes me feel empty."

"I love you too, but I don't want you to feel under any kind of pressure. I realize I was a little aggressive with you in Paris."

"I don't feel pressured. I never did. I just wanted us to take our time in getting to know each other again. These past couple of weeks have been really exciting. You've changed so much, but you're still the same Angelo I fell in love with. Last night, when we made love, I felt a strong connection to you that I can't describe."

"Me too," his eyes swayed with mine.

"Angelo, I've loved you since the moment I first saw you strolling across campus. When Professor Schwartz was going to give the interview to another student for the *American Youth Magazine*, I begged her for weeks to give it to me. She didn't think I had the experience, but it wasn't about that. I had to see you up close, and not just in passing or on the football field. I wanted a moment of your time to myself.

When the magazine went to print with your face graced across the cover, I carried it with me every day so I could feel like you were with me. You were my first love. My first everything, really. When I thought you died, a part of me went to the grave with you. I tried hard to suppressed my sorrows and make my heart understand that you were gone forever, but I never got over you. You're the reason I could never fully love another man."

"Germaine, I'm so happy to hear you say that. It was hard to let you go too. I didn't want to go into the Witness Protection Program, but I feared for my life. Each day that went by without you felt like punishment for all of my wrongs. The minute I saw you in Paris, my heart fluttered with emotions I couldn't describe. I actually cried when you left. I knew I had to face my fear of coming back here so that I could get you back. You are the love of my life, and the only woman who gave me the courage I needed to be myself. You are my strength, my backbone, and my support. You are the only woman I ever cried for or with. I came back here not just to meet my daughter, but I wanted to make our relationship permanent."

Without saying another word, he lowered himself before me, and got down on one knee. My heart pounded with anticipation of what was about to happen.

"Germaine, I talked to your parents, and they gave me their blessing, so did Lisa and Shante. I was hoping for this moment, if not, I was going to take it," he reached into his pocket with a shivering hand, and pulled out a velvet box. He flipped it open, and my eyes watered from the sparkle. It was a huge 3-carat solitaire diamond ring. It was nestled in the middle of the blue velvet cushion. There was no comparison to the half-carat promise ring he'd given me in college.

"Germaine Diane Landry, I want forever with you. Will you please marry me?"

"Yes! I'll marry you."

Angelo's lips slowly curved at the corners and grew into a big smile. As he slid the gorgeous ring on my finger, I could no longer imprison my tears as they streamed down my cheeks.

I threw myself into his arms and he swung me around, my legs twirled in mid-air. I was so happy. I couldn't wait to spend the rest of my life with Angelo. I couldn't wait!

EPILOGUE

2017

The seasons came and went, but my love for Angelo did not fade with the passing of time. We had a love filled with so much passion that after two years of marriage, we created two beautiful babies—twins, Angelo Jr. and Asia.

My relationship with Angelo has taught me that love has a beauty that builds over time, especially when old wounds heal, and lessons are learned. That couldn't have been truer for my sister, Lisa, as well. She has healed from her past, and moved on with her life with Quinton. They married a year after Angelo and I, and they're expecting their first child this spring.

Our parents are very proud of Lisa and me for finding ourselves and our true loves.

My greatest joy these days is being a mother full-time. When I had Angel, I missed out on caring for her when she was a baby since I was in college, and we didn't develop a closeness until Angel was school-age. Now that I finally won the Pulitzer Prize, I've decided to be a full-time novelist and a mother.

The funny thing is, I thought that once my novels became *New York Times* bestsellers, that would be my proudest moment, but giving birth trumped that. Family life is the best accomplishment I've ever received, a true gift from God, and Angelo feels the same way. It's hard to believe that next week, Angelo will be giving away Angel in marriage to Cory. We're so happy and proud of them. They managed to keep their relationship strong, despite their busy WNBA and NBA schedules.

It has been a joy to see how our lives have all come together for the good, even Angelo's relationship with Marcus is much better now. When Angelo is not running his art store in

Georgetown, he and Marcus coach a youth league football team on the weekends. It's a league that they started as a way to help the young men in Baltimore stay out of trouble.

Coaching puts Angelo in a happy place, and reminds him of his dad whenever he's on the field. His brother Chris contributed money toward the youth league, and he visits the team during the off-season from the Washington Redskins.

Of course, Angelo's outreach in Baltimore made headlines in sports. Questions arose about his past and why he used to be in the Witness Protection Program. Thankfully, the news didn't deter the people from Baltimore from showing him respect and support. In fact, the Mayor of Baltimore awarded Angelo with a hero medal of honor after the team recently won their first championship.

As for my mother in-law, Nadine, she stops by to visit her grandbabies often. Although I love being a mother, it can be tiresome, so I appreciate her help. We're learning to accept each other's ways and be respectful. At the end of the day, she loves her grandchildren, and that's all that really matters to me.

I could not have imagined how my life would've turned out after my parents died. All I knew was that I needed someone to love, and for them to love me back. I'm thankful to God that he never forgot about me. For every loss and every trial, he blessed me with twice as much in return. I still remember the day I was singing Jeffrey Osborne, *On the Wings of Love* in the back of my grandparent's station wagon. I know my grandmother would be proud of me. Today I'm flying high above the clouds with the only man I ever loved—Angelo.

Germaine Pearson
Journal Entry: Year 2017

ACKNOWLEDGMENTS

I want to thank my Heavenly Father and Savior for the gift to write. Without writing, I wouldn't know how to mentally cope with these times of distress. I'm thankful I can pray and "write" my way through it all.

To the two special men in my life, my husband who has supported my writing goals since day one. You've comforted me, advised me, prayed with me, laughed with me, and celebrated with me. To my beloved son, the honor student who has many talents- from music and drawing to writing. I am so proud of you! Love you guys to the moon and back! ♥

Thanks to my mother who gives me the courage to keep going. Thanks to my brothers and sisters who support me. My sister-cousin Tish, Uncle Stevie and Tony. All of my family and close friends who have always supported me. If anybody knows my heart, it's you guys. I never have to explain myself to you. You know me and accept me for who I am! I'm always going to keep it real, and be my true self. Love you guys with every breath in me! XOXO ♥

Many, many, thanks to my editor/formatter, Karen Perkins from LionheART Publishing. You were a gem when I needed you at the last minute. Thanks for showing up and helping me out. You were very knowledgeable and patient. Special thanks to my team at Calidream Publishing- cover designers, graphic designers, and digital productions team for putting together my promotional materials. Thanks to my husband for his technical insight and managing my web content.

Many thanks to my beta readers Dejuan Mason and Janice G. Ross. I appreciate the extra pair of eyes and your feedback.

Thank you readers for your support! Kindly leave a review! ♥

ABOUT THE AUTHOR

Selena Haskins is a native Washingtonian who lives in suburban Maryland. Her debut novel, *A River Moves Forward* (2013) was an Amazon Best-Seller in urban-fiction. By popular demand, Selena penned a sequel, *Riding the Waves-the Price of Fame and Fortune.* Selena contributed, "Mirrors Don't Lie" in *Just Between Us-Inspiring Stories by Women*, which still ranks in Amazon's top 10 bestsellers list for inspirational books. *Yesterday Was a Long Time Ago* is Selena's third novel, and fourth book project overall.

Join Selena's social media family via Facebook-@AuthorSelenaHaskins, Twitter and Instagram-@booksbyselena. You may also visit Selena's website for the latest news, book events, interviews, and blogs: www.booksbyselena.com. Enjoyed the book? Email Selena to let her know: selena@calidreampub.com. For book events or speaking engagements, email: media@calidreampub.com

www.ingramcontent.com/pod-product-compliance
Lightning Source LLC
Chambersburg PA
CBHW060408180626
46817CB00007B/2549